THE
DARKEST
DAY

Tom Wood is a full-time writer born in Burton-on-Trent, and who now lives in London. After a stint as freelance editor and film-maker, his first novel, *The Hunter*, was an instant bestseller. StudioCanal and the director of *Taken*, Pierre Morel, are currently adapting *The Hunter* for the big screen.

THE DARKEST DAY

TOM WOOD

SPHERE

First published in Great Britain in 2015 by Sphere
This paperback edition published in 2015 by Sphere

1 3 5 7 9 10 8 6 4 2

A CIP catalogue record for this book
is available from the British Library.

ISBN 978-0-7515-5602-5

Typeset in Sabon by M Rules
Printed and bound in Great Britain by
Clays Ltd, St Ives plc

Papers used by Sphere are from well-managed forests
and other responsible sources.

MIX
Paper from
responsible sources
FSC® C104740

Sphere
An imprint of
Little, Brown Book Group
Carmelite House
50 Victoria Embankment
London EC4Y 0DZ

An Hachette UK Company
www.hachette.co.uk

www.littlebrown.co.uk

THE
DARKEST
DAY

ACKNOWLEDGEMENTS

This book could not have been written without the advice, insight, support and encouragement from Philip Patterson, Danielle Perez and Ed Wood. Thank you to everyone at Sphere in the UK and NAL in the US for doing such continued great work. Thanks also to Will Carver, Mike Hinshelwood and Scott Miller.

Victor was helped through his physical confrontations by utilising a number of the principles and techniques of Urban Krav Maga, as taught to me by instructors Darren Selley, Joe Hallett, Ricky Owen, and co-founder Stewart McGill. Of course, Victor employs such moves a lot more effectively than yours truly ever could and any errors in his method are for artistic licence.

Finally, Adam Bradley, Alex Crook, Becca Pullenayegum, Lidia Teasca, and everyone who lent me their ear during the writing and editing process has my gratitude.

ONE

Alan Beaumont stepped through the automatic door of his office building and down the broad steps to the pavement. The sky above DC was a monochrome of grey cloud. A light rain fell, but a few drops of water were not going to bother him. Damp clothes? Whatever. Messed-up hair? He had no hair to ruin. That was long gone. Nothing had helped retain those once-magnificent curls. Not pills. Not potions. *Nada*.

He used a thumb and middle finger to snap open his Zippo lighter and lit the cigarette perched between his lips. Smoking was perhaps the only real pleasure he had.

He watched the downtown traffic and the pedestrians pass by, all miserable. Good. He didn't like anyone to be happy but himself. It wasn't pure selfishness. Joy was a zero sum game. There just wasn't enough to go around.

He sucked in a big lungful of smoke and held it in as he closed his eyes and tilted his face to the sky, exhaling as the sporadic raindrops exploded on his cheeks, forehead and eyelids.

'You look like you're enjoying that.'

He opened his eyes and looked at the speaker. A young woman stood nearby, dressed in a long cream raincoat, hat and brown leather gloves. She was pale and tall – almost as tall as Beaumont, with wavy blonde hair. Her lipstick was bright red. A bit too much for the office. A bit too suggestive. She must be new then. One of the many drones that serviced the company, he assumed. He had no doubt walked past her a hundred times or more by now. She would know his name, his job, and maybe even how he liked his coffee, but to Beaumont she was no one.

He shrugged and turned away. He was in no mood to chit-chat, least of all with someone whose face he didn't need to recognise. She was a looker, sure; lots of real estate in the bust and hips, but he wanted to savour his damn cigarette alone, as God intended.

'I used to smoke myself,' the woman said, not taking the hint. It sounded like she was from the South. Probably some state Beaumont had been lucky enough never to soil his soles on.

'That right?' Beaumont felt obliged to say.

He edged away from her. It wasn't rude, he told himself. The young woman had intruded on his solitary time.

She did so again, stepping around Beaumont until they were face to face.

'I smoked for maybe ten years,' the young woman continued, undeterred. 'Two packs of Marlboros a day. I had a cigarette in my hand all day long. I started young, you see.

I managed to kick it though. Now, I'll allow myself the occasional cigar. Better than nothing, right? But oh, how I miss a real cigarette.'

She was smiling, but in a sad way, and Beaumont began to feel sorry for her. She reminded him of his daughter.

'You're new, aren't you?' he asked.

She nodded. 'Is it that obvious?'

She smiled in a manner that said the office coven had not welcomed her with open arms. He saw her loneliness and had a strange flash of the future, when he was an old man a couple of decades from now, fat and divorced with a daughter and a son who didn't bother to call him because he had never bothered to take them to the park. Would he be so in need of human contact that he would ignore a stranger's efforts to cold-shoulder him, because any inter-action was better than none?

'How are you settling in?'

She wrinkled her nose and shrugged.

'That bad, eh?'

She didn't answer.

'Say,' Beaumont began, 'would you like a smoke? For old time's sake. It'll make you feel better.'

He forced himself to smile.

The young woman's face lit up as if she'd won the lottery and Beaumont felt even sadder for her. He rooted for the packet.

'No,' the woman said, holding up a palm. 'I'd better not have one. I'll only start again. One's never enough, is it? But I wouldn't say no to a single drag, if you don't mind.'

She gestured at Beaumont's precious cigarette. Beaumont

looked at it too. He wasn't a sharing kind of guy, even if there was a hot chick half his age involved. He glanced up at the tall young woman. He looked at her bright red lips. She didn't appear to be sick. She didn't look like she was carrying some flesh-eating retrovirus. The hope in the woman's eyes tore down any resistance Beaumont had, and reminded him that he wasn't quite as soulless as he'd thought.

There was no reason not to, but if a man was asking to share his cigarette he would tell the fool to take a hike. But it wasn't a man asking.

Maybe if he let her put his cigarette between her lips she would let him ...

He offered the cigarette and the young woman took it between two fingers of her left hand. She brought it up and set it between her red lips with surgical precision, puckering around the filter and tensing them, but she did not inhale. Beaumont watched, entranced.

'That was close,' the young woman said, taking the cigarette away, but this time with her right hand. 'I almost caved.'

Before handing the cigarette back, she rolled the filter between her gloved fingertips for a moment.

'Holding it was enough,' the woman continued, as Beaumont watched.

'Your choice,' he said, taking the precious cigarette back.

A trace of lipstick was smeared on the filter. He took a drag.

The young woman watched him, something in her eyes. She removed the gloves and placed them into a pocket of her raincoat. She held out a palm to catch raindrops and when her fingers were wet wiped them across her lips several times. She took a handkerchief from a pocket and used it to wipe her lips clean.

'Washing away the taste?' Beaumont asked, a little aroused.

The woman smiled at him, but said nothing. She looked pleased with herself. Smug, even.

'So,' Beaumont began. 'What's your name?'

She didn't answer. She just stared.

'Hello? Anyone home?' Beaumont waved a hand before her face and laughed.

No response. No wonder she was having a hard time fitting in when she was bat-shit crazy.

'Right,' he said with a big exhale, erection retreating, and regretting allowing this weirdo to intrude into his private time. He felt the annoyance building inside him, anger making him feel hot despite the cool rain pattering on his scalp.

'All right, honey. I've humoured you long enough. You can stop eyeballing me and be on your way. There's a good girl.'

'Soon,' the woman said, staring.

'Whatever.'

Beaumont turned away, loosening his tie. Damn it, he was really fucking wound up now. His heart was hammering. He reminded himself never to feel sorry for anyone again. Ever. People were scum, always looking to take advantage.

He tried to swallow but his throat felt like sandpaper.

This pissed him off even more. The smoke made him cough. Face red, he tossed the cigarette away. Was it sweat he felt on his forehead amongst the raindrops?

He turned to head back into the office, only to see the young woman still standing there.

'Haven't you fucked off yet?'

'Soon,' the woman said again.

'Listen, you've ruined my "me time", so why don't you—'

Beaumont felt faint and reached out a hand to brace against the woman's shoulder.

'Are you all right?' the woman asked, without sympathy. 'You've gone terribly pale.'

'I . . .'

Beaumont had no strength in his legs. If he wasn't standing straight up with his hand on the woman's shoulder, he wouldn't have been able to stay on his feet. His mouth filled with water.

'Oh,' the young woman said. 'That can sometimes happen if one's constitution is weak. I think we can probably blame the cigarettes for that.'

She stepped away from Beaumont and eased him down to his knees. Beaumont threw up. He watched vomit and blood sluice away in the rain.

'What . . . did you do to me?'

'I can't claim all the credit, much as I would like to. My chemist is quite the genius, no?'

Beaumont didn't answer. He toppled forward, face first, into the pool of vomit and blood. His breathing was shallow, his pulse weak and irregular.

'I'll be on my way then,' the young woman said. 'Adieu.'

The last thing Beaumont saw was his extinguished cigarette, lying on the pavement, soaking up the rain.

The tall woman walked away while Beaumont was taking his final breaths on the pavement. When she had passed beyond the wide-angle lens of the security camera overlooking the entranceway's exterior, she removed her cream overcoat, turned it inside out in a practised move that took five seconds to complete, and slipped her arms into the fire-engine red coat it had become.

Half a block away her patent leather handbag was dumped into a rubbish bin. She dropped the blonde wig into another bin at the end of the street.

Five efficient wipes with a solvent-soaked cotton pad removed the pale make-up from her face. The blue contacts came out next. The clip-on earrings followed. Pads from her bra joined them. As did ones from her hips. She stopped and lifted one foot to her ass. She reached down and twisted off the detachable four-inch heel from her shoe. She did the same with her other foot.

Less than a minute after Beaumont's heart had stopped, she boarded the 1115 bus to Arlington looking like a different person.

TWO

The sky above Prague was a patchwork of blue and white. Thin clouds paled the late morning sun, but enough light fought through to shine from polished cars that lined the road and puddles that nestled along the kerbs. The twisting, cobbled side street was crammed with boutiques and cafés and townhouses. Passers-by were rare and traffic rarer still at this time of day.

A man sat alone at a small round metal table outside an artisan coffee shop. He was tall and wore a charcoal suit beneath a woollen overcoat, black, and black Oxford shoes. His dress shirt was white and his plain tie was burgundy. His black hair was longer than he often had it, at a few inches in length that brushed his ears and reached almost to his eyebrows if he did not push it back from his face. Two weeks without shaving had given him a dense beard that softened his jawline and disguised his cheekbones. The non-prescription glasses were plain and functional and further broke up the lines of his face to a shapeless, nondescript visage. His scarf was brown lamb's wool that was draped, but not tied, over his shoulders and tucked into the thigh-length overcoat, which was undone. He sipped a black Americano from a fine china cup that was as delicate as it was decorative. He made a conscious effort not to crush the little handle between thumb and forefinger.

His table was the central one of a line of three that lay on the pavement before the coffee shop, all painted white and chipped. The table to the left was occupied by two blonde women in fine clothing and jewellery, probably mother and daughter, discussing the weather and where to have lunch after they finished their morning shopping trip. Large bags surrounded their chairs. To the man's right, two older men with lined faces and grey hair talked about how best to ingratiate themselves to their new younger, hipper clients.

The man in the suit would have preferred to sit on one of the flanking tables so as not to be boxed in with no obstacle-laden exit, but the two men and two women had been there before his arrival and both pairs seemed as if they would be staying long after he left. He pretended not to notice that the blonde mother kept glancing his way.

His hands and ears were red and his breath misted before him, but he kept the buttons of his overcoat unfastened and his scarf untied and elected not to wear gloves or a hat, as was common for him.

He wore no hat because, when removed, it meant a greater chance of casting DNA-rich hair follicles into the air to be left behind in his wake. He wore nothing on his hands as even the highest quality gloves reduced dexterity, which he valued above all else. It was more effective to grip with bare fingers, as it was to gouge eyes and tear out throats. His coat was unfastened so a weapon hidden beneath it or within an inside pocket could be drawn without interruption. He was unarmed, as was typical; carrying a weapon was only useful when he had no choice but to employ it, and was a threat to his liberty the rest of the time. But he was a man of habit: an unfastened coat had the added benefits of being easy to discard if required; the scarf was untied so as not to provide an enemy with a ready-made noose, but could be whipped away fast so as to be employed as such by himself against assailants.

He had many enemies, acquired over a professional life that ensured for every foe he managed to remove, a new one would be standing by to take their place. He had learned that survival depended on attention to detail, no matter how small or trivial it might seem before it proved decisive. He had learned to never lower his guard, no matter how safe he might be. Those lessons had been carved into his flesh, ensuring he never forgot them.

He was waiting. Waiting accounted for more than half his work. He was patient and focused. He had to be. He was a man who took his time and valued perfection over speed. He only rushed when necessary, which was rare. There was a certain artistry to his work that he found, if not enjoyable, then satisfying.

He sipped from the little cup. The quality of the coffee was excellent, but not in proportion to the effort it took to hold the delicate cup without breaking it. A shame, but the coffee provided a reasonable excuse for his presence.

On the far side of the road, a narrow-fronted hotel sat between townhouses. A protruding awning and doorman were the only obvious signs of the hotel's existence. There were no fluttering flags or ostentatious trappings on display. The guests liked discretion and they liked privacy and were happy to pay the hotel's exaggerated rates to enjoy both.

The man in the suit was interested in one guest in particular. He was a member of the House of Sa'ad, the extended royal family of Saudi Arabia. He was one of the many princes, a decadent thirty-year-old who spent his family's wealth almost as fast as it could be created. If he were not limited by his father, the prince would no doubt bankrupt them within eighteen months.

Al-Waleed bin Saud toured the world on a permanent holiday, moving from city to city with his humble retinue of sixteen individuals. That retinue included two personal assistants, an accountant, a chef, a security detail of nine and three young women who were listed as interns but did nothing except shop and spend time alone with the prince. He stayed in the most expensive hotels, and only ones that could accommodate his particular requirements. Though he lived an extravagant, hedonistic lifestyle he tried to maintain the image of a respectable, devout, and proud Saudi. To maintain the illusion and to ensure no word of his habits reached his homeland, he shied away from hotels that were too large or too rigid in rules and regulations. He elected to stay where he could bribe staff and hire out a whole floor at a time, whether he needed the rooms or not, for the sole use of his retinue. And he preferred to stay at hotels that could provide suitable extras for the discerning guest, such as prostitutes and narcotics.

Though he embraced every Western decadence imaginable, Al-Waleed helped fund the activities of extremists and fundamentalists from Mali to Malaysia. Though pocket-change to the prince, these donations provided a significant percentage of the funding for several groups known to have committed atrocities and determined to commit more.

The prince was far from the only rich Saudi to support terrorism, but he was one of the most prolific. His donations were often paid in cash or jewellery, making them difficult to trace and even more difficult to intercept. Thus the decision had been taken to terminate his financial support once and for all.

The problem, as was the case for the wider issue of Saudi support for terrorism, was Western reliance on the kingdom's oil. The symbiosis could not be jeopardised. The House of Sa'ad would not tolerate the murder of one of their own any more than they would tolerate one of their princes risking the Western support the royal family needed to stay in power.

So, a compromise had been reached.

The prince was to die, but his death could not lead back to the CIA who orchestrated it nor to the House of Sa'ad who had no choice but to condone it.

Which was the reason Victor had been hired.

THREE

The psychological evaluation included within the dossier theorised that Al-Waleed's support for terrorism was a way of balancing out his excesses with his religious conscience. Victor cared little for such insight. He dealt in usable and exploitable facts. He cared about verified wheres and whens, not speculative hows and whys. The only judgement he trusted was his own.

The two guys to his right stood up and left, leaving much of their breakfast behind and unfinished, only to stop and stand a metre from their vacated table to continue their discussion. One slipped on sunglasses. The other squinted and held up a hand to shield his eyes from the direct sunlight. They interrupted Victor's line of sight to the hotel entrance.

He did not require a perfect view to know when the prince would show because no Rolls-Royce had pulled up outside to provide him with transportation. Hotel records supplied by Victor's employer showed the prince was planning on staying at least another three days. This was typical.

His itineraries over the last twelve months showed a mean duration of four nights for visits to European cities outside summer months. Last night, on arriving, Al-Waleed had partied hard into the early hours, drawing complaints from guests on the floor below. Victor did not expect to see him anytime soon. But he had to wait, just in case. Secondary data was no match for that collected himself.

Which was fine by him. The coffee was good, even if the china too delicate, and the sunshine was pleasant enough on his face to counteract the cold elsewhere. He had a newspaper before him, which he browsed but did not read, to help his cover. He was used to drawing little to no attention, and aside from the blonde woman's casual interest, this morning was no different. Hiding in plain sight was as necessary a skill as any he had acquired. The fewer people who noticed him the freer he was to act and the better his chances of a clean getaway in the aftermath.

He had performed a reconnoitre of the hotel prior to the prince's arrival. He had stayed for two nights in a suite on the same floor as the prince was now staying, and had used his time there to explore its halls and corridors, adding three-dimensional intelligence to the two-dimensional plans he had studied. He had memorised the faces and names and routines of staff members, the position of CCTV cameras, how long it took room service to deliver, how many times the employee would knock and how long they would leave a tray outside before removing the untouched food.

It was simple enough to act the part of a regular guest because, like Al-Waleed, he spent much of his life living in hotels. But whereas the prince moved from city to city out of boredom and a desire for new and ever more exciting experiences, Victor did so out of simple necessity. A moving target was a hard target.

The hotel had a lobby fitted with comfortable armchairs and sofas, but his prior presence there ruled out the lobby as a place to wait. At best, he would be recorded on CCTV cameras, and at worst a keen-eyed member of staff would note him. His study of the hotel had also eliminated it as a strike point, so although the danger of being noted was minimal, he would not go there. He took no risks he did not have to.

The two grey-haired men finished their conversation, shook hands and departed in opposite directions. A waiter collected the cash they had left to cover the bill and began gathering up plates.

Both blonde women had also departed by the time a silver Rolls-Royce pulled up outside the hotel. It was earlier than the CIA-supplied itinerary stated. No problem in itself, but it reinforced Victor's protocol of relying only on his own intelligence.

Three of the prince's security detail stepped out of the hotel entrance a moment later and approached the vehicle. They were all Saudis, dressed in a uniform of smart suits and sunglasses. They looked the part, but knew little about personal protection work beyond what could be squeezed into a two-week course. Still, they were a problem because they operated in groups of three, rotating every eight hours to provide Al-Waleed with continuous twenty-four-hour protection. They were armed too. The prince had diplomatic status and could bring whatever he wanted across borders, including guns.

The prince emerged after the bodyguards had performed a perfunctory check of the locale and climbed into the waiting Rolls. Al-Waleed was dressed in the traditional flowing robes favoured by Saudi men. He was average height and wide in the midriff. One of Al-Waleed's assistants followed. The bodyguards climbed in after him. The last man replaced the valet driver who had fetched the car.

The Rolls-Royce pulled away from the kerb and left the street.

Victor continued to wait. He stood only when the prince's accountant left the hotel about five minutes after Al-Waleed had gone. He was a tall, thin man in his fifties, with a shiny bald head and goatee beard trimmed to razor-straight edges. Like the rest of Al-Waleed's retinue the accountant was a Saudi. He was a friend of the prince's father, sent along to accompany the wayward son on his adventures and to make sure he did not overspend his allowance nor run up debts the father did not want to pay.

Al-Waleed held positions in several Saudi firms owned by the House of Sa'ad, but worked in title only. His lengthy holidays were described as business trips, yet he saw no clients and attended no meetings. Even if he wanted to play businessman, his father would never allow his unreliable son to damage the family's corporate interests. The accountant handled everything. The prince had no personal business ventures, finding such matters tedious; he preferred to occupy his time spending his huge allowance on whatever fun money could buy, and the support of terrorism.

Al-Waleed hated the accountant and what he represented and treated him with appalling disdain. Any task Al-Waleed felt was beneath him would be delegated to the accountant, often purely for the sport of humiliating the man. Thus it fell to him to buy drugs and hire call girls and arrange meetings with terrorist middlemen.

Such middlemen were a necessity, for known members of terrorist groups had good reason to be cautious about venturing out of cover in search of funds. Given the difficulty of hunting down the diverse and disparate terrorist groups, with new ones forever springing up from the ashes of those destroyed in an endless cycle, the war against terror had instead begun targeting their sources of income. Without money, bombs could not be made nor bullets purchased. It was prevention over cure. A philosophy Victor tried to live by himself.

One such middleman was due to arrive in Prague later that day. He was a Turkish banker named Ersin Caglayan who handled the bank accounts of several charities that siphoned funds to jihadi groups all over the Middle East. The prince had met with him a number of times in the past and would again while both were in the country.

Victor watched the accountant while he thought about the problem of killing the prince without the CIA being blamed in the process. Setting up his death to look like natural causes – a freak accident or a heart attack – was out because of the complexity both required on such a hard target. Al-Waleed moved around too much and had too many guards in the way for Victor to plan and exact such a death.

A simple solution, however, was to have Caglayan take the blame.

FOUR

The woman advertised her age as twenty-five, but was at least ten years older. The soft glow provided by the low-wattage lighting helped the lie by smoothing out the fine lines in her face, and generous make-up covered the dark bags beneath her eyes. Victor went along with the deception. Neither did he comment on the fact the photographs on her website must have undergone extensive retouching. There was no need to be impolite.

Still, she was an attractive woman with long dark hair and blue eyes full of life and ambition. She opened the front door to her second-floor apartment on Pařížská Street, off Wenceslas Square, wearing a silk robe and an enormous smile. Her teeth were bleached white and too straight and perfect to be her own.

She advertised herself as an escort. It was a soft, almost harmless-sounding word. Victor understood the need for it in the same way he understood why people like him called themselves mercenaries or shooters or hitmen. He only thought of himself as a professional killer. He had no need to soften his means of employment any more than he had his use of prostitutes.

She took his hand and led him inside without a word, gesturing him to go on into the lounge area while she closed the door behind him. Victor didn't like to give anyone his back, but he was playing the part of a typical client and did as she asked to preserve the illusion of normalcy. A significant part of his life was spent acting; even so, pretending he was just another regular guy while maintaining a permanent guard was a difficult balance to achieve. He never liked to increase his vulnerability if it could be avoided, but sometimes it was better to be a little more vulnerable in the moment to ensure continued survival outside of it. Now was one of those times.

He rubbed his hands together in a sign of nervousness and because they were cold from an afternoon spent following the prince's accountant around the city.

The woman's apartment was small but furnished with expensive pieces in a clean, modern style. It was so spartan he wondered if it served only as a place of business and she lived elsewhere, but bookshelves filled to capacity contradicted that assessment. Maybe she just liked the minimalist approach.

'You know my rate for the hour, yes?' the woman asked as she followed him into the lounge.

She spoke in English, but with a strong Czech accent. Her high heels clicked and clattered on the bare flooring. In them, she was as tall as he.

He had already turned to face her, positioning himself so

he was near to the same wall as the west-facing windows, at an acute angle so as not to be in the line of fire for a marksman across the street.

'Yes,' he answered.

'Then I'd like to see my gift now,' she said with a smile that made it seem as innocent a request as the way she phrased it.

'Of course.'

He withdrew his wallet and counted out crisp banknotes.

She approached and took them from his hand, still smiling, but the smile slipped away as she turned to count the money and put it out of sight on a bookcase between two hardback novels. Historical fiction, he noted.

'I take it you read all the rules,' she said without turning around. 'What's allowed and what's not.'

'I did.'

'That's good to know. I don't like having to repeat myself. It wastes our time.'

'I'm not here to waste time,' he said.

She turned around and regarded him in a different way, as if assessing his desires and perversions from the way he stood and the cut of his suit. Maybe it was a game she played with each client, having long grown used to what makes a man tick.

'What shall I call you?' she asked as she toyed with her hair.

Victor remained silent.

The woman said, 'You can tell me your name, honey. I won't tell anyone, I swear. Discretion is all part of the service, I assure you.'

Victor said, 'Honey will be fine.'

She tilted her head to one side. 'Is that what you want me to cry out in bed?'

'There's no need for you to pretend.'

She smiled. 'I don't think I'll need to with you, will I?'

He'd heard it all before, of course. It wasn't his first time paying for sex. It was sometimes necessary in a life where he could allow himself no real connection with anyone, but could not afford to be distracted by desire for too long. It was one impulse he could do little to control with will alone.

He smiled with her because that's what she expected him to do and he was playing the part of a regular client – a businessman cheating on his wife, maybe, or a politician living out a sordid cliché of a personal life – not a professional killer who used hookers because he couldn't risk a relationship, or even a friendship. Any personal connection created a gap in his defences and at the same time put that person at risk from those who meant Victor harm. The last time someone had wanted to get close to him he had convinced them the feeling was not mutual.

'Aren't you going to offer me a drink?'

He gestured to a small table where a lead crystal decanter sat on a solid silver tray; Scotch, judging by the pale yellow colour of the liquid.

'No,' she said in return. 'I'm afraid that whisky was a present from a dear client. It would be rude to share it with another. I'm sure you can understand that.'

He nodded.

'What do you like?' she asked, and he could feel the

expectation of her words. She wanted to see if she was right in her previous assessment of him.

'I prefer to show, rather than tell.'

This seemed to catch her by surprise. 'That sounds ... promising.' She tapped her bottom lip with a long red nail. 'And there was I thinking you were going to be boring.'

'I can assure you I'm a painfully dull person.'

'I think I'll be the judge of that,' she said.

They stood in silence for a moment.

She gestured with her eyebrows, which had been plucked and drawn back on. 'Bathroom's that way.'

'Yes, of course,' Victor said. 'Clients need to shower first.'

'That's what my listing clearly states.'

'What if I told you I don't like showers?'

'Then I'd politely bid you farewell.'

'No refund?'

She smiled and said nothing.

'Do any clients refuse?' he asked.

'It happens on rare occasions. Most men accept my rules. Most behave as a gentleman should.'

'And what happens on these rare occasions?'

'I show them the door.'

Victor said, 'Even very dear clients?'

She carried on smiling, but did not answer. 'Help yourself to a robe.'

He nodded and circled through the lounge so he did not have to pass in a straight line across the window. His route brought him close to the woman. She brushed his arm as he walked by.

The bathroom was off the hallway. He stepped inside and

shut the door. He slid the little brass bar across to lock it. Not that such a mechanism had any strength to resist a forced entry, but he did not want the woman entering and interrupting what he had planned.

FIVE

Victor pulled the hanging string by the door to turn on the light. An extractor fan whirred into life as the fans got to speed and emitted a quiet hum. He reached behind the shower curtain to turn on the shower. Then he lowered the toilet lid and stood on it so he could reach the extractor fan high on the same wall as the bathroom's small window.

He took a cent coin from a trouser pocket and used it to unscrew the plastic protector from the face of the extractor fan. He felt the change in air pressure as the whirling blades sucked air from the bathroom and forced it outside. The blades were made of plastic and weak, but were spinning fast enough to split skin and maybe damage tendons. He reached into his inside jacket pocket and took out a ball-point pen. Its shell was made from aluminium.

He held it in a tight grip and pushed it between the blades. They came to an abrupt stop.

He heard clicks and creaks and a mechanical whine

before the sound stopped and resistance died with it. He removed the pen and the blades sat unmoving while he replaced the fan's face-plate and screws.

He gave it a couple of minutes for the room to steam up, then began undressing. He did so in a particular way, in a particular order to limit his vulnerability doing so. His balance and flexibility were both excellent, but bending or squatting and standing on one leg all put him at greater risk than sitting down. He first sat on the toilet lid to untie his shoes, perched on the edge, head over hips, ready to spring to his feet if necessary. He untied both shoes before removing them, to spend the least possible time wearing only one shoe. Running or fighting wearing one shoe would be a considerable hindrance, even without the fact Victor had no intention of dying in such an undignified manner. His socks followed because bare feet gripped surfaces far better than soft wool. The jacket and tie were next, which he stood up to remove, followed by his shirt, trousers and then underwear. He placed all the items in an easy-to-carry pile and left them on the toilet seat while he ran the taps to wash himself as requested.

When he had finished washing he turned off the shower and dried himself off on one of the several white towels hanging on a rail and wrapped it around his waist. He saw the rail could accommodate another two towels and tried not to imagine the previous two clients who had been here today before him. He slipped into a towelling robe but did not tie it.

The woman was waiting for Victor in the lounge when he stepped out of the bathroom.

'You take your time, don't you, honey?'

He shrugged and said, 'I think your extractor fan is broken. The bathroom's all steamed up.'

'Oh, that's annoying. Be a dear and open the window for me.'

He placed his folded clothes on an armchair in the hallway and returned to the bathroom and did as she asked.

He heard her say, 'Would you please excuse me for a second?'

'Of course,' Victor said.

He used the time to approach the lounge window, standing side on to the wall next to it and peering outside and over the balcony. He saw that there were no conceivable sniping nests from which a marksman could take a shot, so he allowed himself a few extra seconds to gaze outside at the city.

The view from the window showed a sky blanketed by cloud. No sun was visible. He could see an uneven cityscape of sloping rooftops of red tiles and tall chimneys. A scattering of snow lay across them, thicker on the west-facing slopes and patchier on those facing east. The buildings beneath had an understated beauty with their pale pastel-coloured walls and arched windows. Clock towers and spires poked at the grey sky above. For a pleasant moment he watched the swirling gentle spirals of white chimney smoke rise and dissipate, seeming to join the clouds as though they linked Earth to the heavens. He heard the woman return and turned away from the soothing fantasy.

'Do you like the city?' the woman asked him.

'Yes,' he said, speaking the truth, then added, 'It's my first time here,' which was a lie.

Of all his skills, lying was the one he employed with the most frequency; he spoke more often in lies than truth, existing in a constant state of pretending to be someone he was not – a businessman, a tourist, a nobody. Always unre-markable, always unworthy of attention. It had become second nature to do so because the part he played least of all was himself.

No one saw that side of him other than his victims and the reflection in the mirror of a face that was no longer his.

She stepped closer to him and untied her robe, slipping out of it in an effortless motion that would have been ele-gant if Victor could have ignored the fact she had performed the move countless times. She stood before him in a white bodice. He looked her over as she expected him to.

She parted his robe and eased it off his shoulders. She spent a long time looking at his body and the many scars and marks that covered his skin. He was used to the stares and the questions that followed. He had been cut and burned and shot and torn and bitten and more. He had whole tales memorised for every one of them, explaining away the more prominent scars as the result of a car crash and the lesser ones as sports injuries; if the person enquir-ing knew a scar caused by a bullet when they saw it, he had war stories from a military career that was different to his own.

But when the woman had finished examining him and her gaze returned to his, she did not ask a single question. Which was as rare as it was unexpected. Instead, she said to him:

'I knew that you weren't boring.'

SIX

The tailor had been cutting suits since the Second World War. He told Victor as much while he waited in the fitting room of the low-ceilinged atelier. The establishment was small but stylish, with a long waiting list of elite clientele. It was owned and run by a single tailor who was so short he had to stand on a rickety three-legged stool to measure Victor's shoulders.

'I was a boy cutting fabric for Nazi officers,' the tailor explained, looking as though he might fall off the stool to his death at any moment. 'Can you imagine?'

Victor said, 'I'm not sure I can.'

The tailor snorted. Not quite a laugh, not quite a huff. It sounded to Victor that the man had a chest infection or some persistent pulmonary problem. The tailor did not seem to be any less energetic as a result.

'I smoke sixty a day,' he'd bragged. 'And I've outlived all my boyhood friends who did not.'

Victor offered a hand to help the man off the stool, but he batted it away with palpable disdain and dropped down with a creak of floorboards, or maybe knees.

His fingers were stained by the lifetime of smoking he boasted of. Framed black-and-white photographs adorned the walls of the atelier. They showed the old tailor with clients, maybe even celebrities from yesteryear Victor didn't recognise. In every one the tailor, like his clients, was smoking. One even showed him standing among tobacco plants in some tropical plantation.

The tailor wore a three-piece stone-brown suit complete with pocket square and pocket watch. His glasses were bifocals with thick lenses and the Cuban heels gave him enough height for the top of his shiny scalp to hit five feet if he stood straight-backed, which he did not.

He fetched the bespoke suit from a back room and hung it up on a wheeled rail for Victor to try on.

'I don't understand your reasoning, my boy. You already have a charcoal suit. Off the rack, obviously, but of decent enough quality to avoid outright humiliation. Why pay for another?'

'Do you not want my business?' Victor asked.

'I want you to look your best,' the tailor countered. 'Is that so hard to comprehend? Is your brain not in proportion to your height?'

Victor couldn't help but like the man.

'Charcoal is so unadventurous,' the tailor said with a tut. 'It is but the sickly cousin of black. A pauper to be ignored, not a gentleman to be envied. Black is a colour. Charcoal is a shade.'

'Black is the absence of colour.'

The tailor acted as though he hadn't heard him. 'What about it? Black would be more striking. You'll look good in black.'

'Everyone looks good in black,' Victor said.

The tailor looked hopeful. 'Is that a yes?'

Victor shook his head. 'I only wear black to a funeral.'

The tailor did his best not to sigh. He looked pained. His face was a spiderweb of deep wrinkles. 'But of course. Why would you wear black at any other time? Why would anyone want to look his best? What kind of world is it when someone elects to wear what suits him less? What about a nice navy? It'll be more sophisticated, but still subtle.'

Victor unhooked the jacket and slipped his arms into the sleeves. He said nothing.

The tailor said, 'I wish you had at least gone for a pin-stripe or a colourful lining.'

Suits were important to Victor. He wore one more often than not. A suit gave him an air of authority and respect. In a suit he looked like a man of no small importance while blending in to the masses of office workers, lawyers and bankers found in almost every major city. A suit was ideal camouflage for the urban terrain where he both lived and worked.

Victor buttoned up the jacket and rolled his shoulders.

'It's perfect,' he said, feeling the extra room he had asked for, which made it easier to hide a gun, to fight or climb or run for his life.

The old tailor's eyebrows rose and arched and a curved

fence of closely spaced grooves deepened across his forehead. He wrinkled his nose and blew air out of pursed lips. He did not approve.

'No, no, no,' he said. 'That won't do at all. We need to fix this. It's terrible. The fit is nothing short of an abomination. I'm ashamed of myself.'

'I like it the way it is. This is exactly what I asked for.'

'Then I need to saw open your skull and check you have a brain, my boy. Look here. You don't need all this room across the chest. Are you planning on getting fat? Are you planning on growing breasts?'

Victor shook his head.

The tailor chewed his bottom lip. He looked stressed. Sweat beaded on his forehead. 'Let me bring it in a smidgen. It'll look all the sharper. Please? I can't let you walk the streets like this.'

'I prefer it the way it is,' Victor replied. 'You've done an excellent job.'

'I've embarrassed my name and the name of my father. How about a tiny tuck?' He held a finger and thumb a few millimetres apart. 'Just a little? I promise it will still allow you room to breathe. For me. Please.'

'This is comfortable.'

'*Comfortable?* That's a filthy word if ever I heard one. Barbaric even. If all we cared about was being comfortable then we would be a huge hideous mass of synthetic materials, shapeless and indistinguishable from one another. Sir, if you came in here for comfort then you must have misread the sign above my door. I do not sell comfort here. I sell suits. I sell style.'

Victor remained silent.

'Fine,' the tailor said with a heavy exhale. 'I give up. We'll do it your way and you can walk out of here knowing I shall live my last years in a state of unhappiness and shame.'

'I'm glad we can agree.'

The tailor removed a solid silver cigarette case from his inside jacket pocket and thumbed it open. He held it towards Victor, who shook his head.

'A gentleman should smoke,' the tailor said as he took out a cigarette for himself. He didn't light it. 'And a man who appreciates a tailored suit *needs* to smoke. He must know his tobacco like he knows his fabrics.' The tailor held the unlit cigarette beneath his nostrils and inhaled. 'Suits are my love, but tobacco is my passion.'

'I quit,' Victor said.

'Then start again,' the tailor implored. 'Before it's too late. But only the best. Good cigarettes are like a good suit. Utterly distinct and separate from the mass-produced garbage so commonplace today. No two varieties of cigarette, if made correctly, are the same. They have a range of flavours and feels that titillate the palate. Like a fine wine, almost.'

'Most wine tastes like vinegar to me.'

The tailor looked at him with disgust. 'Your barbarism knows no bounds.'

Victor nodded. The tailor helped him out of the jacket. 'I'm just going to tidy up these threads and the suit will be ready to collect this afternoon. Or you can wait here and I'll do it now. Your choice.'

'I'll wait, if it's all the same to you.'

The tailor shrugged. 'Child, it makes no difference to me what you do. Would you like a drink? Or something to read? I'll be about twenty minutes. I'm assuming a barbarian such as yourself can actually read? I'm probably giving you too much credit, aren't I?'

He asked as though he expected an answer.

'I'll entertain myself,' Victor said. 'Take your time, please.'

The old man nodded and went to leave. He stopped and turned around. 'And a haircut and shave wouldn't kill you ...'

He trailed off, muttering under his breath as he closed the door behind him.

Alone in the measuring room, surrounded by mannequins, hangers and fabrics, Victor stood still, listening to the quieting footsteps of the old tailor as he shuffled away. A moment later, another door clicked open and then closed again. Victor pictured the tailor settling into a comfortable chair to make the final adjustments to the charcoal suit.

He had twenty minutes.

Victor reached into a trouser pocket and withdrew a mini plastic bottle labelled as containing antibacterial hand gel. There was a small amount of ethanol inside, for the appropriate smell, but the bottle contained clear silicone gel. The consistency wasn't quite the same as alcohol gel, but it was similar enough to pass a cursory examination. Not even an airport security guard had ever done more than sniff the bottle, let alone apply some and compare it to a genuine product.

He squeezed a blob of silicone gel into his palm and spent

two minutes rubbing it over his hands, paying particular attention to his fingertips and palms. The gel was cool and oily. It took a further minute to dry. His hands were now coated in a waterproof barrier, invisible to the naked eye, which would prevent the oil from his skin being left behind on any surfaces he came into contact with. No oil meant no fingerprints.

Three minutes to apply the gel meant seventeen remaining.

He replaced the bottle in his pocket and approached the room's only window. The sash window was open a crack and the semi-transparent white drapes rippled in the breeze. Victor pushed them to one side and heaved open the window until it was high enough for him to bend over and step through on to the balcony outside.

SEVEN

The balcony was narrow and overlooked an alleyway four metres below that ran through the centre of the block. It was clean and tidy with no discarded refuse. Everything had been placed by diligent boutique owners and store workers in bins or boxes. The sounds of the city were muted and quiet. Victor stepped up on to the black iron railing that surrounded the balcony and used a palm to brace against the brickwork while he found his balance.

He extended his arms above his head. The balcony above was just out of reach of his fingertips. He lowered himself into a half-squat, then leapt straight up, catching hold of cold masonry with eight fingertips because it was too high to also catch with his thumbs. Without them, he lost 40 per cent of the strength of his forearms, but he pulled himself up with the remaining 60.

When his head had cleared the lip of the balcony, he released his left hand and shot it up to grab hold of one of the iron bars. He then did the same with his right hand and heaved himself up enough to get a foot on to the balcony edge. He brushed down his suit to get rid of dust and pollution.

The balcony was the same as that of the tailor's below, but the window led to a private residence. Victor ducked down so as to reduce the chances of being seen by the two figures – a naked man and woman – moving about inside. They were paying too much attention to one another to care about what might be happening outside the window.

He waited anyway, because he still had more than fifteen minutes before the old tailor returned with his finished suit.

Nine minutes later the two figures in the apartment stumbled from the lounge and disappeared into a bedroom. Victor sidestepped to the far edge of the balcony. A metre further along the exterior wall was another window. This one was open a few inches.

Victor sat on the balcony railing and pivoted round. With one hand holding on to the railing he stretched out the other arm until he could grip the windowpane and slide it higher to create a larger opening. When it was high enough to fit through, he gripped the sill in one hand, released the railing, and swung himself across. He pulled himself up and into the bathroom.

Six minutes left. It was going to be tight.

The bathroom was humid from the shower. The floor was wet in places. Victor avoided the puddles and footprints and eased the door open.

He could hear grunts and the knocking of a headboard against a wall. Outside the bathroom door he found a pile of clothes on the same armchair he had used the previous afternoon.

In a pocket of a suit jacket he found the accountant's smartphone.

It was locked, as expected, but Victor removed the SIM card and inserted it into a credit-card-sized scanner attached to a second-hand phone he had bought for cash that morning. He activated the app and waited while the scanner extracted all of the data from the SIM and copied it on to the empty SIM in his phone. The scanner had been supplied by Muir, his CIA handler.

In his freelance days he had worked with a range of brokers, most of whom he never met or learned their identity. It had been rare to work directly with a client. Both they and Victor preferred to use professional intermediaries who understood discretion and knew how to put the right people on the right job. At other times they would be associates of the client in some capacity. They might be individual free agents or members of intelligence agencies or executives of private security firms or sometimes board members of multinational corporations with a cutesy brand image and beyond-ruthless business practices. In his earlier days he had worked for brokers and clients whom he knew, as they in return knew him, at least as well as anyone could. For years he had avoided any personal connection with his work, and it had helped keep him alive far longer than he had believed he would remain breathing. In recent times the majority of his work had come from individuals within the CIA, even though the wider organisation maintained a termination order for him. The arrangement was a good one, and not only for the intermittent donations to his bank account. His handlers kept him off the radar of the rest of the agency. That alone was worth maintaining the relationship. The jobs he received were infrequent and often dangerous, but that danger was offset by the lack of CIA contractors hunting him. They also paid well.

It was as good a business relationship as Victor could hope to have with anyone.

After a short pause the screen changed to denote the new SIM was now a clone of the accountant's.

One of the perks of working for the CIA was access to such technology.

He removed the accountant's SIM from the scanner and replaced it inside the smartphone he had taken it from. He slipped it back into the same pocket.

Four minutes remaining, if the tailor wasn't faster than expected with the adjustments.

Victor crossed the lounge to the bookshelf and found cash placed between two historical fiction hardbacks.

He put some extra cash between the books to cover the cost of the broken extraction fan and exited the apartment the way he had come in. It sounded as if the accountant was almost finished.

Lowering himself out of the window, he inched along the sill until he could stretch one hand across to grab hold of the balcony railing while he supported his weight with the other.

Less than a minute after his return to the fitting room the door opened and the old tailor came in.

'All done,' the tailor said as he hung up the suit. 'And

when I say all done what I really mean is the abomination is complete.'

Victor said, 'I'll need a tie as well.'

'Let me guess,' the tailor said with an exaggerated sigh, 'something plain? Nothing with even the remotest hint of style? Something insufferably boring?'

Victor raised an eyebrow. 'How did you know?'

EIGHT

Muir had supplied a lot of intelligence regarding Al-Waleed and the accountant, but what the CIA hadn't been able to supply was the time and place of the meeting with the Turkish banker, Caglayan. That wouldn't be arranged until the day of the meet, and with only a short amount of warning. The CIA, via the NSA, were more than capable of intercepting phone calls or emails or any other method of electronic communication, but Caglayan trusted no one, least of all a spoilt Saudi prince who donated money to terrorists to ease his conscience. The Turk would use a prepaid mobile phone purchased that day to contact the accountant, and insisted the accountant did the same. Then, only Caglayan and Al-Waleed himself would be present to make the drop off. The Turk would not tolerate the presence of the prince's retinue.

It was almost impossible to intercept such communications, which was why Victor had needed to clone the accountant's new SIM card. When Caglayan sent a message to the accountant stating the time and location for the meeting, Victor received the same message.

The dossier Muir had supplied on Caglayan contained almost as much intel as the one on the prince. Most of it was as inconsequential, but the salient facts were that the Turk was a sadistic, vengeful man suspected of the torture and murder of rivals and betrayers. He was the type who would respond to an attempt on his life with extreme violence. When both Caglayan and Al-Waleed were found dead with all the forensic evidence suggesting they had shot one another, the narrative would suggest a deal-gone-wrong between a terrorist sponsor and terrorist middleman. Muir was more than happy for an individual as unpleasant as Caglayan to be collateral damage in the prince's assassination.

The meeting was to take place in the basement of a disused office building on the corner of a city block that was in the process of regeneration. The ugly decades-old concrete from the middle of the last century was being torn down and replaced with a sleeker, modern construction. The basement was accessible through the main building or via a side entrance that comprised a wooden gate and through it a doorway.

Victor approached the gate at nine p.m. as instructed in the original message. With little warning, he had not been able to conduct a proper reconnoitre of the area or plan an attack strategy. He would have to improvise.

The street outside the basement entrance was wide and empty. On the opposite side of the road was the rear of a large office building. It was a modern structure, five storeys high, with windows that did not open. Victor liked that. There would be no marksmen sitting out of sight behind high-powered rifles. But maybe someone was waiting on the roof. Victor could see no one, but the sky above was dark and the street below was well lit by street lamps. A sniper on the roof would be all but invisible.

Victor, meanwhile, would be exposed and vulnerable, though only for a short time, because the basement entrance was ten metres from an intersection. But it was still enough time for someone with a rifle to spot him, take aim, and shoot before he made it into the safety of the building.

The taxi arrived on time, pulling up outside the basement entrance as per his specific instructions. He was pleased to see the firm had sent a big people carrier – again as he had asked.

He turned the corner on to the street after a ten-count, imagining if there was a sniper overlooking they would have already settled behind their scope, reticle hovering over the taxi, ready to shoot whomever climbed out of the sliding doors.

Victor walked fast because he knew he would pass through the scope's magnified viewfinder. His appearance would surprise any sniper, who would have to re-aim, by which time he would be through the door and out of sight.

The wood was old and warped and covered with cracked and flaking paint, but had a new magnetic locking mechanism activated with a keycard. The door had been left ajar.

He pushed it open and stepped through. No shot sounded. No searing pain consumed him.

Either the deception had worked, or there was no sniper to deceive. Prevention over cure.

On the far side of the entrance was an antechamber with a single flight of metal steps leading down to basement level and a trade elevator to lift heavy goods. A single light flickered on a moment after the door opened. He saw the motion detector high on one wall. The light fixture was hidden behind a bulbous shade that looked as ugly as it was out of place. The walls were breeze blocks covered in white gloss that had dirtied to almost grey. They looked as though they had never been cleaned. The ceiling soared above Victor's head. A card reader to unlock the door glowed green. Insulated wires and pipes created a maze on the wall to his right, leading to a row of enclosed circuit breakers.

The taxi would leave after a few minutes when it was obvious the fare was a no-show. He felt guilty for wasting the driver's time.

The steps were steep and narrow. Wooden handrails ran on either side of them, the varnish worn down in places to bare wood. At the bottom of the steps the entrance chamber narrowed and then opened out into a room that served as a junction for the two halves of the basement. A narrow-fronted elevator provided access to the main offices above ground. Adjacent to it was an even narrower staircase leading to the upper floors. Under the stairs was a door plastered with labels and signs warning of the danger of electrocution on the other side. Much of the floor was taken up with a haphazard pile of unused pallets, broken chairs and unwanted tables. On the far side he could see a door with fat copper pipes snaking into the wall next to it. No sign denoted the purpose of the room beyond, but Victor pictured a massive gas boiler system.

A set of glass double doors led to an area where the renovation work had been completed. A floor plan had been tacked to the left-hand door. He spent a moment memorising the image, noting the uneven walls and protrusions that created odd angles and areas that could be used as cover and concealment if necessary. The beige carpeting in the refurbished room was new and unmarked. Victor could detect the scent of fresh paint and cleaning chemicals. The air tasted metallic.

The main office space comprised two areas of similar size arranged in a rough L-shape. Half a dozen large desks were dotted about the first area, with room for maybe twice that number. There was also a small kitchenette, complete with sink, cupboards, refrigerator and coffee machine. A leather sofa sat before a coffee table nearby. Unlike the rest of the furnishings, the sofa appeared to have been there forever. The leather was worn and frayed, but still looked comfortable. Victor imagined stressed workers slumping on it in exasperation or taking a nap while everyone else was out to lunch. For all the dangers of his profession, being chained to a desk five days a week seemed a far worse kind of hell. It might prove even more dangerous too – at least he knew he would not miss when he pushed the muzzle of a pistol against his temple to end the misery.

No sign of Caglayan. No sign of the prince.

Victor backtracked and entered the second half of the basement, accessible through the other set of double doors. This half was in the process of being renovated. No floor plan had been fixed to the wall to show the layout, because that layout had yet to be finished. On the other side of the open doors were neat piles of building materials – cement, tools, piping, shelves and boxes of screws and nails. Opposite, leaning against one wall of an adjoining ante-chamber, was a huge mound of waste material that had been stripped out from the depths of the basement – insu-lation, dry wall, ceiling tiles and rolls of soiled carpet. Plastic hazard tape had been stretched across the pile and tied to pipes on either side to keep the whole lot from falling over.

The antechamber opened out to a corner of the basement with no light fixtures. It was illuminated by a free-standing lamp that struggled to push back the gloom. The area had no floor in places, the dark holes marked off by hazard tape, the weak light failing to reach the bottom of the foun-dations below. A cold draught found Victor's ankles. Yellow-painted stepladders leaned against one wall next to a fire escape on the other side of the chequerboard floor.

Fluorescent strip lights ran along the ceiling of the central corridor, flickering into life as soon as Victor crept through the opening. Pipes and cables were fixed to the ceiling above them. The corridor was about three metres wide and twenty long, with several closed and open doors and doorways, some with plastic sheeting hanging before them to limit the transfer of dust and fumes, leading off to unused rooms yet to be furnished or areas that were little more than con-struction sites.

The corridor opened out on to a large area in a partial state of construction. As with the area at the other end of the antechamber there were no permanent light fixtures here. More free-standing lamps were spread out to light the space in a dim white glow. Victor's shadow stretched out far behind him.

Holes in the floor were marked with tape. In some places plastic barriers provided temporary walls around areas that had no flooring at all. Pillars held up the ceiling, some covered with new dividing walls. Steel pipes and copper pipes ran from ceiling to floor in places. Replacement piping was stacked and laid out on the floor nearby, ready to be used to reroute the existing systems to free up more space. Plastic sheeting suspended from girders on the ceiling sealed off areas by their level of renovation.

No Caglayan or Al-Waleed here either. The whole basement was empty. Victor drew his handgun – an FN Five-seven – because he knew he'd walked straight into a trap.

A second later, the lights went out.

NINE

Victor was moving before the assassin appeared, knowing he was exposed and vulnerable to multiple points of entry. He threw himself to the floor as a shape moved in his peripheral vision, silhouetted by ambient light shining through the high windows. Average height, but slim and lithe and female.

He had no time to consider this uncommonality because suppressed automatic fire echoed as the shape swept a submachine gun his way.

A spray of bullets cracked masonry and pinged off steel pillars. The burst was short and controlled – a snapshot at his diving form, halted as soon as he had made it into cover.

He waited a beat to test the assassin's intentions and to take a sample of her resolve. Would she hurry to catch him out while he was prone, or wait until he showed himself again?

The second option proved to be correct as he heard no

footsteps. This enemy was patient – not one to act in haste and leave herself vulnerable.

In the darkness he had seen little other than her outline, but it had been enough to note she wore no thermal-imaging goggles.

He edged towards where she had appeared, creeping on his stomach. The floor was uneven. The concrete was cold. He detected the quiet crackle of plastic, his own exhales and the rustle of his clothes and scrape of his shoes on the floor. So close to the floor the near darkness hid him well but limited his line of sight. Victor rose on to one knee so he could see beyond the clusters of pipes and pillars and hanging wires to view the assassin's previous firing point. Had she moved too or remained in cover? If she was good, she would have moved. She would know no position to be perfect, to be impregnable.

Victor swept with the gun, seeking a route the assassin might have taken to another firing position. He saw a wall of vertical pipes, and a scatter of sacks and crates that would have provided spots of cover between there and the original position. Victor would have taken that route, settling behind the pipes and finding a gap through which to fire.

He dropped just as rounds burned through the air above him.

He raised his gun to fire blind – not to hit, because he did not believe any measure of chance could direct a blind shot across twenty metres and send it between dense pipes capable of causing ricochets, but to convince the shooter he had such delusions.

In his head, Victor kept track of the rounds fired – one, then three, five – fourteen remaining in the magazine, with one in the chamber. Losing track meant running out of ammunition at the worst possible moment. People died that way. Victor knew this because he had made sure they did.

Then, after he had used up half the FN's magazine to cement the deception, he leapt up, sprinted, dodged around the pillars, heading left, then right, taking a short zigzag until he had covered the empty ground, his heart rate soaring to send blood to his pumping limbs. Rounds chased him, slicing off wood and cutting through low-hanging cables as he ducked below them, but the pillars and darkness combined for near-perfect cover.

Victor turned and braced against the pillar, eyes fixed along the FN's sights at the area to which the assassin had withdrawn. If she retreated Victor would spot her, but if she edged sideways, she could remain unseen in the crowd of crates and pipes and other obstacles. The pillars there provided a great deal of protection. Victor's gaze turned to every swirling cloud of dust or echoing noise.

Rounds pinged off the pillar before him. He fought the instinct to duck or back away, eyes searching the darkness for the light or rippling gases from the suppressor.

Plastic sheeting shredded next to Victor's arm. He twisted and backed away, responding to the distant muzzle flashes with shots of his own. A round sparked off a pillar and ricocheted through the shoulder pad of his jacket. He dropped low behind an unfinished wall to reload the pistol with his second magazine.

He rose up a fraction, still squatting low, and tried to locate his attacker. She wore black attire, which meant she was almost indistinguishable from the darkness behind her. Utilising the protection of the low wall, he fired a spread of rounds, spent cartridges bouncing and clinking off the wall, and dropped back behind its cover. The figure in black fired in return, the sub-machine gun's suppressor reducing its sound and flash. Rounds sliced the air above Victor's shoulder. He popped up to fire back, not risking staying up to get a good aim, but the missed shots struck near enough to persuade the assassin to retreat into better cover herself.

She fired as she moved, the burst of rounds hitting the unfinished wall protecting Victor. He used an arm to shield his eyes as dust swirled above his head and fragments of concrete rained down over him.

Another burst followed, and another, continuing the destruction, disintegrating concrete in a relentless barrage. When it stopped, Victor was covered in a layer of dust and rubble. He held his breath, unwilling to breathe – then the inevitable cough or sneeze would follow and give away his exact position.

He swept dust from his face and inched along the floor, on his back, moving in a straight line to maintain the concealment for as long as possible.

His body responded to danger like anyone else's. Hormones were released. Instincts kicked in. Ancient man only needed to run away or stand his ground. Physiological responses prepared him for this. For Victor it was more complicated than that.

He breathed, deep and slow, filling his lungs with air

between each deliberate exhale. The controlled breathing fought the autonomic nervous system, counteracting the adrenaline in his blood that sought to boost his heart rate to better supply his muscles with the oxygen and energy needed for effective fight or flight. The problem with the system was a high heart rate meant a reduction in fine motor skills. Ancient man didn't need those to flee from a sabre-toothed tiger or pummel a rival. Ancient man had no cars to hotwire or locks to pick and guns to aim.

A round punched a hole in a nearby barrel and diesel trickled out. Victor cupped his hand beneath the flow. He smeared it over his face and arms and any area of exposed pale skin. It darkened him, but only a little, and the slick coating caught the light and made him more visible – at least until he gathered up handfuls of ash and dust to throw over the diesel. It was far from perfect camouflage, but it might take his enemy a second longer to spot him and that was all the time he would need.

He backed off until he reached one of the exterior walls and headed down the connecting corridor, intending to circle around and flank the woman. The corridor was narrow with awkward obstacles of rubble and an uneven cement floor covered in a layer of dirt and junk before it opened into a large room. Gleaming galvanised steel pillars supported the ceiling above Victor. Crates and pallets of building materials were piled in neat stacks or strewn in equal proportion. Spilled oil shone in the dim light, bright on sections of piping and uneven surfaces. He stalked, fast but controlled, rounding the obstacles and ducking low-hanging wires bowed by their own weight.

When he reached the previous area, he crept forward into the darkness and the shafts of ambient city light bisecting it. Dust and mould spores swirled through the light, not drifting in lazy patterns as they would if they had not been recently disturbed by a passing figure interrupting the flow of air.

His enemy was near.

He glimpsed a ripple of black in the darkness and lowered himself to one knee, waiting and listening. The ripple became a blur and he tracked ahead of it with the gun's iron sights, but not squeezing the trigger, unwilling to give away his position on a shot that had only a small chance of hitting its mark.

He moved, fast and low, while the assassin ducked back into cover. When she reappeared, she had moved too and they exchanged fire, gunshots loud and echoing despite the suppressors, bullets clanging and clattering off metal and thumping into masonry. A ricochet made Victor back off. He turned side-on to reduce the width of his profile and reloaded the FN, slipping the three-quarters-empty mag into a pocket, not wanting to discard the few remaining rounds any more than he wanted his enemy to hear the magazine clattering on the ground.

The assassin had no such qualms. It was the second time Victor had heard her reload. He doubted the woman had brought more than three magazines. Ninety rounds was a lot of ammunition to carry just to kill one man. Would the pressure of knowing she had used up two-thirds of her ammunition coerce her into doing something rash?

It did.

She left the cover of some crates and darted closer to a wall of pipes between them. Victor squeezed off a shot, but the woman was weaving fast and slid the last few metres.

Less distance and fewer obstacles meant a better chance of a hit for both of them, but the assassin's fully automatic capabilities gave her the advantage.

She waited until Victor appeared again and let loose with a burst that rattled the metal around him. Sparks and bullet shrapnel struck his arm and shoulder. He dropped down again, no time to target a shot without risking a skull full of lead, but he saw enough of the assassin's position to plan his next move.

Victor shuffled along until he was at the edge of a tall pile of sacks of cement, creeping around them to come at the woman's flank. He popped out of cover and squeezed off a couple of fast shots that missed, but gained his enemy's attention.

She didn't return fire now the angle was tight – eager not to waste her remaining rounds – but Victor knew the angle could be lessened by the shooter moving parallel along the wall of pipes.

He waited, picturing the assassin doing what he would do. This time when Victor edged out of cover he did so in a crouch, because the protection provided to the assassin by the pipes did not extend to her shins and feet at this end.

She realised her exposure and was moving away an instant before Victor opened fire.

He jumped up to track her, but she had already made it into cover and was turning his way. She was as good at predicting his actions as he was hers.

He had lost the element of surprise and given himself away at the same time to a better-armed opponent.

Now he was exposed and vulnerable and if he failed to out-manoeuvre her he was as good as dead because he was never going to outshoot her. He ducked back into cover and backed off. When he had moved what he judged to be far enough, he rolled on to his front and rose on to one knee, head low.

And exploded into a sprint.

Automatic gunfire echoed through the building as he dashed between pillars, metal sparking behind him, the air hot with lead as he swerved and ran, fast and unpredictable, difficult to hit, half-unseen due to the darkness, shielded by the pillars.

When he had reached the end of their line, Victor threw himself to the ground and slid on the cement for the final metres, tearing his suit, grazing his elbows and knees, but reaching a doorway and, beyond it, the city.

But he didn't escape.

TEN

Instead, he waited a second, rose, and using the doorframe as cover, adopted a firing position. His pursuer was a phantom – blurring darkness against darkness – swift and noiseless, but was lured into believing Victor was fleeing and she was pursuing; the attacker, in control.

He shot her with his last two rounds, the bullets striking her in the chest for a double tap.

She contorted and dropped, the gun falling from her hand. It clattered on the hard floor.

He approached. Cautious, despite what had to be fatal wounds, but without delay. He wanted answers before she died. She lay on her back, her head, arms and torso still and unmoving while her legs writhed. He could hear pained breaths that were machine-gun rapid. Her right hand was pressed over the twin holes in her chest.

'Who are you working for?'

She didn't answer. She groaned and tried to angle her

head to see him. He saw the tears glistening in her eyes. The bone structure of her face was prominent – defined jawline and cheekbones – without looking unhealthy. He wasn't sure of her ethnicity from appearances alone. Her skin was only a little darker than his, and he was pale, but he detected a hint of Persian in her facial features: arching eyebrows, full lips and large eyes. Those eyes were as dark as his, and her hair even darker.

'Caglayan?' he asked. 'The prince?'

She had an athlete's body, slim but strong. She had been raised well. The good nutrition showed in her height and shoulders.

Victor said, 'If you don't tell me, I'll make the pain worse.'

She didn't speak. Her rapid breathing grew louder as he neared.

'A lot worse,' he added. 'At this moment you might think that's impossible, but you should believe me when I say there can always be more. If you tell me everything I want to know then instead I can make it all go away. No more pain. No more suffering.'

'Okay,' she spat between breaths and he stopped. 'I'll tell you.'

'I'm waiting.'

'Please,' she said, 'I'm just a shooter.'

'Trust me when I say that you don't want me to become impatient.'

Victor took another step, now close enough to see there was no blood seeping out between the fingers of her right hand.

He couldn't see the other hand.

He was moving before that hand snapped up, the dim light catching the hard lines of a small backup pistol.

She shot at him as he ran, the barks of each unsuppressed shot loud and echoing, the muzzle flashes illuminating his surroundings in a strobe of bright yellow light.

He made it into cover and the shooting stopped. He heard her climb to her feet, now recovered from the winding impact of blunt force trauma caused by his two bullets striking an armoured vest.

It had been a stupid mistake to have fallen for the same trick he had used on her, lured into believing he had been in control. Underestimating an opponent was something he should never do. He withdrew a folding knife and opened the blade. Not much use against a gun, but it was better than nothing at all.

He heard her approaching footsteps.

'You're out,' she called. 'I saw the bare metal of the gun barrel. The slide was back. You would have reloaded if you could.'

He didn't respond. He concentrated on plotting his escape route and the odds of her hitting a fast-moving target in the dark with an inaccurate backup weapon.

Then he dismissed running for it because he heard the scrape of metal as she retrieved her primary weapon from the floor. She may be low on rounds but all she would need was a single burst.

'You're lucky that cab went by when it did,' the assassin said. 'Otherwise you would have taken a seven-six-two in the back.'

Victor said, 'There's no such thing as luck.'

'Regardless, you're out of it,' she said. 'Now, we're going to switch roles. You're going to answer my questions.'

Victor was a little surprised because he thought she only wanted to kill him. If she wanted to interrogate him, that gave him options.

'So let's go grab a coffee and talk. I could use an espresso.'

She laughed. It echoed. 'It's a bit late for caffeine. Besides, I don't think I want to date you.'

'Your loss,' he said. 'I'm a riot.'

'I like that you can keep your sense of humour at a time like this, but I'm afraid to say it's not going to change the fact that I'm the only one who will be walking out of here.'

He heard the sound of metal on metal as she reloaded her primary weapon, followed by her approaching footsteps. He pictured her sidestepping to get a line of sight because those footsteps scraped a little. It was no surprise that she was keeping her distance and wouldn't round the corner close enough for him to attack. She had already proved herself a good operator. Better than him so far, because she had two guns and he had none.

But then he saw he didn't need one, because for her to get a line of sight on him she would have to pass by the taped-off piles of building waste.

He rolled the knife around in his palm so the blade was facing up and then darted forward, covering the short amount of open space and flicking out the blade, slicing through the thick tape with an upward motion.

He kept moving because he knew he had exposed himself

and heard the dull whip-crack sound of a suppressed shot as he sprinted away.

The round punched a hole in a nearby wall, but no others followed it because without the tape to hold the pile of waste in place the weight of brick and concrete shifted and slipped and became an avalanche of collapsing material that fell into the assassin as she rushed to follow him.

He heard the echoing rumble of the collapse and her cry of surprise and alarm, but didn't look back – he wasn't going to be fooled by her play-acting twice – and dashed through the rest of the basement level. The collapsing building waste would only injure her at best, and might have done nothing more than distract her. He wasn't going to risk investigating either way. She was still armed and he was not.

A kick knocked fire doors open.

It wasn't often Victor thought himself fortunate to be alive, but cold night air hadn't felt so good in a long time.

He ran out into the street and kept running.

ELEVEN

Prague was a low-rise city. From only five storeys up Victor felt on top of the world. The cold morning air reddened his cheeks and numbed his hands. A thin layer of snow covered the flat roof and coated the hardy potted plants that formed a roof garden.

Footprints and a cleared bench showed the chill didn't keep office workers from using it in such weather. Between the benches, a plant-less pot showed fresh cigarette stubs. The garden occupied about a quarter of the roof space. A low barrier of metal tubing fenced off the rest of the roof. Victor placed his footsteps in or over those of previous visitors and stepped over the barrier to approach the roof's south side. He shuffled his steps to distort the prints left in the unbroken snow.

Vents and boxy air-conditioning units stood in a cluster. He rounded them and moved with caution until he was in position. He peered over the waist-high parapet and down to the street below.

On the far side of the street was the gated entrance leading to the basement where he had been ambushed the night before.

You're lucky that cab went by when it did, the assassin had taunted less than twelve hours before. *Otherwise you would have taken a seven-six-two in the back.*

She was referring to a 7.62 x 52 mm bullet: a high-velocity rifle round. A useful one for an urban environment because the rifles that shot it weren't as long or as difficult to position and transport as those that fired larger rounds. He pictured her assembling it from component pieces taken out of a briefcase.

Somewhere out there Al-Waleed bin Saud was flying to his next destination on a charter jet according to a coded email from Muir. Caglayan had disappeared.

Muir wanted answers. She wanted to know what had happened and what Victor intended to do to rectify his mistake.

His mistake.

Victor had elected not to reply. He didn't know what had happened. He had been set up and ambushed. It wasn't the first time. It was doubtful it would be the last. And he wanted answers beyond those his employers were able – or willing – to provide.

He had no interest in fulfilling his obligation on Al-Waleed when someone had almost killed him. His priority was to stay alive first, and get paid second.

He squatted low, imagining the assassin doing similar, maybe steadying the rifle with a bipod resting on the parapet. He saw no indentations in the snow for the bipod feet for the same reason he saw no footprints on the roof.

It had snowed overnight.

Victor inched forward to correct the perspective of a woman behind a rifle. How long had she been up here, waiting? He could not be sure. He had not seen her prior to the attack in the basement while he had performed routine scans of the area, but as he had noted at the time he had not had the window for thorough reconnaissance. The message with the time and location of the meet had only arrived an hour beforehand, and Victor did not know where or how she had gained her intelligence.

It had required no prior preparation for Victor to gain access to the building and its roof. It was an office building with no security greater than a bored guy behind a desk. Victor had walked straight by and taken the elevator up to the top floor and followed the signs to the roof. She could have done the same, or booked an appointment with someone in the building to provide an excuse for her presence, or she could have pretended to be a cleaner, or paid a bribe, or gained entry through any manner of distractions or bluffs.

It had been cold last night, and the woman was slight and had not worn any winter clothing. Like him, she opted for agility over comfort.

Using his knuckles, he brushed aside snow in a circle around him. He did so with a light touch to remove only the top layer of new snow. Nothing.

He widened the circle. Cellophane crackled. He removed a glove and picked the cellophane out of the snow with the nails of his thumb and forefinger.

It was crumpled and torn from its original box shape: three inches long by two wide and half an inch in depth. He recognised the shape from his days as a smoker. Though he had never littered like this.

He searched through the snow around where he had taken the cellophane from but found nothing further.

The roof was a big place. He could not search through every inch of snow. Besides, the assassin could have tossed any stubs off the roof.

He remembered yesterday's wind, fierce and cold, blowing south. He hadn't paid sufficient attention to estimate the wind speed, but that's where weather reports came in. He looked over the parapet. He stood and brought his right thumb and index to his lips. He inhaled and moved his hand away, extending his index finger and parting it from his thumb in a flicking motion. He pictured a cigarette tumbling through the air, veering to his right and falling under gravity's pull, but the wind blowing it back. He pivoted as he watched the imaginary butt arch back over the parapet and on to the roof.

Victor found it lying beneath the top layer of snow, next to an air-conditioning unit.

He used his nails to retrieve it by the burnt end. It was moist but not wet because the temperature had not yet risen enough to cause the overnight snow to melt.

A trace of mauve lipstick smudged around the filter end.

In the darkness, he had not noticed the assassin wearing lipstick – he had been too focused on staying alive to take in such details – but there was about half an inch of tobacco above the filter. No smoker threw away so much unless they had to – say because they needed both hands to operate a rifle now their target had presented themselves. That would also explain why she had overlooked the stub blown back on to the roof. She had been distracted by thoughts of killing Victor.

He broke off the ash from the tip and smelt the unburned tobacco. He hadn't smoked for a couple of years but at that moment was tempted to start again.

He pushed the thought from his mind, breathed in the scent one last time, and dropped the butt into a pocket of his new suit trousers.

A taxi took him across the city and two buses brought him back in a circuitous route. He walked the rest of the way to Wenceslas Square, seeing no sign of a female assassin stalking him. He didn't know if she was still on his trail or if she had fled or was preparing to strike again. The only thing he knew for certain was that she was alive because no mortuary in the city had received a corpse crushed by falling building material.

The old tailor grinned when Victor returned to the low-ceilinged atelier and moved to greet him with a youthful deftness to his step.

'You've changed your mind,' the tailor began with a glimmer of hope in his eyes. 'You've seen sense, finally, else have been reborn and resurrected into a man of taste. Yes?'

'Not exactly,' Victor answered.

The glimmer faded from the old tailor's eyes. 'You don't want me to adjust your suit?'

Victor shook his head. 'I assure you I'll consider it if I could have your opinion on something.'

The tailor looked at him with suspicion. 'That sounds like a bribe to me.'

'That's because it is.'

'Very well, let's have it.'

'You said before no two varieties of tobacco are the same. Was that hyperbole?'

'It was not.'

Victor produced the cigarette stub. 'Then can you tell me anything about this particular cigarette?'

He handed the stub to the tailor who first examined it in his palm, then held it beneath his nostrils to smell.

'This is no ordinary cigarette,' the tailor said. 'This is a work of art. These are crafted with love and rolled by hand. Not some godless machine.'

The tailor squeezed some unburned tobacco into his palm, then pinched and rubbed it between his fingers and smelled his fingertips, one by one, before holding the butt under his nostrils.

'This is a particularly good blend of tobacco, strong and sweet. An aftertaste of chocolate, I think. This is the Château Lafite of cigarettes. Hand-rolled from only the finest leaves, perfectly dried under only the hottest sun.'

Victor listened.

'From the West Indies,' the tailor said. 'Almost certainly. Dominican, would be my guess.'

'Guess?'

'Please, child. They don't come with a serial number.'

'Don't you need to light it?' Victor asked.

'You ask for my expert opinion and then question my methods?'

'I'm sorry. Thank you for your time.'

The tailor made a small nod to accept the apology. 'And your suit?'

'Maybe the jacket can be brought in a little.'

Victor had never seen a man look so happy.

TWELVE

Janice Muir ran every day, either on a treadmill or the old-fashioned way. Sometimes she ran twice a day. She did so for health and sanity, not for a figure. She had always been thin. Her mother told her she would look better with a few more pounds on her and her mother might well be right, but Muir didn't care. She had never been vain, never cared for fashion, and she was too old to start caring now. Her health came first, her work came second. There was no room for a third concern in her life. Guys didn't seem to understand that.

She finished up her evening workout, showered and changed into her work suit. She would change again when she was back home, this time into some loungewear or maybe straight into her PJs – it was rare she wore anything but smart business attire, running clothes or PJs. She didn't get the chance to go out much and was never comfortable in civilian attire. Muir liked her outfits to match her mood and she was almost never in the mood to wear jeans and a strappy top.

She headed to the parking lot where her cobalt-blue Acura sat reverse parked. She thumbed the bleeper only when she was a few feet away and climbed in, dropping her gym bag on to the passenger seat.

Something felt wrong when she started the engine, but she only realised what when she engaged her seat belt and checked her rear-view mirror, seeing—

The dark silhouette of a man in the back seat.

Despite her long years with the CIA, despite her training, she hesitated, but only for a second.

Her hand snapped towards the gym bag, towards her nickel-plated SIG Sauer.

She had it out of the bag, cocked and ready before a further second had passed. She swivelled, aiming the gun, and—

Recognised the man.

'Hello, Janet.'

'*Christ*, you asshole. I almost killed you.'

'No you didn't. The SIG's empty.'

She hesitated, then realised it weighed less than it should. She thumbed the catch and withdrew the magazine. It was indeed empty.

'How did you . . . ?'

'That's not important.'

Muir creased her brow and placed the empty SIG back in her gym bag. 'I think we're going to have to disagree on that.'

She knew him only as Tesseract, a code name designated to him because no one knew his real name. She had met the man a handful of times before and each and every time she had been frightened, although she liked to think she had hidden the fact. He had almost killed her on their first meeting. It had been the only time in her career with the CIA that she had believed she was going to die. That fear had never gone away.

'But what is important is how you answer my question,' the man whose real name she didn't know said. 'Was it you?'

'Are you talking about Prague?'

He nodded.

'No,' she said. 'Whatever you're talking about had nothing to do with me.'

She saw him studying her. She knew if he didn't believe her then she would not live much longer.

'Okay,' he said. 'I believe you.'

Muir couldn't hold back the sigh of relief, but she was still annoyed. 'That's because I'm telling the truth.'

'Which is why I believe you.'

'I thought you knew me well enough by now to know that I'm not looking to set you up.'

'I don't delude myself into thinking I can ever really know anyone.'

'How depressing for you. And I really mean that,' Muir said.

'I can see that you do. Can you see that I don't care?'

She ignored the rhetorical question. 'Could we not have done this via email or even the phone like normal civilised human beings?'

'I'm far from civilised, Janice. I thought you would know me well enough by now to know that.'

'Why don't you tell me what happened.'

Tesseract did. He summarised the events from his perspective, knowing Muir would have seen reports. She listened without interrupting as he described his confrontation with the assassin.

After he had finished, she said, 'Is this personal? Is this about you?'

'I don't know,' he replied. 'I have more than my fair share of enemies. You know that. I live each day expecting it to be my last. I know there are people out there hunting me. Right now, they're trying to track me down, and sooner or later they always do. I don't know who will find me next or when or how they'll do it, but it's inevitable.'

'So that's a yes then?'

He shook his head. 'Prague doesn't feel like one of those times.'

'It doesn't *feel* like one?'

For a few seconds she was worried her surprised tone came across as sarcastic, but he didn't react.

'Yes,' he said. 'It doesn't feel like it.'

'I didn't take you for the kind of guy who went with instincts over logic.'

'Instinct is unconscious logic that's hardwired deep in the mind.'

'Okay,' she said. 'Then explain this feeling to me.'

'I'm a difficult man to find. If someone wants me dead their best bet is to come after me when they know where I am. That's usually soon after I've earned their wrath. They wait, I'm gone.'

'So you're saying you haven't pissed anyone off recently?'

He didn't comment on the swearing. Muir hoped he appreciated she was toning down her profanity level for his benefit.

'I've been a good boy, yes.'

'And it's inconceivable no one from your past has tracked you down?'

'That's not what I said. It's *unlikely*, which is why I'm here. And enemies of mine tend to work in groups or send teams. A lone shooter is rare.'

'You didn't really believe it was going to be me, did you?'

'Of course not,' he said, toneless.

'Then why come here?'

'To make certain. And to find out who supplied the target.'

She hesitated. 'That's classified.'

'I expected more from you, Janice.'

'Come on, you know I can't talk about that kind of thing. We've been through this before. You know how the agency works.'

'No,' he said. 'I don't. But I'm not agency, you just use me to do the jobs that are too dirty for even the CIA to go near.'

'That's not exactly how we see it.'

'I don't care what you tell yourself so you can sleep at night. What I do care about is not being sold out so you can protect some bureaucrat from a possible senate hearing a decade down the line.'

'I protect you too,' Muir said.

'Not right now you're not.'

'I'm not sure what to say to that.'

'Then this is where we part ways.'

She took a breath. 'I don't think that's necessary.'

'I think you've shown what you deem necessary so as not to be misjudged.'

Muir said, 'Now you're being immature.'

'I beg to differ. I told you before: I'm not an employee. I've told you before of my intolerance for withholding information.'

'Related to the job,' she was quick to add. 'You know everything I do. I've always been full and honest with you about anything operational.'

They sat in silence for a few seconds.

'Someone wants me dead, almost certainly because of my last job. Therefore I need to know who assigned Al-Waleed bin Saud as a target.'

Muir said, 'That's not relevant.'

'What is relevant though is that I know your nine-month-old Jack Russell is diabetic and she'll do anything for a belly rub.'

Any fear Muir felt melted away, leaving anger behind. She didn't try to hide it. 'I won't ask how you know that.'

'Good,' Tesseract said. 'Because I won't tell you.'

'But I will ask why you felt the need to know?'

'Insurance. Don't pretend you don't have any, Janice. Don't pretend you don't know exactly what to say to me to save your life if I had a gun to your head right now. You're far too smart not to have prepared for the moment when I turn. You think it's inevitable, don't you? I'm a hired killer. No morality. No loyalty. You'll never trust me, and that's the way it should be. Like I said, you're too smart not to have insurance. You're also smart enough to know that pretending otherwise is a waste of both our time.'

'Is that why you told me about Daisy? You're threatening me?'

'I'm being honest. I'm reminding you before I walk away that no matter how bad it gets some day from now, no matter how much pressure you're under, do not hang me out to dry. I'm reminding you that no matter what you fear in this world, you need to fear me more.'

Her voice was low: 'You don't need to remind me. I know exactly what you are.'

'No, you don't. Pray you don't ever find out.'

He worked the door release and climbed out of the car.

THIRTEEN

Victor had crossed fifteen metres of asphalt before he heard Muir's voice behind him, shouting:

'*Hey.*'

He stopped, turned. He watched her jog over to him. Graceful, efficient movements. Hurried, but not rushed. She wore a brown leather jacket over her work clothes. He recognised the jacket from the last time he had seen her. It flared at the waist, giving her the illusion of shape. She was narrow in width and depth.

'You waited longer than I thought you would,' Victor said.

'Yeah, well, it's hard to call after someone when you don't know their name, right?'

She had the flat accent of a Midwesterner. Maybe she had come from somewhere with a regional accent, but many years in the homogeny of the heartlands had smoothed out any local intonations.

He didn't answer.

'You're right,' she said. 'I should be as honest with you as you are with me, but I'm in a difficult position here.'

She edged closer. The last time he had seen her she had been thin and unhealthy. Now, she was still thin, but she looked better. Her skin and hair spoke of plenty of rest and enough of the right kinds of food. The small amount of extra fat in her face smoothed out some of the lines and made her seem younger than she had then. She didn't wear a lot of make-up, at least during the day, but she knew how to make it work for her. She looked uncomfortable in civilian attire. She would work long hours in a business suit. Time out of it would mean loungewear or pyjamas or workout gear. She wouldn't own a lot of dresses. He didn't imagine many heels in her closet.

'You chased after me just to say that?'

'No, I'm telling you that although I can't – won't – pass on personal information about the client, I will pass on your concerns.'

'Not good enough,' Victor said, and began to turn.

She reached out to stop him, but stopped herself an inch before her fingers came in contact with his arm. He looked at the fingers, picturing grabbing the index and forefinger in one hand and the ring finger and little finger in the other hand, and using the strong muscles of his upper back to rip the hand in two pieces, right down to the wrist bone.

'Sorry,' she said, snapping the hand away as though she had read his mind.

She was scared of him, he knew. Which was the way it should be. He didn't seek to frighten, but if he ever met

Muir and he saw no fear in her eyes he would know he had walked straight into an ambush.

'But will you let me speak for a second?' she said. 'I'll pass on your concerns and I'll have him contact you. Maybe directly you can work this thing out.'

'No,' Victor said. 'I'll meet him, face to face, in one week's time. On O'Connell Bridge in Dublin, Saturday, twelve noon.'

She regarded him, close and searching. 'Why do you want to meet him in person?'

'Same reason I met you in person.'

The breeze blew her hair across her face. She pushed it back behind her ears. 'So you could tell if I'm lying?'

'That and, if you were, so I could kill you.'

She inhaled and swallowed. 'I can't allow you to kill the client.'

'That's for me to decide.'

'I'll have to tell him you said that.'

'Do so. If he has nothing to hide, there's nothing for him to be worried about.'

'Okay,' Muir said. 'I understand, but I guarantee he'll feel the same way. Why Dublin?'

'I like Guinness.'

She looked at him like she didn't know if he was joking or not. Which was the point.

Victor said, 'Please stress to the client the importance of punctuality.'

'Right. And I suppose I should tell him to come alone?'

'He can bring as many guys with him as he likes. Tell him it won't make any difference.'

FOURTEEN

Victor had never been in Ireland on a cloudless day, but the sky above the city was as blue as he had ever seen it. The temperature was pleasant enough. Sunglasses and T-shirts were plentiful, even if shorts were not. He was on the south bank of the River Liffey, enjoying the sun on his face and the wind in his hair. As capital cities went, Dublin was as clean as any he had visited. On a roof five storeys up, the air smelled as fresh as countryside.

He liked Ireland. He liked that of all the countries of Europe, Ireland was one of the handful he had never worked within as a professional. That made it as safe to operate in now as anywhere could be for him.

Victor had a great view of the O'Connell Bridge and the streets that fed into it. The bridge was greater in width than the river it spanned. It had six lanes for traffic, separated by a central reservation on which stood wooden and metal boxes of flowering plants. Ornate lamp posts were spaced along at regular intervals. Connecting Dublin's main thoroughfares, the bridge was often busy with traffic, but not today. It had been closed to vehicles.

Thanks to Victor's view, he could see every one of the team. He counted eleven threats in all. They had spread themselves out – four were positioned on the south side of the river to watch each of the four roads that fed on to the bridge; three were doing the same job on the north side of the river; the other four were spaced out along the bridge itself with two on the west side and two on the east.

The client had yet to arrive.

Either the client had listened to what Muir had to say and deduced that Victor was going to kill him – which was a distinct possibility – or he had decided Victor was the kind of problem he didn't need in his life. At that moment, it was hard to know which of the two explanations formed the justification for the presence of an eleven-strong team.

They were watchers right now, but he could tell they were more than mere pavement artists. They were all men, which he hadn't expected. Multi-sex teams made far better shadows. It was easier to hide in plain sight as part of a couple than as an individual.

Over half were not Caucasian and those that were had tans from time spent in sunny climes. These facts led Victor to believe they weren't locals but ex-US military, which had a disproportionate percentage of minority representation – which suggested that the client was as well. The client knew who he was dealing with. He wouldn't trust his life to outsiders. Military men tended to put more faith in their own kind than intelligence operatives. Likewise, spies trusted other spies more than they did grunts or jarheads. The watchers were easy to spot because they arrived early to settle into their spots and they didn't leave them again. They did their best to act inconspicuous, but there were only so many ways one could hang around doing nothing. They would have vehicles nearby, but there were few places to park in the vicinity, and none provided a good view of the bridge. So they had to be on foot, and in the open. They couldn't hide. It would be a waste of manpower to have still more. If the client had brought an eleven-strong team to protect him, he wouldn't have left men behind that could be better employed in his defence.

Victor had half-expected to find a watcher on the roof where he now crouched, but the client or whoever was in charge of his security had decided it was better to have the whole protective detail on the ground, where they could be employed in a range of tasks. Positioned on a roof might be useful for seeing Victor coming, but no good for doing any-thing about it.

Unless he planned to kill the client with a rifle. It was interesting that they hadn't accounted for that. Or had they?

The lack of watchers on rooftops implied they hadn't been able to get rifles into Ireland for snipers, which could reveal a lot about the client and his influence or lack thereof, but it was as likely they didn't want gunplay on the streets of Dublin, whatever Victor's intentions or their own. If he were to die, they would smuggle him into the back of a moving van and take him somewhere remote and quiet. No need to upset the locals.

Victor's plan was working so far. It was ten minutes to

midday and he had spotted the entire team and assessed their capabilities. They were good. They had positioned themselves well and done as good a job as could be expected at remaining unseen.

Professionals, but not the best.

Which again suggested ex-military. They had spent their lives training for battle, not for urban surveillance. If it came to violence, they would be more dangerous as a result, but it shouldn't come to that if everything worked out as Victor had planned.

He wore khaki trousers and a denim jacket over a black T-shirt emblazoned with a faded motif of a band he didn't recognise. A camouflage baseball cap covered his hair. All had been purchased from charity shops and dirtied in puddles. Non-prescription glasses completed the look.

The disguise was basic, and wouldn't fool anyone who knew his face and was looking out for him, but it would be enough here.

With five minutes to go before midday, the client arrived.

FIFTEEN

He walked on to the bridge from the south side of the river. Victor didn't spot him straight away, but he saw the muted reactions from the watchers. They didn't look at him, but they couldn't help tense with readiness. Professionals, but not the best.

Upon seeing this, Victor identified the client within a minute. A military man, straight of back and gait, tough and wary. He wore civilian attire: jeans and a black bomber jacket. He was tall and strong, with coal-black skin and a shaved head. He had his back to Victor while he walked along the middle of the bridge, so it was hard to estimate his age until he stopped in the exact centre.

He turned around on the spot three hundred and sixty degrees, examining all the lone men standing nearby or passing. When he realised Victor wasn't there, he backed up and leaned against the stonework. He touched his chin to his collarbone and said something into a lapel mike. Victor was at the wrong angle to read his lips, but he didn't need to.

He was younger than Victor had expected: from this range, he looked to be no older than forty. There were no signs of grey in the stubble on his face or head. This was a man who had not absorbed all the excesses of civilian life. If Victor had expected him to have grown soft giving orders from behind a desk, he was wrong.

Two minutes to twelve. Victor didn't move. He figured the client would wait five minutes, but from the agreed time. He wouldn't fly across the Atlantic to leave again without giving Victor a chance to show. But he wouldn't hang around longer. Victor had instructed Muir to inform the client to be punctual. If Victor was late, it would communicate that he wasn't going to show, and that would smell of a set-up. The longer the client stood exposed on the bridge, the easier a target he made of himself.

So Victor had seven minutes. There was no need to rush. In fact, Victor needed to wait until the last minute.

The client stood with all the patience that could be expected of a man waiting to meet a professional assassin. He was anxious. If he hadn't been, Victor would have expected a trap. He was prepared for one regardless.

At one minute past twelve he headed for the roof door because it would take him three minutes to get down to the ground floor and on to the street outside. It would take a further minute to reach the client.

When his watch showed the time to be three minutes and forty-nine seconds past midday, Victor was walking through the main entrance and on to the street outside.

He was going to walk straight along the street and on to the bridge where the client waited and the watchers weren't going to see him.

The client had been standing next to one of the ornate lamp posts, on its north side, making a headshot difficult from where Victor had been waiting. Deliberate positioning, no doubt. The man was also wearing that large bomber jacket. The temperature did not warrant it, so Victor pictured an armoured vest beneath; lots of layers of Kevlar reinforced by ceramic plates to protect the heart and lungs, both at the front and back.

Even with the body armour and the lamp post impeding his line of sight, Victor could still have made a kill shot, had he wanted. The client knew enough about him to know Victor was capable of such a shot.

But he didn't intend to kill the client, at least not until after he had spoken to him.

Besides, this guy wasn't the client. But they wanted Victor to think that.

It had almost worked too. Everything about the team and their positions and the 'client' had been right, except the black guy in the bomber jacket had made a single mistake. He had ignored the other watchers while he had walked along the bridge, but as he had taken up position next to the lamp post he had glanced at one of them.

It was a reflex action, hard to control. He hadn't glanced at the others. He had glanced at one in particular because one in particular had significance.

The real client.

He was on the bridge too. He had been one of the first to

arrive, which had been a smart deception. He had exposed himself early and by doing so had caused Victor to all but ignore him. Until now.

Outside the building Victor was even harder to see than when he had been crouched, high up on the rooftop – because he stepped into a huge crowd of people.

Right on schedule, a march was heading towards O'Connell Bridge. The crowd of protestors numbered several hundred, which was a good chunk less than estimates on the organisation's social media page had suggested. It didn't matter.

He would have been invisible in a crowd half the size.

They were a mix of ages, more women than men, holding home-made placards and printed banners denoting their cause: opposition to austerity measures and cuts to frontline services. They were loud and raucous, but good-spirited, moved by passion and social responsibility, not anger.

Victor slipped amongst them, joining their chants and whistles.

He sidestepped until he was next to an old guy with a beard to his waist. 'I'll give you fifty euros if I can carry your placard for five minutes.'

The old guy said, 'You can carry it for free, lad,' and passed it to Victor. 'My arms are killing me.'

As they approached the bridge, he saw the watchers panicking. They hadn't expected a crowd of protestors. They hadn't checked for such things. They should have found out why the bridge was closed to vehicles. They should have thought harder why Victor had chosen this location on this day at this time. Professionals, but not the best.

They would waste precious seconds discussing and arguing and going through options. Their attempt at deception would work against them now. By the time they had decided whether to close in on the real client or withdraw with him, it would be too late.

The crowd reached the bridge and Victor spotted the client still present, staring at the crowd. Not searching for Victor, but trying to decide what, if anything, it meant. That he didn't withdraw was significant. It meant he was determined if nothing else.

The watchers did their best to find Victor in the crowd, now realising that he must be among them, but even having studied and memorised every one of his features, he was as good as impossible to spot in the dense mass of protestors.

Pedestrians and tourists moved out to the bridge walls to avoid the march. The watchers were now scattered and ineffective. They could no longer keep track of each other and their boss, let alone scout for Victor. He handed the placard back to the old guy with the beard.

'Thank you, sir.'

With dozens of people now on the bridge between the client and Victor, it was impossible to keep the man in sight at all times, but the client was doing the sensible thing and remaining stationary, waiting for the crowd to pass.

As Victor neared the client, he changed his trajectory to walk behind the man with the beard and placard, ensuring the client wouldn't see Victor's face as he covered the last few metres.

A moment after the man with the beard and placard

passed the client, Victor took the client's arm and said, 'Come with me.'

Before the client could react, Victor pushed two knuckles of his free hand against the small of the man's back. Knuckles were more convincing than using fingertips as a fake gun – bigger, more solid – and the client didn't resist.

He took off his camouflage baseball cap and placed it on the client's head, pulling the brim down low to help conceal his face. Victor then ripped away the lapel mike and veered back into the centre of the crowd, taking the client with him.

Victor kept his gaze forward. He wanted to know where the watchers were and what they were doing, but any head movement created the risk of drawing their attention.

They maintained pace with the rest of the protestors until they had left the bridge on the north side. He headed right on to the pavement that flanked the road running alongside the river.

He guided the client across the road and between parked cars and around pedestrians.

'Where are you taking me?' the client asked.

'You'll know when we get there. Stop talking if you value your spine.'

After a few seconds, an alleyway opened up between the commercial buildings.

'Turn here,' Victor said.

The client obeyed.

When they were out of line of sight of the adjoining street, Victor pushed the client against a wall and patted him down, finding a wallet and phone but no gun. The man stood still while Victor checked him and took the phone.

'There's no need for any of this,' the client said. 'That's my personal cell.'

Victor didn't respond. He crushed the phone beneath a heel. 'This way.'

He led the client along the alleyway for another ten metres, until he came to the faded back door of a commercial property with a 'TO LET' sign.

The door was unlocked because Victor had picked it earlier. He opened the door and pushed the client into the room beyond.

SIXTEEN

The property had been an internet café, until it was driven out of business by smartphones and wireless technology. There were no terminals, but the cheap desks and chairs remained. The air was dusty and stale. There was no active electricity supply, so no lights, but enough sunlight found its way through the whitewashed windows for Victor to see the client and for him to be seen in return.

'Can I take off this ridiculous hat now?'

The client's voice was a deep growl. His accent suggested the East Coast, maybe a native of Virginia or Maryland.

Victor nodded.

The client removed it from his head and placed it down on a desk.

Up close Victor saw scars on the client's neck. They were old and faded but still distinct against the rest of the tanned skin. They were burns marks, protruding out from the collar of his polo shirt. He had grey eyes and the weathered skin was marked with deep crow's feet and ice-pick scars from acne or pox decades before. He looked tough and capable; a former military man who, though long out, had not allowed himself to weaken. His posture was straight and rigid. He didn't fidget. His hands stayed by his hips, in loose fists. There was no wedding band and no pale ring of skin where one had been removed prior to this meeting. His clothes were good quality garments, but there were no designer labels signalling significant disposable income. The Ray-Bans were the most expensive item on his person. His watch was for telling the time on a battlefield, not a display of wealth. He wore the experience of combat on his face and triumph in the set of his shoulders.

The client spent a moment examining the room. He seemed content enough to give Victor his back to do so. He then nodded to himself before facing Victor. He looked to Victor's hands.

'You don't have a gun.' He seemed more curious than surprised. 'Do you?'

Victor said, 'Do you think I need one?'

'Never thought I'd fall for the old fingers-in-the-back trick. Guess I must have lost a step in my advancing years.' The client paused. 'I told Muir that twelve men would be more than enough to handle you.'

'Then why did you bring only eleven?'

A sigh. 'One got sick on the way over. Some stomach bug. Shitting and throwing up every which way. No plan's perfect though, right? You must know that better than anyone. But, I have to say, I can't see he would have made the difference, can you?'

'Not really.'

The client appeared to consider this, then nodded. 'Okay. I think we both know you've proved your point. It was a real nice demonstration out there. My guys dropped the ball with the march, sure. But you played it perfectly. I understand the message: you can get to me no matter what. But, as I said outside, there's no need for any of this. We're not enemies. We're on the same side here.'

'That's impossible,' Victor said. 'I'm the only one who's on my side.'

The client cocked a sardonic smile and shrugged. 'Whatever. Muir informed me what happened in Prague. You fucked up. That was supposed to be nice and quiet and clean. That's why I hired you. I heard you were good at this kind of thing. Muir told me you were the best.'

'Muir should also have told you to watch your language when you're with me.'

'Oh, she did. She told me all about you and your little quirks. But what I'm doing is ignoring her advice. Do you honestly think I give a shit about your delicate sensibilities? I'll talk however I want. You don't like it, you know where the door is.' He gestured. 'But you're not going to walk out of here because you don't like my use of language, are you, son?'

'I think you're forgetting who's in charge here.'

He shook his head. 'Save the thinly veiled threats. I didn't have to fly three thousand miles. I didn't have to meet you. Until today, you had no idea who I was and I could have kept it that way. But I didn't. I'm here, aren't I? I'm here as a courtesy to you and to Muir as well. Some thanks would be nice, don't you agree?'

'I'm overwhelmed with gratitude,' Victor said.

The client smirked. 'Fine. Why don't we get down to business? I'm sure you're as keen to get out of here as I am. I'm sure both our time is too precious to waste with this merry-go-round. Why exactly did you bring me here?'

'To ask you one question,' Victor said. 'Did you send her?'

'No,' the client said, strong and resolute. 'I did not send her.'

Victor watched his eyes, which remained forward and unblinking. Victor believed him.

'So it's about you,' the client said. 'Your past catching up with you. And quite a past you have, don't you?'

'You don't know the half of it.'

'Whatever. We're done. I won't be using you again. You've got too much baggage to be an effective operator. As was proved in Prague.' He gestured to the door on the other side of Victor. 'Excuse me.'

He didn't move. 'When my past catches up with me, I know about it.'

'I don't know what that means and I don't care. As I said: we're through. And I'm gone. This is a waste of my time.'

The client stepped within arm's reach, expecting Victor to move. He remained where he was.

Victor said, 'If she was there for me, why didn't she try again?' The client waited. 'If it was my past catching up with me, why did she let me go?'

'Muir said you escaped.'

'Barely,' Victor said. 'But if she tracked me to Prague, why hadn't she tracked me down beforehand? Why hasn't she since?'

'How would I know?'

'I don't know either.'

'You're not making any sense. And I'm getting bored.'

'This won't take much longer,' Victor said. 'If I were her primary objective then she could have moved on me at some other point. If she was sent by someone I've angered before now, then why did she wait until that exact moment to strike?'

'Go on,' the client said.

'Maybe I'm not her primary objective. Maybe I was only a target because of who I was after.'

'You're saying she was there to protect the prince.'

'I'm saying that makes more sense.

'Okay,' the client said. 'I'm listening.'

'She's five feet nine inches tall, right-handed, one hundred and fourteen pounds, early thirties, dark hair, olive skin, brown eyes, Middle Eastern, probably Persian heritage but with the calcium-rich bones of a Westerner. My guess is she is American. Maybe her family emigrated during the Iranian revolution. My guess is she's one of yours. She can work the field as well as I can. She knew my approach and I only knew she was on to me a second before I would have been killed. Who is she?'

The client exhaled and shook his head. 'I ... I can't be sure on that description alone.'

'Maybe you can't be sure, but you have a good idea. We don't have to guess though. Here—' Victor took a sheet of paper from his jacket pocket and unfolded it. 'Take a look at her face.'

The client took the paper from Victor's hand and held it

under a shaft of light for a better look. His expression changed straight away but he went on studying the drawing Victor had sketched of his attacker for a long time. When his gaze returned to Victor, he looked sad.

'Shit,' the client said. 'She is one of mine.'

SEVENTEEN

'I mean,' the client was quick to clarify, 'she used to be one of my people.'

'Who are you?' Victor asked.

The client handed the image back. 'My name's Jim Halleck.'

He held out his hand. It was strong and worn and coarse. Victor looked at the hand suspended between them and kept his own near his hips.

Halleck let his hand fall back to his thigh. 'No reason why we can't be friendly.'

'There's every reason.'

'Whatever. Muir said you keep your name to yourself. She refers to you as Tesseract.'

'It's a code name I can't seem to shake.'

'Better than no name. Guess I'll do the same as Muir and call you Mr Tesseract.'

'I'd prefer you didn't.'

Halleck shrugged his shoulders. 'You're not exactly leaving me a lot of choice, are you?'

'What are you, CIA?'

'Not exactly. I'm as much CIA as you are. Affiliated, but not officially. I run my own task force. A small, elite crew. We're independent, but connected with all the usual suspects. We work with the Pentagon, DIA, CIA, NSA, Homeland Security, FBI, and foreign intelligence services as well as with the CIA.'

'The Activity?'

Halleck shrugged a hand, dismissive. 'That's an out-of-date label. The Activity doesn't exist any longer. At least, not how it used to be. Now, it's branched and split off into many different unacknowledged black-ops units. Some of the originals are still around, somewhere.'

'And you control one of these offshoots?' Victor asked.

Halleck nodded and scratched the back of his neck.

Victor said, 'Tell me about her.'

Halleck said, 'She went rogue three years ago during an op in Yemen. At the time we thought she had simply gone AWOL. It happens. People cut and run from the intelligence community like they do from the army. Not often, but there you go. Then she turned up, twelve months after she vanished, as a freelance shooter. We've tried tracking her, of course. But obviously she knows a lot about how we work and how to stay off the radar. Recently, she's been hitting targets close to home: CIA assets and agents in the Middle East and Europe. She goes by the handle Raven.'

'What's her real name?'

'Constance Stone. You were right, what you said. She

grew up in the US but her father is Indian, of Persian descent. She was originally CIA, a star of the Special Activities Division. A career operative, straight out of college. No military background, not that you'd know. I worked with her and saw her talents were being wasted. I offered her a job with my unit and trained her up and she became my best operator.'

'Why did she go rogue?'

Halleck shook his head. 'I don't know. Why does anyone move from the public sector to the private? It pays better.' He looked back at Victor from over one shoulder. 'Isn't that your story too?'

'I'll keep my story to myself, if it's all the same to you.'

'I already know your story.'

Victor said, 'Keep telling yourself that.'

Halleck turned round and leaned back against a wall. He rolled his shoulders to loosen some tension. He'd been standing up for a long time.

Victor said, 'Why would she be protecting Al-Waleed?'

'You're suggesting it isn't merely a coincidence?'

Victor remained silent.

'Al-Waleed has been on our list of problems for a long time. As far back as when Raven worked for me.'

Victor was shaking his head before Halleck had finished. 'No, she hasn't been sitting idle for three years waiting for you to make a move on him. She knew when and where the kill was going to take place. So her intel is up to date.'

'That's impossible.'

'If it were impossible we wouldn't be having this conversation now. She'd found out somehow that the prince was a target and I was the shooter. Either you have a leak or she still has access to your data.'

'Shit,' Halleck said. 'But why? Why would she protect him?'

'Because she's freelance. Because, like you said, the private sector pays better. If she knows who you plan to assassinate, she can make a pretty penny helping to prevent that happening. If someone was going to kill you, how much would you pay to make sure they failed?'

Halleck looked away.

Victor said, 'Have you lost any people recently?'

'Killed? No.'

'Or captured unexpectedly while spying?'

Halleck exhaled. His lips were tight.

'She's selling your people out. She's sabotaging your operations. Why?'

'For the money, like we've established.'

'What did you do to her?'

'What are you talking about?'

'She's coming after your unit any way she can. Maybe she's cashing in at the same time, but if she's as good at staying under the radar as you've suggested, then bringing herself out into the open like this is incredibly risky. She's not going to do that unless she has a very good reason. So, I'll ask you again: what did you do to her?'

Halleck swallowed. 'Not to her, her boyfriend.'

'Continue.'

'She had a romantic relationship with one of my men. He was on her team in Yemen. They were going after a terrorist cell . . . ' He paused, and looked at the ceiling. 'But the intel was bad. She narrowly escaped. Her lover wasn't so lucky.'

'She blames you?'

'My sources were reliable, but no one is one hundred per cent, are they? It was bad luck. She didn't see it that way. Like I said before, she went AWOL.'

'And now she's back for revenge.'

'That's your conclusion, not mine. But if you're right, she has lists of our deepest agents and blackest of black operations. She's already got one of my men locked up for life in a Shanghai prison and sabotaged the Prague job. Who knows what she's going to do next?'

Victor paused for a moment because he heard footsteps in the alleyway outside and pictured Halleck's men, but ignored the sound when he also heard children laughing.

'How did she know I was to be Al-Waleed's assassin? I shouldn't be on any list.'

'The CIA is a spy agency second and a bureaucracy first. Everyone is on a list. We have lists of lists.'

'Why haven't I been told about this threat before?'

'Because until you identified her, we didn't know who she was and who she was after. In case you failed to notice, she's good. I trained her, after all.'

'Which is more likely: a leak, or Raven still having access to your files?'

'A leak. I don't believe any of my guys would, but even if Raven was any kind of hacker, there is no way she'd know her way around our system now. A lot changes in three years.'

'Find the leak.'

'Oh, I plan to. And I'll deal with it, don't you worry about that.'

'I never worry. When you find out who is doing this, pass me their details.'

'Hold on there, friend,' Halleck said with raised palms. 'If someone is selling us out to Raven, then they'll get what's coming to them. But through the courts. I'm not handing them over to a cold-blooded killer. No offence.'

'None taken,' Victor said. 'But I don't plan to kill them. I only want to use them to get to Raven. In the meantime I want her file. I want every sliver of intel you have on her.'

'Why?'

'I would think that was obvious.'

'You're going after her?'

Victor nodded. 'Of course.'

'Even though you don't think she was targeting you directly?'

'That's my judgement based on limited evidence. It's going to take a lot more to convince me. If I'm a target, I want to know about it and I want to know why and most importantly, I want to eliminate that threat on my terms. I have enough people to look out for without adding Raven too.'

'If you go after her, then even if you're not a target, you will end up as one.'

'I have to act like I am anyway. Making it a reality doesn't make a lot of difference.'

'Okay,' the client said with a nod. 'I'll have Muir pass on Raven's particulars.'

'No. I deal with you directly. I don't want an intermediary.'

'What do you have against Muir?'

'Nothing. But I have plenty against information being shared beyond those who need to know.'

'I'm not sure I'm comfortable with that arrangement. I went to Muir in the first place. I know her. She should stay in the loop.'

'I don't care what you think. You sent me to kill a target and now I have one of your former assets after me. You owe me. So we do things my way.'

Halleck considered this. 'Doesn't sound like I have a lot of choice.'

'That's because you don't.'

'And what if Muir feels like I'm stepping on her toes if we cut her out?'

'She's a grown-up. She's a professional. She'll get over it. I'm sure her psych screening didn't highlight any irrational tendency towards jealousy.'

'Okay then. You'll deal with me and me alone.'

'I have a question about Raven,' Victor said. 'Before she went rogue, did she have any assignments in the Dominican Republic?'

'Yes, maybe three years ago now. One of her last jobs before she went dark. Why?'

'Did she work alone or with local assets or any former agency people out there?'

'Yeah, a local asset. Why?'

'Anyone she might have connected to; any reason for her to go back?'

'She hasn't been back there since. We know that.'

'Who was the asset?'

'Jean Claude Marte. He's a fixer. Passports. You know the sort of thing. He's in real deep with the cartels down there. Does all their documents. You probably know a dozen such guys.'

'Two dozen,' Victor said. 'What's his cover?'

'What do you mean?'

'I mean: Marte doesn't own a shop called Forgers R US. I mean: what's his day job? What kind of business does he run that's legitimate?'

Halleck thought about this, eyes going up and to the left, accessing memories that hadn't needed recalling for maybe three years. He said, 'If I remember correctly, he was a tobacconist.'

Victor opened the door. 'Email me everything you have on Raven by midnight tonight. I'll do the rest.'

'You know,' Halleck called after him, 'this whole not explaining yourself thing is really quite annoying.'

'I know,' Victor said. 'But that's half the fun.'

EIGHTEEN

The Dominican Republic occupied almost two-thirds of the island of Hispaniola in the southern Caribbean, sharing the island with its neighbour, Haiti. Victor travelled by boat from the isle of Grand Turk to the north, having flown to Jamaica, and then on to the Turks and Caicos Islands before disembarking in Haiti.

The port was little more than a seafront, squalid and half-derelict through neglect and natural disaster. Children, underdressed and undernourished, played in the streets, their bare feet shielded with dead skin, thick and cracked. They seemed not to know of their poverty, kicking punctured footballs and chasing after stray dogs and cats.

He took a bus across the border to the town of Monte Cristi on the northwestern coast. A short domestic flight in a twin-prop chartered Cessna had brought him to the capital of Santo Domingo.

The circuitous route had added a day to the journey, but

even without the imminent threat posed by Raven, he did not like to travel via direct routes if it could be avoided. She was far from the only enemy he had, and even associates like Halleck and Muir might one day turn on him. They already knew or suspected he would be heading to the country. Travelling there on a direct flight would expose one of his aliases with only the simplest of checks.

The Cessna pilot was a seventy-year-old American, a former naval fighter pilot who insisted Victor sit up front in the co-pilot seat while he recounted stories of the many air raids he'd taken part in during the Vietnam War.

'What brings you to the Dom?' the pilot asked him.

Victor said, 'The women.'

They flew in a more-or-less southeasterly direction, over the lush greenery of the Cibao valley and then flying above the peaks of the Cordillera Central mountain range, passing through wisps of pure white cloud.

'Look me up next time you're in Monte Cristi,' the pilot told him as they shook hands. 'I'll take you to a whorehouse that you'll need dragging away from.'

'Sounds delightful,' Victor said.

Jean Claude Marte was a hard man to find. Both Christian name and surname were common in the Dominican Republic. He had been a tobacconist three years ago, but only as a cover. A name, an out-of-date face and profession were not a lot to go on.

Halleck had supplied Victor with the same photograph of the man Raven had been given three years ago. The photograph had been out of date then. It was a copy of a Polaroid. Marte was playing poker in a hot, smoky room.

He was distinguished from the other poker players by the red ring that had been superimposed around his face. Halleck could not tell Victor when the photograph was taken, but it was easy enough to guess it was at least ten years old. The Marte pictured was a thin Haitian with dark skin highlighted white under a bare bulb ceiling light. Age was hard to determine: the picture was poor quality, a copy, or even a copy of a copy; the exposure was poor; the smoke acted as a filter. Marte could have been anywhere between twenty and forty, based on appearances.

Now, that made him at least thirty, but he could be in his forties. Not a helpful age range to hunt someone down. But he had done so with less before.

He fuelled up with a late breakfast of traditional Dominican fare: fried plantain with eggs and salami. The portion was so big he could only finish half of it. He assured the distraught bar owner it had been delicious.

It was hot and humid. He wore a cheap linen shirt with the sleeves rolled up to his elbows. A T-shirt would have kept him cooler, but the ugly raised scar on his right triceps was too noticeable, as were the tan-less marks to his left biceps. He bore the evidence of many wounds, and though his ethnicity alone made him stand out, the scars marked him as more than just a tourist or aid worker. They invited curiosity and questions and were as identifying as finger-prints. He had scars on his lower arms too, but cosmetic surgeons had helped disguise them, and the hair on his fore-arms made them less noticeable.

He carried no weapon. It was almost impossible to sneak one through airport security and never worth the risk trying. He had no contacts in the Dominican Republic from whom to acquire one and no stash to draw upon.

He waved a hand to usher away flies and tried not to breathe in as he passed an open sewer. It was too warm to drink coffee, but he saw nowhere he trusted to purchase it from regardless.

He spent the day wandering around Santo Domingo, seeking out tobacconists. He spoke Spanish and made small talk with the people who sold him hand-rolled cigarettes. He lit up as he left each establishment, drawing smoke only into his mouth to encourage the tobacco to burn. He exhaled without first inhaling, and extinguished the cigarette. When the smouldering had stopped and the butt cooled, he smelled the remnants, then threw away the rest of the cigarettes.

After the third tobacconist his mouth tasted disgusting and he had made no progress either with the tobacconists or the cigarettes.

Beyond the modern hotel complexes and skyscrapers lay the old town of Zona Colonial. He walked down narrow alleyways only a fraction wider than his shoulders, past bright painted doors and under windows guarded with wrought-iron bars. He walked by buildings ruined by hurricanes, earthquakes or the unyielding degrade of time.

He carried a satchel and a guidebook to look like a tourist. He had broken the spine of the guidebook in several places and thrown it at his hotel room wall a few times to give it a well-used appearance.

His Spanish was good, but he was not familiar with the African influences of the local dialect and failed to understand some vocabulary, and sometimes struggled with the different grammar and syntax. Asking questions about Jean Claude Marte was proving problematic.

The streets were teaming with Dominicans, Puerto Ricans and Haitians, but also many migrants and tourists. He saw locals wearing baseball jerseys and caps with the logos of Dominican and American teams. The Yankees seemed to be the most popular.

Cigar and cigarette sellers were almost as common as gift shops and souvenir stalls. No one seemed to know a Jean Claude Marte, despite a liberal spending of funds. Victor carried a supply of Dominican pesos but also a substantial amount of US dollars.

He found himself in a square busy with locals, tourists and pigeons. Cigar smoke fragranced the air. Victor took a seat on an upturned plastic crate in the shade of a mahogany tree to let a boy of ten or eleven clean his shoes. They needed no attention, but the boy worked up a sweat scrubbing and wiping them until they looked new. The boy was shirtless and Victor could see every one of his vertebrae like the peaks of a mountain range.

While he worked, Victor's eyes swept the area for signs of watchers. A man in mirrored sunglasses stood next to a bronze statue of Christopher Columbus and drank from a plastic bottle of sugar cane juice. After a minute, the man screwed the lid back on to the bottle and walked away.

When the boy had finished he rattled a tin cup of peso coins. Victor dropped in some coins, and then a folded one-hundred-dollar bill when the boy wasn't looking.

Stone buildings surrounded the square. Arched walkways led off in several directions. To the south lay the double archway entrance of the Catedral Basilica Santa María la Menor. He stepped out of the heat and into the interior. There were a few tourists as well as locals inside. He admired the stained-glass windows while he waited to see who followed him in.

No one did.

He performed counter surveillance while he wandered around the shops and boutiques as any tourist might, stopping on occasion to peruse wares as part of the cover. Jewellery items made from amber or larimar stones were common.

He walked by outdoor cafés where tourists sipped fruit juices and cocktails. The old city had many squares where centuries-old colonial buildings stood proud and elegant, giving him an excuse to loiter in apparent admiration while scanning for watchers or shadows.

A skinny Dominican man in denim shorts and a yellow T-shirt approached him, announcing himself as an official tour guide. The man had bare feet and a huge smile. His hair was slicked back from a broad forehead. The beard was short but untrimmed with sparse and ragged growth up to his cheekbones. Small eyes peered at Victor from below eyebrows that were thick and wild. The nose was long and crooked through injury or unfortunate genes. His neck was dense with muscle but his shoulders were narrow. He was fit and strong, but only through hard work. Nature had made him weak, but hard work and hardship had overcome that disadvantage.

He had as close to zero body fat as anyone not starving to death could hope to achieve. His forearms were a maze of protruding arteries and veins made more prominent from the thump of rushing blood. His small hands were tanned and rough, nails bitten and torn down.

He was no guide. He was a hustler, out to scam tourists. He was perfect for Victor's needs.

'What's your name?' Victor asked.

'I am the great Sylvester.' He grinned. 'You may call me Sylvester.'

'How much do you charge, Sylvester?' Victor asked.

'Fifty dollars for the whole day,' he answered with another huge grin.

'You mean I hand over fifty dollars and you take me to the market and I just happen to lose you in the crowds and never see you again?'

The grin faded. 'I would never—'

'Spare me,' Victor said, and took fifty dollars out of his wallet. 'I need documents. A passport, that sort of thing. I hear there is a man named Jean Claude who provides such items. Do you know him?'

'Maybe I have a friend who does?'

'Well, turn that maybe into a definitely and I'll pay you another hundred when you introduce us. Deal?'

Sylvester stuffed the fifty dollars into a pocket of his shorts and nodded.

'Meet me at the Fortaleza Ozama in two hours. Bring your friend.'

NINETEEN

After leaving Sylvester, Victor kept moving. He didn't like to stay still, especially in a new town. He was a stranger here, ignorant of the rhythm of street life and melody of the inhabitants. Exploring meant acquiring knowledge that could prove useful, even essential, to both the task at hand and the more difficult job of staying alive.

He liked the city, despite the locals hassling him to buy snacks or worthless souvenirs. Everyone seemed to smile, as if even the most mundane of daily activities brought genuine joy.

With half an hour left before he was due to meet Sylvester, he walked down a pedestrianised street lined with cafés, bars and shops. He followed the street to the seafront and spend a while gazing at the bay. He turned into a tree-lined street where grand colonial buildings towered above him.

A trio of musicians played merengue music as they

strolled along the boulevard. Dominicans sprang into impromptu dance as they passed by. He smiled and clapped in the same way he had seen tourists do. A local girl tried to take his hand so he would dance with her, but he shook his head and moved on. A roadside stall sold coconuts. For an extra dollar the seller let Victor use the machete to chop the top off one and he sipped the juice from a straw as he continued on his way to the grounds of the sixteenth-century Fortaleza Ozama.

Victor waited on the fort's battlements, next to a deactivated cannon that faced the river and pirates and invaders from the previous millennium.

Sylvester arrived alone, and late.

'He won't come here,' Sylvester was quick to explain. 'You must go to him.'

'That's not what we agreed.'

'I could not persuade him.'

Victor said, 'You called yourself the *great* Sylvester.'

The man shrugged. 'He won't come to you.'

'You mean you were not willing to share the money I gave you.'

Sylvester shrugged and repeated, 'I could not persuade him.'

'Let's go,' Victor said.

Sylvester led Victor to where a sun-bleached old VW Beetle was parked under the shade of a palm tree. Sylvester unlocked it with a key while Victor waited on the kerb to look out for watchers. No one seemed to be paying them any attention.

Metal squealed as Sylvester wrenched open the driver's door. 'Get in.'

'Where are we going?'

'My friend lives out of town. Like all the other cartel people.'

'Where out of town?'

'A village near the plantations,' Sylvester replied. 'Fifty or so kilometres north. Only half an hour if we are lucky.'

Victor regarded the Dominican. Being led away into the unknown was not his style, but he had little choice. He wasn't going to find Marte without some help. He pulled open the passenger door, which made even more noise than the driver's had a moment before.

'Don't worry,' Sylvester said with a grin. 'The car is as safe as the houses.'

'If you've set me up in any way,' Victor said, gaze locked on Sylvester, 'I'm the worst enemy you'll ever have.'

Sylvester said nothing, but the grin slipped away from his face.

'You do know that I'm telling you the truth, right?' Victor said.

The Dominican didn't answer and climbed into the Beetle. Victor climbed in too. He was surprised when the car started on the first turn of the ignition.

They set off northeast, leaving Santo Domingo behind and heading into savannah. They passed *gua-gua* buses of tourists on excursions to the Cordillera Central mountains. After twenty minutes on the highway they headed off on to narrow roads winding through villages and sugar and tobacco plantations. Here people used mules as much as cars for transportation. Sugar plantations seemed to be everywhere.

They drove past market stalls set up along the side of the road selling fruit and sugar cane to passers-by, slowing down as the road became narrow with parked vehicles and mules. One stall sold leering carnival masks. It was noisy with locals and tourists alike bartering for better deals.

A traffic cop in mirrored sunglasses waved them over.

'What's wrong?' Victor asked.

'Do not sweat,' Sylvester said. 'He's just seen your foreign face.'

'Bribe?'

Victor's guide only smiled and dropped out of the vehicle to hand over money to the smiling cop, who patted him on the back as if they were friends, before leaving.

'All fine. Only ten dollars.'

'A bargain,' Victor said.

The sun sank down towards the horizon. Dust clouded and swirled in the breeze against a backdrop of blazing orange. Flamingos so bright they seemed to glow pink stood in the glassy waters of a shallow lake.

Sylvester stopped the Beetle on the outskirts of a ramshackle collection of buildings that formed a village in the centre of endless fields of tobacco.

Sylvester climbed out and Victor followed him into the village. Here the buildings were made of wood and painted in faded and cracked pastel colours. The streets were narrow and winding. Cars were rare. Two women hung out laundry on a line over a small balcony. One waved as he passed. Teenagers danced merengue to music emanating from their mobile phones.

He passed an area of grassland where spray paint had been used to make crude baseball markings. The grass had been worn away to bare dirt where every base was marked. A yellow house surrounded by a wall stood on a small hill overlooking the rest of the village. Generators rumbled and coughed fumes into the air. The power supply on the island was inconsistent at best and many relied on their own electricity instead. He passed young women who rolled cigars on their thighs from tobacco leaves while they laughed and joked with one another under a string of twinkling fairy lights.

They ducked under the low archway to enter the bar. Victor nodded to the patrons who looked his way and they nodded back, appreciating his manners. He knew a little of Dominican etiquette. The few dozen men and handful of women drank rum and coconut milk from dappled glasses. The chairs and tables were all made from dark-stained mahogany. Dominican rap music thumped out of speakers. Colourful paintings of famous national boxers hung from the walls. In one corner a blue Hispaniolan parrot cleaned itself inside a gilded brass cage. He could smell seafood cooking: shrimps grilling and kingfish frying.

Sylvester said, 'Wait here,' and went to speak to the bartender.

A bowl of mangoes, oranges and passion fruit sat on a nearby table. Victor selected an orange and used a thumbnail to pierce the skin in a line that followed all the way around its circumference. He peeled that half away and took a bite from the flesh beneath. With his free hand he stroked the chin of an iguana that lay on the same table.

A man said something in Haitian Creole as he passed towards the exit. Victor had no idea how the words translated but a drunken slur was the same in any language.

After a minute had passed, Sylvester waved Victor over and he approached the bar, where he used a napkin to wipe his fingers and deposit the orange skin. The man tending the bar had braided hair, brightened by colourful beads. He wore a necklace of blue and black amber stones.

'You want passport?' the man asked.

Victor nodded.

'You have money?'

Victor nodded again.

The man with the braided hair nodded too and said, 'Come with me.'

'Go with him,' Sylvester added. 'But pay me first. One hundred dollars, please.'

'Fifty,' Victor said. 'Because you didn't bring him to me as agreed.'

Sylvester scowled but didn't argue. He took the fifty dollars and settled on a stool. He waved a young woman over from where she sat at the end of the bar and ordered himself a drink.

The man with the braided hair and amber necklace guided Victor into the back of the bar and through the kitchen, which was so hot and humid Victor had trouble catching his breath. His face was damp with sweat by the time they had exited the back of the bar into a dusty court-yard behind the building.

114

Several dirt bikes and quads were parked in the court-yard. Near to them five Dominican and Haitian men sat at a bench, finishing a meal of white rice, red beans and fish, and drinking mango juice. None of the Haitians looked the right age or build for Marte.

One stood, a large Haitian in a white vest darkened with sweat and grime, and went up to the man with braids. They exchanged whispered words.

'You want the passport?' the Haitian asked Victor.

'Yes.'

'Show me your money.'

Victor said, 'Where's the forger?'

'I'm the forger.'

Victor looked at the man's hands. They were large and strong.

'No, you're not.'

The man with braids headed back to the bar. Victor would have followed his movements but he kept his gaze on the Haitian, because behind him the other four men stood and approached.

Victor heard the bar's back door shut. He didn't hear, but he sensed the lock engaging from the inside.

'Show me your money,' the Haitian said again as he took a machete from the tabletop.

TWENTY

There was no one else in the courtyard apart from Victor and the five locals. The only exit, a narrow covered alleyway, lay behind the men. Two storeys above, a woman hung out wet laundry and watched proceedings. Of the four guys from the table, two had knives drawn. Both were cheap and unsharpened, but still capable of splitting skin and arteries and piercing organs.

The machete was a crude but effective weapon designed for chopping and splitting. With a good swing it could slice a coconut in half or bury itself deep enough in a skull to perform a partial lobotomy. This particular weapon was old and rusted and the blade looked dull, but the Haitian was strong enough to make up for the neglect.

'I have five hundred dollars on me,' Victor said. 'You can have it.'

'Good,' the Haitian said. 'Hand it over.'

'But I'll double that if you tell me where I can find Jean Claud Marte.'

'You have the other five hundred on you?'

'No,' Victor answered. 'It's in my hotel room.'

'What do you want with Marte?'

Two questions asked by the Haitian and neither included the word *who*.

'I want to ask him some questions,' Victor explained. 'All you have to do is tell me where to find him and you can earn yourself another five hundred dollars.' Victor took out his wallet and threw it at the ground between himself and the Haitian, who stood a little in front of the others. 'That's your first five hundred. Five hundred and thirty, to be exact.'

'The rest?'

'I've told you already. It's in my hotel room.'

'Maybe you're hiding it.' He gestured at Victor's shirt. 'Secret pouch or belt.'

'There is none.'

The Haitian pursed his lips in consideration.

Victor said, 'You don't want to do what you're thinking about.'

'Which is?' the Haitian asked with a smirk.

'Don't,' Victor said.

The big Haitian adjusted his footing in a sign of nervous energy. The others were even more anxious: pacing back and forth, clenching jaw muscles, spitting, or scratching.

They were armed and in a position of strength through numbers, but they were just criminals, not professionals. Adrenaline was hyping them up and might make one try something rash before their boss had decided how best to proceed.

Victor continued looking around, never letting one of the locals out of sight for more than a few seconds. He acted passive because he did not want to provoke them into action through a challenge, but he needed them to be aware he was not their average victim. Weakness would only increase their confidence and therefore the risk they would turn to violence if they failed to get their way.

'Take the five hundred now,' Victor said. 'And earn another five hundred the easy way. Don't make this into something it doesn't need to be.'

The Haitian stared at him; his unblinking eyes were bloodshot.

'Well?' Victor asked, when it seemed the big guy would say nothing further.

'I'm thinking,' he said.

This seemed to be a challenging process, given the pinched expression he wore.

The next closest man spat out a glob of saliva that landed on Victor's shoe. A rope of it stretched from the man's lip.

Victor looked at his shoe and then to the man in an acknowledgement of the taunt. 'Thanks, they could use a polish.'

The man smirked in return. Victor did not know if he had been understood. It didn't matter.

The Haitian in the white vest swallowed and clarity seemed to enter his bloodshot eyes for the first time. He smiled.

'No,' he said. 'No five hundred. We search you.'

'You'll find nothing,' Victor said.

The Haitian stepped forward. 'Then I'll be angry.'

The other four locals may not have spoken English, but they understood their boss's tone enough to know what the decision had been. They neither tensed with readiness nor became focused with aggression.

The Haitian came forward, machete raised to threaten more than attack. At least for the moment.

The other four approached too. The two with knives stopped ahead of the two without.

'Okay,' Victor said with a sigh. 'Okay. The other five hundred is in my belt.'

He unbuckled and slid it out from the belt loops of his trousers. He wrapped it around the buckle until it was a tight ball. He held it in one hand and gestured to the big Haitian.

'Here,' Victor said. 'It's in a secret pocket.'

The Haitian smiled in triumph and reached with his free hand for the belt, which—

Victor snapped out, holding on to one end, so the buckle was sent flying into the Haitian's face.

It ripped open the skin of his left eye socket. Blood smeared across his cheek and temple. He staggered away, clutching his face with his free hand while he swung the machete back and forth with the other.

The two with knives darted forward.

Victor feigned an attack at the first, only to whip the belt at the second as he lunged to intercept. The buckle caught him on the side of the skull and he fell face first on to the floor.

A blade glinted in the dim light.

Victor blocked the incoming wrist with a forearm, then released the belt to grab hold of the arm in both hands and swing the guy into the closest wall. He managed to react in time to get a hand out to stop his face colliding with the brick, but not fast enough to stop Victor twisting the blade from his grip and throwing it away.

He blocked a punch from one of the two unarmed Dominicans, caught the wrist before it could recoil and pulled the man closer and into an arm bar, arm locked out, elbow facing upwards.

A second forearm strike broke the joint.

The man wailed, and again tried to punch, but with his other fist. Victor parried it with a shoulder as he turned on the spot, coming outside of the guy's arm. He stamped on his instep, and then swept that injured leg out from under him.

The guy went down hard.

Thick arms grabbed him from behind, pulling him down into a headlock. Victor turned to his assailant, positioning his left foot between the guy's legs for stability, and sent a palm strike into the groin that became an uppercut to the man's chin. The grip loosened and Victor threw him away.

He parried an incoming punch and trapped the arm between elbow and ribs, leaving the man exposed and vulnerable to the counter strike that hit him in the sternum. Victor released him so he could stagger back, doubling over, airless and stunned.

The Haitian roared as he charged, machete swinging in a wide arc.

Victor knocked it from the big man's grip with a downward forearm strike to the wrist and it skidded away across the floor.

A punch to the abdomen knocked Victor back into a wall. He blocked the next blow with a raised forearm, then another as the Haitian tried to overwhelm him with strikes. Victor responded with an open-palm blow to the side of his attacker's face and he staggered away.

The Haitian raised his arms to parry Victor's next strikes, but instead he went low, wrapping his arms around the man's thighs and taking him to the ground.

The wind was knocked from the Haitian's lungs and in that instant of stunned paralysis Victor grabbed hold of the back of his own head and drove his elbow down – using all the strength and mass of his upper body – against his enemy's sternum.

The whole ribcage compressed until the remaining energy had nowhere else to go.

Ribs snapped.

The sound reminded Victor of breaking branches as a boy. The Haitian made a soundless cry.

Victor stood. The man lay as still as he could to avoid the agony of moving with multiple broken ribs. Tears welled in his eyes with every shallow breath.

Victor glanced around to check the other four were finished, then placed a heel on the Haitian's destroyed ribcage.

'Where's Marte?' Victor said as he began applying pressure.

TWENTY-ONE

There were no sentries outside Marte's yellow house and no signs of any other forms of security because up until now it had never been needed. He was an untouchable, feared and respected and protected by the cartel.

Victor entered through an unlocked back door. Inside the yellow house, the hallway was well lit by light fixtures and lamps. The air was humid and hot despite ceiling fans thrumming overhead. He breathed in the scent of grilled shrimp, cigarette smoke and incense. The chatter of multiple conversations fought in his ears along with the clink of glasses and scratch of cutlery on earthenware and hiss of juices on searing metal. He separated out the overlapping sounds into four – then five – voices. There could be more though; present but not partaking: drinking or eating or cooking or just listening.

He stepped with measured footfalls along the hallway, keeping close to one wall because the bare floorboards were old and would no doubt bend and creak under his weight. As he reached deeper into the house and closer to the voices he detected another sound: a clattering scratch, faint but rapid. He recognised the sound and pictured someone cleaning a pistol, the small brush pushed and pulled along the barrel in rapid motions to scrape away gunpowder residue.

At least one potential enemy had disarmed himself as a result. The gun may have been out and in hand, but it would be unloaded. He could not tell for certain about the others, but cooking shrimp or eating from a plate with cutlery or drinking from bottles of beer would restrict their ability to respond.

When he reached the entranceway, he saw the problem. The inhabitants were spread between two rooms – a kitchen and dining room separated by a breakfast bar and half-wall. He could not take all of them by surprise at once nor keep watch on them all at the same time.

He was considering his options when he heard a toilet flush upstairs. There had been no lit windows on the first floor a moment ago so either the bathroom had no window or the person had not been in there at the time.

Victor moved past the entranceway and into the stairwell, standing in the gap beneath it with his chin near his chest so he did not have to squat down.

After forty seconds he heard a door open upstairs and footsteps grow louder. The stairs creaked and groaned as the person descended – a heavy person, overweight or large with bone and muscle. The rhythm of their steps suggested they were drunk or had some disability affecting their movements.

The person came into view. He was a giant, the dome of his head almost touching the low ceiling. Victor saw a brief profile of the man as he turned into the entranceway and then his back. He lifted weights or trained in some other physical activity that had strengthened his arms, shoulders and back. He appeared healthy, so Victor deduced he had been drinking.

Four long steps brought Victor up behind the giant. He timed his footfalls with the man's own, disguising the noise while the man's great size hid Victor from those in the room beyond.

'*Aleo*,' shouted someone.

The giant responded with a grunt, then a wail as Victor kicked him hard in the back of the knee, folding the leg and dropping the giant down low enough for Victor to wrap an arm around the man's neck, pit of the elbow above the Adam's apple, forearm and biceps applying simultaneous pressure to both carotid arteries.

For a second everyone in the rooms was too stunned to react. In that instant, Victor took a snapshot of the layout and the inhabitants: two men sitting at a table in one corner, bottles of beer and playing cards and gambling chips on the table surface; another slumped in an armchair, smoking a cigarette. He could only see two in the kitchen: one at the breakfast bar eating, the second by the stove, but he knew there was at least one more out of his line of sight.

Victor said, 'Be cool or he dies.'

It was hotter in the dining room, with the heat from the men adding to the heat coming from the stove. Ceiling fans pushed around a haze of cigarette smoke. The men wore T-shirts or vests, and shorts. Trainers or sandals covered their feet. He saw three handguns for three men – stripped on the table, lying on the floor by one's feet and resting on the arm of an unoccupied sofa. A poor show, even by criminal standards.

A glowing bare bulb hung from the ceiling. Insects buzzed around it and remains of others were fused to the surface. Next to the table, a tall shaded lamp added to the illumination. The floorboards were bare and in as poor condition as those in the hallway. Cracks and chips were scattered across the painted walls. A frame hung skewed on one wall, without a painting. A thin curtain shielded the only window and rippled in the flow of air.

The two at the table looked related, sharing similar builds and facial features. One had a shaved head, the other an Afro. The man in the armchair was a lot older but a lot tougher too. He was a little under six feet tall with a slim, wiry frame. His head was shaved and a sparse beard covered his chin and jawline. He was in his late forties and well preserved, despite the smoking habit. He had the look about him of someone who had been through hardship but had triumphed despite great odds. He was the leader, Victor was sure. Men like that did not take orders well.

The one at the breakfast bar was the youngest, in his early twenties but a grown man. Half a dozen empty bottles of beer stood in a parade line near to his plate.

The giant's strength was incredible. With one hand he almost pulled Victor's arm away, but Victor increased the pressure of the choke by using his free hand to push the man's head forward.

In seconds he had weakened and Victor eased off the pressure to stop him losing consciousness. If he did, Victor would struggle to keep him on his feet and he couldn't risk losing his combined human shield and bargaining chip. The others would not know if their friend had passed out or died.

'We are cool,' the one in the armchair said.

'Hands where I can see them,' Victor said. 'Those in the kitchen, get in here now.'

The three before him raised their hands. The others were slow to move despite the hostage because they were wary and unsure of Victor's intentions and waiting instructions. The two he had seen came shuffling into the dining area, hands up and palms showing.

'And the other one.'

'Who?' the one in the armchair said.

Victor tripled the force on the giant's neck. He gasped and his face contorted, eyes pinched shut, skin reddening.

'He hasn't got long,' Victor said.

'*OKAY, OKAY. Lucian, get in here.*'

The man with the cigarette gestured with his head and a youth rushed into view from the kitchen. He was tall and thin; long arms without a hint of muscle definition hung from his T-shirt. The light shone off a face slick with adolescent oil.

'Get out,' Victor said. 'You're too young for this.'

The kid stayed put. He squared himself, defiant. His eyes were wide and staring. His nostrils flared.

Again, Victor increased the pressure on the giant's carotids.

'Tell him to go,' Victor said to the man in the armchair.

He did, but even ordered by an authority figure, the kid didn't hurry. By the time Victor heard the back door open and then bang shut, the giant was almost out. He eased off to keep him conscious. The giant was no longer trying to fight, unable to free himself and too scared to keep trying and encourage Victor to increase the pressure. Pain compliance was a powerful tool.

'What do you want?' the smoking man asked.

'Put out the cigarette.'

The man shrugged and snubbed it out in a metal ashtray balanced on the armrest. 'Is that it?'

'Where's Marte?'

'You're looking at him. Or at least you're looking at the man who uses that identity. The real Marte, the man you no doubt have been looking for, died a long time ago.'

'Why the deception?'

The man shrugged again. 'No reason beyond insurance. People who ask for me usually do so because they seek to do me, or those close to me, harm.'

Victor, choking the giant to near death, remained silent.

Marte sat up. 'Why don't you release him?'

Victor tried, and failed, to read anything more in Marte's eyes. The giant tensed.

Marte gestured at Victor. 'There is no need to be concerned with reprisals. You'll find my manners are a good deal better than your own.'

Victor glanced at the other men in the room. They were as anxious as before, but he sensed a readiness too. Maybe they had heard Marte speak like this before and knew what would happen next. Or he could have slipped them some predetermined code.

Victor knew a prelude to violence when he saw it.

He saw it begin almost thirty seconds before anyone made an aggressive move. He recognised the slow preamble as an orchestrated routine.

The guy on the sofa leaned forward, as if for comfort, but Victor understood the action. Whether it had been conscious or not, it was impossible to spring up fast when sitting slumped with head far out of line with the hips.

The two at the corner table were already both looking his way, but subtle adjustments to their poses gave away their intentions. The one who had his back to him was twisted round as much as his spine would let him. One hand rested on the back of the chair, the other on the table surface, while the one facing him had both palms on his knees, ready to explode up to his feet.

'Well?' Marte said.

Victor nodded, because now he knew what his enemies were going to do, he knew what he would do in response. There was nothing to gain in waiting any longer.

'Manners,' Victor said.

Marte smiled once more and his men attacked.

TWENTY-TWO

Victor wrenched the giant's head into a neck crank, not killing him but taking him out of the fight with damaged ligaments, torn tendons, ripped muscle, and hyperextended vertebrae. He heaved him forward, into Marte, turning to go for the one on the sofa as he sprang out of the seat.

Victor shot out a stomp kick at the guy's leading knee. The leg folded backwards the wrong way. He collapsed on to the sofa, screaming.

A spinning roundhouse kick knocked the gun out of the hand of the guy with the Afro as he grabbed it before standing.

With his own gun lying useless in pieces, the second man at the table went for a takedown, but with no real technique, charging into Victor and going low, the top of his skull colliding with Victor's abdomen, arms wrapping around his thighs.

Victor shoved the head down and to one side as he was pushed back, then, wrapping his arm around the guy's head and locked off with a gable grip, put the guy into a face bar, his wrist bone tight across the guy's nose and cheek. When Victor squeezed the head against his sternum the man screamed louder than the guy with the broken knee because the skull was thick and strong and could resist the enormous pressure Victor applied with the blade of his forearm, but the nose and cheekbone could not. The cartilage in the nose flattened first before the weak bone splintered and crushed and the prominent cheekbone cracked.

Victor threw the man to the floor and grabbed a seat cushion from the sofa to use as shield as the guy with the Afro attacked again, this time stabbing with a kitchen knife. The blade pierced straight through the foam cushion, and Victor folded and wrapped the cushion around the hand and wrist, trapping the knife and pulling the guy closer and into an elbow.

His head snapped back and teeth pattered the ceiling.

A sweep took him from his feet. He landed hard, semiconscious, face smeared in bright blood. Victor raised a foot to stamp his heel on to the guy's temple, but instead lowered the foot back where it had been. Killing Marte's men was not the plan, but resisting the instinct to finish him off tested Victor's willpower. He'd been taught to always neutralise a threat on his terms if possible, and if not at the first available opportunity.

Now though his priority was to secure Marte's cooperation. Killing his entire crew might encourage that, but it had an equal chance of securing defiance. And while those crew members were still alive they could be used as leverage in a way a corpse could not.

The Haitian appeared as unaffected by the violence as he seemed unafraid that no one stood between him and Victor. Which made him a good actor or insane. He was at Victor's mercy.

'How much money you want?' Marte asked as he regarded Victor with an indifferent gaze.

Victor held the gaze. 'To do what?'

Marte gestured at his five men, all alive but out of the fight and writhing in pain with crippling injuries. 'How much do you want to go on my payroll instead of these useless fucks?'

'You can't afford me.'

Marte sat back in the chair and said, 'Then what do you want?'

'You know why I'm here. I'm looking for information. That's all. I want to know about a woman. She goes by the handle Raven.'

'No you don't. That kind of knowledge will get you killed.'

'We all have to die sometime.'

Marte said, 'But why rush towards it?'

'I prefer to meet death on my terms.'

'Then you're a fool if you believe you can decide your end.'

Victor shook his head. 'That's not what I said. And you're avoiding the question.'

'You have yet to ask me a question.'

'Where is she?'

Marte smiled because he believed Victor had acquiesced too early, which made him feel in control of the conversation. Which was how Victor wanted him to feel.

'Why would I even know? You think she trusts me? You think she trusts anyone?'

Victor said nothing.

Marte used a palm to wipe sweat from his face. Victor could feel the perspiration coating his own skin, unable to evaporate into the humid air.

Marte swallowed. 'And what do I get in return for this information you desire?'

Victor said, 'It's more a case of what you don't get.'

He looked at the five men moaning on the floor. Marte did the same, but with contempt. He sucked on his lower lip.

Victor said, 'Do you still think I have no manners?'

'Who are you?'

'I'm two people,' Victor answered. 'I'm either no one or I'm the worst enemy you'll ever have.'

'The cartel runs this island. They protect me.' He used a thumb to point at himself for emphasis.

'Then where are they now?'

'You can't touch me,' Marte said, defiant.

'I can do whatever I choose.'

'If you do, they'll take your head,' Marte sneered, drawing an index finger across his throat.

'It's right here,' Victor said. 'What are they waiting for?'

Marte reached for his packet of cigarettes.

'Don't,' Victor said.

Marte looked up at Victor and then to the cigarettes. He kept his fingers on the packet for a moment in silent debate, but then withdrew the hand. Which meant Victor no longer needed to break it.

He took two steps and stamped down on the right hand

of the guy with the Afro, who had been reaching for the gun Victor had kicked across the floor. The man wailed through his smashed teeth. Victor picked up the pistol and tucked it into his waistband.

'I only want information about Raven,' he said. 'This never had to get ugly. I would have paid you well. You might even have gained yourself an ally in the process, which would have been particularly useful to you as you're going to end up losing one.'

Marte considered this.

'What's to think about?' Victor asked. 'You don't have a choice. Any delay, any withholding, is only going to end up being bad for you, not me. I have all the time in the world.'

'She'll kill me for betraying her.'

'She won't,' Victor said.

Marte sneered again. 'And why wouldn't she? She demands loyalty. She will not forgive this betrayal.'

'She won't kill you because I'm going to kill her first.'

'But why? What has she done to warrant your wrath?'

Victor said, 'Does it really matter to you why?'

Marte looked at the ceiling and shrugged. 'I suppose not. I doubt the reasons of a man like you would make any sense to me. I always liked her, though.'

'I'll tell her you said so if that makes you feel better.'

'A little.' Marte sighed and examined his hands, as if looking for some answer only they could give. When he looked back to Victor he said, 'I don't know where she is. She would never tell me that. So I can't help you.'

'You're a fixer. She's a killer. So you got her documents, passports, things like that. Yes?'

'That's right,' Marte said.

'I want the names of those identities. Copies or any photographs, if possible.'

The Haitian shook his head. 'No copies. No photographs. She had me burn any evidence.'

'And you kept nothing for insurance in case she turned on you?'

'She would never turn on me.'

'What makes you so sure?'

'Because she has honour,' Marte said. 'Unlike you.'

Victor remained silent.

Marte studied him. 'You're really going to kill her?'

'As sure as night follows day.'

'And you believe you are capable of such a feat? People have tried before.'

Victor said, 'Everything made of flesh can, and will, die. Raven is no different.'

'You make it sound so simple. You make it sound so very easy.'

'She's not bulletproof, is she?'

Marte smirked, then nodded, to himself as much as Victor. 'Okay, you win. I'll write you a list. Every identity I've ever created or sourced for her. Will that do?'

'If you miss out any names, or if any of that information proves false, or if you try and warn her—'

'I know,' Marte said with a heavy sigh. 'I'm scared of her, yes. But now I'm scared of you more.'

Victor said, 'Then you're smarter than you've acted so far.'

TWENTY-THREE

Before leaving the island, Victor called Halleck from his hotel room in San Domingo and read out the aliases Marte had supplied to Raven in the last twelve months.

'I've got a hit,' Halleck said when he called back. 'Angelica Margolis flew into LAX three days ago on a flight from Paris.'

'That doesn't help me a whole lot,' Victor replied. 'The US is a big place. She could be anywhere by now.'

'There's more. A private landlord in New York ran a credit check on Miss Margolis three months ago.'

Victor said, 'Tell me the address.'

It took two whole days to reach New York. Flying direct would have taken a little over five hours, from San Domingo to Miami, Miami to New York. But Victor didn't travel in straight lines, least of all when entering the United States. He caught a flight from the Dominican Republic to Jamaica, and then to Nicaragua and then Mexico. He crossed the border into the US in a rental car. Then domestic flights bounced him across the country until he disembarked in Newark, New Jersey.

He walked through the airport terminal. People saw him, but they didn't see him. They went about their business, not paying attention to the man in the charcoal suit who walked among them. His height would have made him stand out a little, but the lowered chin and lax posture shrank him enough not to be noticeable. The bland clothes, pale skin, cheap haircut and non-prescription glasses meant features that might otherwise be considered appealing seemed ordinary. He neither walked fast enough to catch the eye nor slow enough to generate annoyance. His expression was neutral. No one would wonder what he was thinking. No one would smile at him.

The only thing that could be considered notable were his eyes, which never stopped moving.

Outside, while waiting for a cab, he stood near a professional couple in sharp suits and lots of hair product as they argued with obvious passion about nothing Victor could understand. In his experience, relationships made people miserable. He didn't understand what kept people together when they were unhappy. He was used to being alone. He reminded himself that wasn't the same as being used to loneliness.

The cab driver wanted to talk about baseball. Victor was no sports fan. They settled on politics as a middle ground. To make the ride as smooth as possible Victor agreed with everything the driver said.

By the time they had passed through the Lincoln Tunnel

the weariness of two days spent travelling was catching up with Victor. He had the driver drop him off outside a hotel, waited until the cab had turned off the street, and walked for three blocks until he found a hotel that felt right. They had plenty of rooms available. Victor asked for one on the second floor.

He placed his attaché case on the bed and performed a sweep of the room, looking for anything out of the ordinary and memorising the layout, position of furniture and objects that might be useful as improvised weapons, should they be needed. The window opened a fraction and he let in cold, polluted air. Sirens sounded somewhere in the distance in a muted, half-strangled whine. A thousand lit windows stared back at him.

He would have lingered to enjoy the view, but a sniper could be at any one of those windows.

The wardrobe was set into the wall and could not be positioned in front of the door. Instead, Victor used the heavy desk as a barricade. It wouldn't stop a determined assault, but it would buy him time to slip out of the window. Two storeys up wasn't a long way down; high enough so someone could not heave themselves up with any degree of ease, but not so high that Victor would have to spend a significant amount of time scaling down when his life depended on it.

He lay on top of the cover, still wearing his suit and shoes, and slept.

When he awoke, it would be time to go to work.

TWENTY-FOUR

The address Halleck had given Victor for 'Angelica Margolis' corresponded to a rundown tenement in a bad neighbourhood in the Bronx. It took Victor two hours to make the forty-minute journey because he spent extra time on counter surveillance to reduce the chances he was being shadowed.

He knew enough about Raven to increase his odds of spotting her, but she knew more about him. She had tracked him down before he even knew she existed.

The neighbourhood was a mix of dilapidated social housing and the commercial enterprises that served the residents – thrift stores, pawnbrokers, fast loans, 99c stores and ambulance chasers. Every one had security gates ready to be rolled down. No ground-floor window was free of bars. Drug dealers hung around on the corners of alleyways and in the shelter of doorways. An abandoned church was boarded up and falling down. Graffiti marked any area of defenceless brickwork. Razor wire protected every low wall.

Victor walked by a disused basketball court. The backboards were cracked and the hoops were missing. A homeless guy slept in one corner under a blanket of nothing but damp cardboard boxes. Victor could see a hand-scribbled sign near to where the man lay and just about made out the word *veteran*.

To the south, multibillion-dollar skyscrapers were backlit by a pale afternoon sun.

He circled the block on which the tenement stood, taking the pavements opposite, checking out the locale for signs of anything out of the ordinary. No one waited longer than they needed at any bus stop. No construction workers or repairmen were busy doing nothing. Watchers disguised as dealers and degenerates would be hard to identify, but he trusted the genuine loiterers would do that for him. They would scatter if they noticed someone who didn't belong amongst them, suspecting cops.

There were a few anonymous vehicles parked in the area – a dirty red Impala, a midnight-blue panel van with a delivery-company logo on the side, a modified Dodge pickup, and a rust-spotted grey cargo van – but he saw no people waiting inside any.

Watchers could be hidden in the back of either van, but the cargo van had no rear windows and the panel van was parked side-on to the tenement, so anyone in the back wouldn't be able to watch it.

Victor saw why Raven had picked the area for a safe house. It wasn't because she was short of money. Professional killing paid well, and for the best the rewards were huge. Raven was good enough to get high-profile contracts.

If she wanted to she could afford to live in five-star hotels, as Victor did more often than not. The area offered other advantages beyond money.

For all the dereliction and obvious criminal activity, he had not seen a single cop. With more crime than there were cops to combat it, there weren't enough resources available to serve those who hung on to the edges of society. Residents here would keep to themselves and even if they did become suspicious of the comings and goings of a certain individual, they were not going to rush to inform the police any more than the police would rush to investigate.

A landlord here would be happy to take cash payments for rent and a few extra bills in return for ignoring a lack of references or credit history. She might not even need to show any ID at all. She could keep her safe house operational with a minimum of funds and maximum of anonymity.

Victor found himself nodding as he made his way down the alleyway at the back of the building. There were trash cans and dumpsters and piles of garbage bags. A teenage girl was sitting on the ground examining her nails. When she heard him approach and looked up he saw she had a black eye. She scrambled to her feet and ran.

When she had gone, he examined the fire exits and windows and plotted escape routes should he need to make a fast exit. He was here on reconnaissance, but the only thing he had to lose by planning for the worst was time, and that was one thing he had in abundance.

A woman was leaving her ground-floor apartment as he headed for the stairs. Her greasy hair was tied back with a rubber band and ash fell from the cigarette between her lips as she dragged a pushchair through her doorway. The baby it contained was crying. She didn't look at Victor once.

There was no sign to say the elevator was out of service, but Victor always took the stairs if the option was there. Maybe not if the alternative was forty flights of stairs, but stepping into an elevator was as close to volunteering to trap himself in a steel coffin as he was ever going to get. There was no telling who or what was going to be there when the doors opened again. The last time he had been inside an elevator, the doors had opened to reveal an assassin who had come closer to killing him than anyone had before or since.

Victor flexed his left hand as he reached the top floor. He wasn't surprised Raven had chosen to rent an apartment on this floor and not one below. Having people above as well as below was no fun for anyone, least of all assassins looking for security and privacy. As such, he expected to find her safe house would be a corner apartment, so she would only have neighbours to one side. Windows on two walls gave snipers more options, but armoured glass or even blackout blinds could negate that threat, and more windows meant more means of escape.

He made his way down a narrow corridor to the front door of Raven's safe house, which occupied the building's southwest corner. Had their roles been reversed he would have chosen the same one. South-facing windows would reflect the most available sunlight, making it harder for watchers and snipers to see through.

Her front door was coated in resilient green paint like the

rest of the front doors. And like them it had been used enough to have gained scratch marks around the keyhole and scuff marks where it had been toed open, though less than the other doors. Which made sense. Raven was using it as a safe house, not a residence. She wouldn't be here anywhere near as often as those who lived within the building. If he conducted a building-wide comparison study of scratches and marks he knew he could form a rough estimate of how much time Raven spent here, but he didn't need to know her life in that much detail when all he planned to do was end it.

He was surprised to find only two standard locks securing the door, but he reasoned her primary layer of defence was the anonymity the apartment provided. The kind of enemies that would find her safe house would not be defeated in their intentions by any lock, no matter how sophisticated.

Victor had been picking locks long before he took his first contract as a professional killer. He had learned to shimmy open car doors before he had learned to drive. He had mastered the intricacies of raking tumblers long before he owned a property key of his own. If he had to, he could crack a safe with nothing more than graph paper and a pencil. The two standard locks fitted to low-cost urban housing were nothing he hadn't beaten countless times as an adolescent delinquent. He had Raven's front door unlocked in less than ten seconds.

He turned the handle and stepped across the threshold.

TWENTY-FIVE

Two men sat in the back of the midnight-blue panel van. They used upturned beer-bottle crates as seats. Not comfortable, but practical. If a cop insisted on taking a look in the back he would see nothing to catch his attention. The windows of the van's rear doors had been treated with one-way film. They could see out. No one could see in. The film was similar to that used in sunglasses and the outside world was darkened as a result. On a grey winter day that darkness was pronounced, but they could see enough to do their job. That job was to watch.

But they were not using the rear windows to watch. They had parked across the street from the tenement building. Parking with the one-way windows facing the building would be too suspicious to such a careful professional.

Instead, they used a camera. The lens of the camera looked through a hole in the van's side panelling. That hole was covered in glass and treated in the same way as the windows in the rear doors and disguised within the delivery-company logo. It was almost impossible to see unless someone knew where to look for it and was standing no more than two feet away.

One of the men watched a screen and operated the camera's zoom and focus. He whispered observations to the second man, who noted everything because neither man knew exactly what was required of them but they knew enough to know that they were not to cut corners. This was a serious business. The price for failure was absolute.

'Subject has entered the tenement,' the first man said.

'Manner?' the second asked.

'The same as when he arrived: relaxed.'

'Is he carrying anything?'

'If he is, it's in his pockets. His hands are empty.'

The second man nodded and scribbled on his notepad with a 2B pencil. His shirt pocket had another two for when the first grew blunt. There might not be time to sharpen it. The graphite might snap. Pens were not much better. They could stop working for no good reason. Pencils could write when wet or on wet paper and pretty much any surface. He preferred pencils. No contest.

A phone rang. The first man answered it. He didn't need to say hello or state his name or ask the caller how he could help. Only one person knew this number.

The caller said, 'Is it him?'

'I think so.'

'Can you track him when he exits?'

'I would advise against that course of action. Subject is observant and paranoid. If we follow, he will make us.

Repeat: he will make us. I suggest bringing in Bravo Team to establish surveillance at Point Niner and wait for him to show.'

The caller said, 'Your advice is noted. Proceed as planned. Follow the subject as soon as he leaves the building. Do not let him out of your sight.'

'Understood.'

The call disconnected.

'Better get ready,' the first man said.

The second climbed behind the wheel.

TWENTY-SIX

No intruder alarm had been fitted. Victor saw no cameras or microphones or motion sensors in the hallway he stepped into, but that didn't mean they weren't there. He knew how to hide them so that only a search that would take hours to complete and leave the apartment in ruins would uncover them. If he knew that, so could she. He had neither the time nor the necessity to do so. Once he killed her, any recordings of him in her safe house could be found at his leisure. Or even ignored, because they were no threat in the hands of a corpse.

The lights were off throughout the apartment, and the drawn blinds made it dark. The air was cold too. Even colder than on the streets. No heating had been on today to take the chill from the air, and no sunlight had been able to spill through windows to raise the temperature in line with that outside.

Victor let the door fall shut behind him, stood still and

breathed in slow, shallow breaths to let every sound reach his ears unobstructed. Even without the darkness of the apartment limiting his vision, hearing was more important. Light could not penetrate walls.

He heard traffic outside, the ticking sound of pipes at work, and a television or radio emanating from the apartment beneath or next door – he couldn't be sure which. He stood statue-still in the darkness for several minutes until he was certain he was alone.

He hadn't expected to find Raven inside, but it would have made things easier if she was hiding, or better yet asleep and vulnerable.

He explored the safe house, moving from room to room in a slow, methodical manner. There were few furnishings and only those that fulfilled the most basic requirements of someone who needed to sleep and eat and lie low and nothing else. The lounge was almost cavernous, furnished only with a single foldout camping chair and table. A second foldout chair was still in its packaging. The three pieces had come as a set, but she had set up only what she needed. There was no television or sound system or any other electronic device. Aside from the folding chair and table the only other item was a paperback novel. It looked new and unread. The spine was still intact and the pages not unfurled.

He had never heard of the author or the title, but it had been published within the last two years and what fiction he read was picked at random from second-hand book stores, often by the box, so if anyone studied his reading material they would find no indication of personality or taste. Raven might pick new books in the same way. He could learn nothing about her from a single novel she had not yet read.

The kitchen had no toaster or kettle or microwave or other labour-saving device. In a cupboard he found a set of three rugged iron camping pans – small, medium and large. In another he found a twelve-piece crockery set. The only food he found was an unopened box of cereal. There were enough carbohydrates contained within to keep a person alive for a long time.

In a drawer, a cutlery set had been aligned with neatness and order. It was the only true sign of personality so far, but he had expected to find some indication of a need to have everything in its place, accounted for and ordered. Like himself, she was fastidious in her need for order. His had grown out of a need to survive and a knowledge that the smallest detail, the smallest mistake, might make the difference between life and death. In the neat, ordered layout of the cutlery he saw that she was the same as him in that way as she was in others and he wondered how else they would prove to be alike.

He did not enjoy discovering the similarities between them because it would make her harder to kill. But better he find out in advance than when his life might depend on it.

He found soap in the bathroom, but no toothbrush. He imagined she bought a new one with her every time she stayed, disposing of the old one and its traces of DNA.

The apartment had a single bedroom, which contained nothing but a sleeping bag. It was a quality item. He assumed it had been brought from the same store as the chair and table set and the items in the kitchen. He wondered what lie she had told the person who served her. He squatted down to smell it. There was a trace of female scent within the synthetic material. He had read that smell produced the most powerful memories.

He was a little surprised to find no gun. But, like the toothbrush, she must bring a weapon with her and take it away again. With the limited security offered by the front door, she did not feel it prudent to leave a weapon, no doubt illegal, behind.

An idea came to him. He returned to the lounge and picked up the paperback novel. A sticker on the front jacket showed it had been in a promotion. He had to fight the compulsion to peel the sticker away. Had it been his own he would have done so before he had walked out of the store. Raven hadn't felt the same need, but it seemed as though she hadn't read the book either.

He balanced it by the spine in the centre of his palm and let the pages fall open. They did not do so in an even manner, parting to about a third of the way through instead of the middle. The book was in far too good condition for Raven to have read up to page 100 of a 311-page paperback novel.

There were no pencil or pen marks on the page, no words circled or underlined. He read both pages. It was almost all dialogue between two characters, discussing another character. Victor had no idea what the story was about. He took the book into the kitchen, flicked a wall switch to send power to the oven, and turned dials to operate it. A fan whirred and a light came on. He switched off the ceiling light so the only illumination came from the oven, leaving the room dark and glowing in soft orange.

Sitting down next to the oven, he positioned himself and angled the book so the light shone across the pages in a horizontal manner. With no other light reaching the pages, the texture of the paper was obvious – rough and fibrous. It had a moonscape quality of tiny hills and shadowed craters.

Except in three places.

On page 100 the first word on the first line had a faint horizontal groove beneath it, where pressure had been applied. Victor placed the nail of his little finger into the groove. It was a good fit for his, or the index finger of a medium-sized woman. Towards the bottom of the page, the first word of the twenty-eighth line had a similar groove. On the same line was another, deeper, groove, under the word *met*. It was the fourth word on the line.

He pictured Raven opening the book to page 100, placing her fingernail under the first word and counting down to the twenty-eighth line, then across to the fourth word. She had been given the name of the book and a six-digit numerical code – 100, 28, 4 – resulting in a single word, or maybe another code comprised of three letters – m, e and t.

He retried balancing the book by its spine in his palm in case it fell open to another page, but without success. At first it seemed odd that she had left the book behind, given its significance, but he reasoned she would need to use it again for further communications with whoever had given her the first code. Bookstores were a lot rarer than they used to be and there was no guarantee she could buy another copy when she needed to.

In his earlier days in the business he had sometimes used newspapers and similar codes to communicate with those it was too risky to meet face-to-face, but he had never done so with novels.

He thought about the word *met*, and what it could mean, and what *m-e-t* could stand for. He was no sports fan but he knew of the New York Mets. Met was also a common name for the Metropolitan Museum of Art. Or met might signify a pre-determined course of action like a meeting or could be a code word for something or someone.

But on its own it couldn't reveal much information. Unless the numbers that led to it were also significant. He flicked back to page 100 and then turned back pages until he came to the start of the chapter: 15. Today's date was the fifteenth.

100, 28, and 4. He didn't understand what the numbers could represent. A grid reference, maybe. Or the 4 might denote the time of the meeting or handover or whatever else. 100 could be for the street, but there was no way of knowing whether it meant E 100th Street or W 100th Street.

He had no more time to ponder it because two federal agents kicked open the front door.

TWENTY-SEVEN

There were no preceding footsteps, so they had to have approached with stealth or caution, but he heard them shuffle outside the apartment door an instant before it was kicked open.

'*Federal agents*,' shouted one. A woman.

The voice carried weight and resonance and confidence. It was the well-practised shout of someone who believed in the absolute authority and righteousness of the words. She sounded to Victor like the real thing.

Which was a serious problem. He would have preferred it to be a bluff, and the woman a killer trying to catch him off-guard. Killers were easier to deal with. There wasn't any grey area. It was always a simple case of killing them before they killed him. He could lie in weight and ambush the first one, disarming him or her of their gun and perhaps using them as a human shield while he shot their partner before torturing anything useful out of the one alive before finishing them off.

152

Government agents were different. It was all grey area. There were no black-and-white decisions. Killing them was to be avoided at all costs. The fallout would be huge. No expense would be spared in the attempt to bring him to justice. Killing drug lords and arms dealers and corrupt spies and fellow assassins might bring him to the attention of law enforcement, but killing government agents who were doing their job would unleash a whirlwind of retribution. Also, they were not going to be an immediate threat to his life, which meant killing them would be hard to justify to what remained of his conscience. He would if he had to – if it came down to taking their lives or spending the rest of his behind bars, but only then.

There was nowhere to hide in the apartment, so he raised his hands, said, 'Don't shoot,' and stepped out into the hallway.

Both agents had him in their gunsights in an instant. The one on the right was the woman he had heard. She was young, with olive skin and jet-black hair pulled back into a ponytail so tight the hair at the top of her forehead was thinning. She wore a grey trouser suit and stared at him with the same authority and confidence he had detected in her voice.

The man next to her was tall and well built. He had a thick neck and a solid, angular jaw. His hair was clipped military-short and his skin was tanned and smooth. He looked a few years older than the woman. His gaze was locked on to Victor with a more evaluating quality.

Neither had expected to see him.

'Who the fuck are you?' the man demanded.

Victor kept his hands above his shoulders. He stood passive, but unafraid. 'I'm saying nothing until I see some ID.'

'We don't have to show you shit.'

'Then this conversation is going to take a very long time.'

The woman stepped forward. 'We're from Homeland Security. I'm agent Guerrero. This is agent Wallinger.'

Victor said, 'I didn't ask your names. I asked to see your ID.'

'Don't make us arrest you,' the man said.

'Arrest me if you want to. But I've done nothing wrong so I'll be walking within the hour and you'll look like an idiot in front of your boss.'

The man glared. The woman took her left hand from her right and lowered her gun. 'I'm going to put this away and take out my ID. Okay?'

Victor nodded.

She inserted the pistol back into a black leather holster attached to her belt on the right hip. Then she reached beneath her suit jacket and withdrew a badge booklet, also black leather. She opened it up and held it out for Victor to see.

'It's dark,' he said. 'I can't read it from here. Step closer.'

She did. The man adjusted his aim on Victor, looking as though he would like nothing more in the world than to paint the wall with the contents of Victor's skull.

The woman stopped out of arm's reach and he examined the badge. Occupying one half was a golden Homeland Security badge. On the second half was a photograph of the woman before him. *Agent Miriam Guerrero*. The photograph was a few years old. Guerrero's hair was thicker at the front. It was genuine as far as Victor could tell, not that he had ever come this near to a Homeland Security ID before. But if they were pretending, they could have shot him by now. There was no need for a continued deception.

Victor gestured to the man. 'His turn.'

The man did nothing but stare at Victor and hold his aim.

'Let's make this easy, shall we?' the woman named Guerrero said to the man.

'Fine,' he said in return.

He put his gun away and showed his ID to Victor with almost the exact same movements that Guerrero had. Maybe they were even trained how to identify themselves.

Guerrero looked to Victor. 'Now it's your turn.'

'My name is Jimmy Marino. I'm a credit enforcement agent.'

He showed the ID. It was fake, but the best money could buy. They would need to being up the identity from the DMV's database to see that Victor's picture did not match Mr Marino's. If they could tell it was fake by eye alone then they were the best anti-fraud agents in the whole country.

'You mean you're a debt collector,' Guerrero said.

'Miss Margolis is behind with her rent. The landlord hired me to get his money.'

Wallinger handed the driver's licence back, then said, 'Company ID.'

'I don't carry any. I'm a one-man band.'

Guerrero said, 'Business card then.'

'I work on personal recommendations only.'

Wallinger looked him over. 'So, let me get this right,

you're a debt collector who works for himself, who doesn't carry business cards because he only works on personal recommendations?'

'That's what I said.'

'Why do I think you're in a more *organised* kind of activity?'

Victor said, 'I don't know what you're talking about.'

Wallinger said, 'Then let me make it more obvious: I think you're mob. I think you're an enforcer. Would I be close?'

'I don't know why you would think that, Agent Wallinger. You must be a naturally suspicious person,' Victor said, gaze even, but with just enough arrogance in his eyes to help Wallinger along the wrong path. Any path that led away from Victor's true profession would do, but Wallinger had already made a wrong assumption. It would be wasteful not to exploit it. 'Or are you suggesting I'm involved in organised crime because I have an Italian surname? Because that would make you a bigot.'

Wallinger frowned but kept his lips tight.

'I've committed no crime,' Victor continued. 'You're the ones who kicked the door open. I used a key supplied by the landlord. If I wasn't meant to be here you wouldn't have had to wreck the door, would you? You could have simply walked inside.'

'Whatever,' Wallinger said.

'Where's your warrant?' Victor said, even though he knew they didn't need one to enter private property if they had reasonable suspicions of criminal activity or a threat to national security.

'We don't need one,' Wallinger said, looking smug.

'We're going to look around,' Guerrero said and gestured to the floor. 'You, don't go anywhere. We'll be right back.'

And they were, in less than a minute. There wasn't a whole lot to look at. Victor did as instructed and stayed in the same spot.

Wallinger said, 'There's a good boy,' on his return, as if talking to an obedient dog. The taunt had no effect on Victor but he narrowed his eyes and flexed the muscles of his jaw because that's what Marino the debt collector would do.

'What are you guys doing here?' Victor asked.

Neither answered.

'The door's going to need repairing. I'd like to be able to explain why when I'm asked about it.'

They ignored him. Wallinger adjusted his belt while Guerrero typed out a message on her phone.

'What's Angelica done?'

'Who says she's done anything?' Wallinger asked.

'Two Homeland Security agents kicked in her front door. You wouldn't do that for a parking ticket.'

'Maybe we just need to ask her some questions.'

'So you didn't think to knock?'

'Maybe she's in danger.'

Guerrero said, 'When did you last see Miss Margolis?'

'I've never met her before.'

'Do you have any idea where she might have gone?'

'If I did, I would be there now. I wouldn't be wasting my time here, would I? I've got a job to do.'

'Okay,' Guerrero said. 'You're free to go.'

'I didn't realise I hadn't been.'

Wallinger frowned at him.

'You know,' Victor said. 'If you tell me what this is all about then maybe I'll be able to help.'

Guerrero said, 'A minute ago you said you didn't know where we could find her. If you're withholding information from us then that's obstruction of justice and you'll go to prison.'

'Why would I withhold information from you?'

'So you can collect the debt she owes before we get to her.'

'Ah,' Victor said. 'Now I understand.'

Wallinger said, 'What do you understand?'

'Angelica wouldn't be able to pay the debt once you track her down, so you're not looking to protect her or ask her questions. She won't be able to pay off her debt because she'll be in custody.'

Wallinger and Guerrero didn't respond. They didn't need to.

'Look,' Victor said. 'I'm just a guy working on commission. There's no way I'm going to get in the way of a federal investigation for my cut of Miss Margolis's outstanding rent. Look at this place; do you think I'm going to get rich off fifteen per cent of three months' arrears? You honestly think I'd risk prison for a few hundred bucks?'

He smiled at the ridiculousness of it all. Guerrero smiled too. Wallinger shrugged and shook his head.

'Exactly,' Victor said, exaggerating the syllables. 'And I got to say,' he added. 'You scared me to hell when you guys burst in here waving guns around. I'm not used to that kind of thing.'

Guerrero looked apologetic. He probably reminded her of some little kid in floods of tears because she had charged into someone's family home. 'We have to work on the assumption that there are armed and dangerous people inside and enter accordingly. If there are, then we're ready for them. If not . . . well, someone like you might get shook up a little as an unfortunate consequence.'

Victor pursed his lips and blew air through them. 'I don't know how you do it.'

'We're well trained,' Wallinger said.

'You'd have to be.'

They stood in silence for a beat before Guerrero tapped Wallinger on the arm and gestured for the door. Then she handed Victor her card.

'If you find out anything—'

'I'll let you know.'

They headed to the door.

'Say,' Victor called after them. 'Since I'm going to strike out with this collection, I wonder if you could help me with my next one.'

'No chance,' Wallinger said. 'Do your own damn job.'

Guerrero added, 'I'm afraid we're not able to assist in commercial matters.'

'Fine,' Victor said. 'I'll remember you said that if I hear about Margolis's whereabouts.'

They stopped and turned his way.

'Fine,' Guerrero said. 'Shoot.'

'I've only got a couple of questions,' Victor explained. 'Are the Mets playing today?'

Wallinger said, 'What kind of question is that?'

'No,' Guerrero answered. 'They're not playing today.'

'Okay, thanks.' Victor nodded. 'What about if I told you a six-digit number? What's the first thing that comes to mind?'

The look they gave to one another told Victor they had no idea even before she turned back to him and said, 'Sorry, not a clue.'

'What about a five-digit number?'

She looked at him like he was an idiot. 'Zip code, of course.'

'Of course,' Victor said.

TWENTY-EIGHT

Victor left the building ten minutes after Guerrero and Wallinger had exited the apartment. He didn't know if they would be outside waiting for him, making themselves obvious to let him know he was going to be watched in the hope of scaring him into a mistake, or incognito so they could find out what he was up to. He left through the main entrance anyway. If he slipped out of the back they would become suspicious of him if they were not already, and if they were then they would only become more determined to find out what his real intentions were.

He saw no government-issue vehicles on the street outside and no other signs they were present. The street was the same as it had been when he arrived except the rust-spotted grey cargo van had gone. The other vehicles he had seen earlier were still present.

Now that Homeland Security were on to Raven and the apartment safe house it was no longer viable as a strike point. But he had another option: 10028 was the zip code for the Metropolitan Museum of Art. It was located on the Upper East Side. He could be there in twenty minutes, but he couldn't risk a direct route and didn't have the luxury of time for proper counter surveillance if the number 4 meant four p.m. Maybe Victor was being shadowed. Maybe he wasn't. There was no way to be sure, given the short time frame.

It made little difference to his behaviour. He always conducted himself as if enemies were close. Guerrero and Wallinger were looking for Raven, not him, and it seemed as if they believed his cover story. They also seemed to be operating alone. But that didn't mean they couldn't have called in backup – local cops or other cooperating agencies.

He saw no one on the street who hadn't been there when he had entered Raven's building.

Apart from the two figures now sitting in the front of the midnight-blue panel van.

The vehicle was a new model Ford. The windows had a dark tint. The vehicle sat on the kerb, unremarkable apart from the fact it had two people inside. At this range, he could not make out any details, but the height and breadth of shoulders indicated two men. He saw their silhouettes and not much else. Two men sitting inside a parked Ford van was common enough, apart from the fact that the silhouettes had not been there fifteen minutes before. They weren't moving either. They sat stationary, without any arm movements. If they were talking, they did so without large gesticulations or head movements. They did not look at one another.

They could be bored, or they could be focused. There was a simple way to find out which.

Victor approached the dirty red Impala. It was parked about fifty metres from the van, on the opposite side of the road. He went down on one knee and removed a shoelace, folded the string in half and tied a slip knot across the centre of the folded lace, creating a loop.

He stood and pulled the two loose ends to shorten the loop and extended the lace until it was taut, with the loop in the centre. He then pushed the loop into the corner gap where the driver's door met the chassis. With a sawing motion he worked the lace through the gap and behind the door until the loop was over the locking mechanism. He pulled both ends of the lace at the same time to tighten the loop around the mechanism and then pulled upwards to unlock the door.

He climbed inside and rethreaded the lace into his shoe while he watched the panel van in his driver's side mirror. The reflection of the silhouettes was now too small to identify any telling movements even if they made them. The silhouettes blurred and distorted to one dark mass.

He sat a while longer. They couldn't see him watching via the wing mirror any easier than he could see them. He waited because if they were shadows he wanted to make them nervous. And if not nervous, anxious. The longer he waited, the more questions would be conjured up in their minds. Had they been spotted? What was he going to do? Where was he going to go?

Once he pulled away, they would fall into shadow thinking. They would be concentrated on following him and staying hidden. The questions would fade away from priority, but the effect would still be felt. They might be less patient or more obvious.

They were. Exhaust gases were condensing from the Ford before Victor had pulled out all of the way from his space. Too soon. Too eager. Nervous or anxious.

Which was good, because it answered his own question without further need to confirm what he had suspected, but bad because he had picked up a tail. At this time, he had no idea who they were. Wallinger and Guerrero or colleagues of theirs seemed most obvious, but he couldn't afford to assume.

He was suspicious of Halleck too, of course. The man had wanted his own people to assist and Victor had turned down the offer. Not that it had been an offer. Halleck had made it clear he didn't trust Victor, and he was right not to. So it made sense that he would put his own people in the field too. But Victor didn't know their greater intentions. Were they on his tail only to observe, or did they have other orders?

The panel van stayed back the textbook distance of two car lengths. Victor drove around for fifteen minutes, turning at random and changing lanes when the mood took him. The Ford stayed with him the whole time. He pulled into a parking garage to test their orders. It would have made as good a place as any to make a move on him as they were going to get, but they didn't follow him in there. They waited until he drove out again and continued following. Just watchers then. For the time being, at least.

He did nothing to indicate he had made them, and if they

were Halleck's people, they would think he was performing routine counter surveillance.

But he couldn't be sure Halleck had sent them. Halleck had been right when he baited Victor about his past. There were numerous individuals and organisations out there that wanted his head. He was never surprised when someone tracked him down. He was as hard to corner as anyone, but unless he lived off the land in some faraway corner of nowhere, then there was always the risk of exposure. And he wasn't prepared to give up everything just to stay vertical.

He ditched the Impala a few blocks later. He didn't like confining himself in a vehicle unless he had to. Besides, he wanted to know more about his shadows. Were the two in the van the sum total, or were they part of a larger team?

He set off north, because he needed to head south. The panel van passed him by and disappeared into the distance. He had walked for a couple of blocks when it began to rain. It came down straight and hard. Buses passed by on the street before him, sending waves through the flooded road that crashed against the kerb. Cars followed, some with lights on, all with wipers struggling to cope with the down-pour. Pedestrians without umbrellas hunched and hurried, dodging around those that had planned ahead and could walk with a smug slowness. A taxi, too close to the kerb, sent up a spray that showered unfortunate passers-by.

Victor walked at a slow pace. The rain darkened his over-coat and flattened his hair. He liked the weather. He liked rain. He always had. Rain helped him stay alive. It helped identify watchers and shadows. People walked faster in the rain or didn't walk at all or stayed indoors. Streets were less busy as a result, creating fewer potential threats to evaluate. Almost no one loitered in the rain, even if waiting for someone special. People sought cover, not the best vantage points. Anyone who did not huddle under awnings or in doorways stood out, and a watcher who wanted to stay dry himself, or at least wanted to appear as someone who did, limited his ability to watch and follow in doing so.

Victor walked at a slow pace despite the rainstorm, because if someone else matched his pace it was as good as signposting his or her intentions. An umbrella would have kept the rain away, but only at the expense of tying up one hand and limiting his vision. Soaked with rainwater was always preferable to being soaked with his own blood.

Some tourists had been caught out and were a comical spectacle, underdressed and unprepared. Victor would have felt sorry for them but they were smiling and laughing at their own misfortune and how ridiculous they looked and Victor remembered when he was a boy and rain was nothing but fun.

As a child puddles had begged him to splash through them. Soaked to the skin had been something to achieve, not avoid. Watching the wisps of steam rising when indoors had inspired his imagination to thoughts of wizards and spells.

A lorry rumbled past and Victor slammed the door in his mind shut. If he could, he would erase any memory of his young life. Memories of that time were a distraction he had to fight against. Thinking about the past meant not paying attention to the present. He had too many enemies to ever risk indulging in nostalgia.

Thousands of raindrops pelted the road surface and

pavements every second. He wondered if there was a pattern to it, some formula, some rhythm – algorithm – known only to nature. The intermittent wind swept patterns through the rain. Headlights glowed on the road surface.

A young woman used a plastic carrier bag as a rain shield as she ran along the pavement. She wore a dress, thin and white. To be courteous, he looked away until she had passed.

When he looked back, a man was standing on the pavement opposite, positioned near to the kerb, not under the shelter of any awning or doorway, hair flattened by the downpour.

TWENTY-NINE

The man was Hispanic. Short, with a neat black beard. He wore a thigh-length leather jacket and beanie hat. About thirty-five. The man was turning away as Victor's gaze reached him. Then the man walked a few paces as he fished a phone from a pocket of his leather jacket and thumbed the screen.

He looked familiar. Victor had to work on the assumption there were no coincidences, that every familiar face was a shadow or watcher or killer. He could not afford to think otherwise. He would not allow himself to believe otherwise.

Maybe he had seen the man at the airport and been followed here, or maybe Victor had seen a similar-looking man in a leather jacket and beanie hat. Victor's memory was superb, but it was impossible to remember every face. No one had a genuine photographic memory.

Victor moved on. He walked until the end of the block,

slowing to make sure he didn't reach the kerb while the crossing light was shining, so that when he stopped he had an excuse to wait and look around. The Hispanic man hadn't followed. Victor couldn't see him at all.

Which could prove he was a no one. No threat. Or he had backed off to avoid suspicion.

Victor headed into a coffee shop and stood in line to order an Americano. The coffee came in a fine china cup sat on a saucer. Both had decorative glaze. He sipped from the cup. The coffee was a delight, near espresso strength, yet almost sweet. The best he had tasted in recent memory.

The coffee shop labelled itself as a modern bakery, but the styling was old and rustic and more European than American. It was called Clayton & Bale. A made-up name, he was sure – one that sounded quaint and authentic and not like some soulless corporation. It was staffed only by young white women. The ones he heard speak were from Australia. Maybe they all were. There was a padded bench opposite the door and plate-glass windows. He picked a spot next to two old guys who were complaining to each other about the price of the coffee while ogling the staff. Neither looked at Victor as he sat down.

To his left was a long serving counter where a barista worked the coffee machine and customers salivated as they perused the selection of cakes, muffins and other treats. A quick glance told him there were no threats inside. The clientele were either below working age or beyond it. The only people in the right age bracket for watchers were a couple of men who had been sitting down before Victor had entered. As he hadn't known where he had been heading until he had walked through the door, there was no way his enemies could have headed him off.

They wouldn't wait long. They knew he was a hard target. They couldn't be sure why he had entered the coffee shop. If he had done so only to exit through the back, they would lose him. They wouldn't allow that to happen.

If the Hispanic man was no one, then this precautionary measure would prove a pointless exercise and a waste of Victor's limited time to get to the Met. But there was no such thing as being too careful. He suspected Halleck had sent men to babysit him, but that didn't mean Homeland Security weren't keeping an eye on him or even a third party had tracked him down. There was no point rushing to deal with the threat posed by Raven if it left him exposed to another.

After a minute, a man he hadn't seen before entered, but he looked like he was one of Halleck's men. This one had the same kind of look as the ones Victor had seen in Dublin: same square build, same style-less attire, same cropped hair. It wasn't a uniform, and it wasn't anything deliberate. At least, not deliberate in a conscious sense. It was because the team had been together a long time. The men had started to dress like each other, acting like a tribe, forming their own subconscious identity.

There had been a time when SAS soldiers had favoured moustaches outside of the fashion of the wider populace. People who respected and relied on one another had a tendency to homogenise their behaviour. Which helped Victor. It would make them easier to spot, but of more use was the fact these guys were a close-knit unit. If they became his enemies, they would grow emotional when he started killing them. They would want revenge. They would make mistakes.

But only if it came to that. Victor didn't trust Halleck, but he wasn't going to start executing his men on the off chance. Even as a preventative measure, which Victor was a fan of, he wasn't going to kill this guy. At least, not in a crowded coffee shop in broad daylight. For one, he didn't need to. And two, Victor liked the guy. He did everything so wrong he couldn't help but feel sorry for him. He paused in the entranceway to look around the room. He fidgeted while he pretended to look at the food available. He didn't know what to order when one of the Australians asked him what he wanted. He sat in the wrong place – near to Victor and not near to the door. He didn't touch his drink. He did everything he could not to look in Victor's direction.

He may have been with his teammates a long time, but he wasn't one of their best. He might be an exceptional shot or tactician, but his shadowing skills were non-existent. This guy was closer to a civilian than a professional. It would be bordering on cruel to kill someone so clueless. Victor was no sadist.

He finished his coffee and headed back outside. He had seen four so far in total, counting the two in the van and the man on the phone. He needed to find out if there were more.

The rain had stopped by the time he left again.

Ahead lay a bus stop with a waiting bus and line of people boarding. To his right, across the street lay the entrance to a subway station. Either were viable options to create distance. He crossed the street because a taxi pulled up in front of him and the passenger climbed out of the right back door.

The station was old and hot and smelled of sweat and pollution. For someone of Victor's height, the arched ceilings of the passageway seemed low and almost claustrophobic.

He reached the platform and headed left to the end, so when the train arrived he boarded the first door, behind the driver. There were several seats available, but he stood with his back to the driver's door, giving himself a clear view of the entire car and everyone travelling with him – in particular, those who had boarded the car with him. He watched people through his peripheral vision, checking for tells in age, clothing, body composition and behaviour for potential shadows or threats.

Age was the first indicator, and he dismissed anyone too old to keep up with the physical demands of the role and anyone too young to have acquired enough training and experience to actually do it. People of the right age, but too out of shape to have the requisite stamina and agility were then dismissed. Impractical clothing was the next tell; anything too tight and restrictive or too eye-catching would not be worn. Two people, a man and a woman, met the criteria, but the man was drunk; he had a red face, wide staring eyes, and kept swallowing. The woman – neither young nor old, slim and toned, wearing loose clothes and flat shoes – was playing with her hair and trying to meet Victor's eye.

He ignored her attempts to catch his attention and remained vigilant as the train pulled away and accelerated. He stood with his feet a little further apart than shoulder width and used his left hand to brace against the forces trying to push him off balance.

So far, it seemed he had escaped unnoticed, but he could not shake the feeling that he was being followed still. The nagging doubt could be his unconscious's way of communicating some sight or sound or smell that Victor had not noticed, but that been detected and processed nonetheless. In his experience, if something felt wrong, more often than not it was wrong. He had to spend his life assuming and preparing for the worst-case scenario. For him, optimism was wilful ignorance.

If he had been followed into the station, the shadow would have boarded the same train as him, but even after he'd established that there were no threats in the car he continued to evaluate anyone who boarded when it stopped at the next station and the ones that followed. A good shadow never let their mark out of sight, but a good one never sought to get closer than necessary. Boarding the same car presented a huge increase in the chances of Victor identifying that person.

A better tactic would be to board a different car, and then change into the same car at one of the other stations.

In a similar situation Victor would not change cars until the second or third station to be as inconspicuous as possible whilst not leaving the mark out of sight for too long.

No shadow boarded at the second station.

One did at the third.

THIRTY

It took Victor almost a minute to be sure because the shadow was a lot better than the one in the coffee shop. Five people boarded: two women and three men. One of the men and one of the women were together: a retirement-age couple. Victor ignored them. One of the men was so overweight he required two seats. Victor discounted him too. The remaining man and woman were in the right age bracket and wore the correct kind of clothes.

The man entered through the door right next to Victor and came as close to Victor as he allowed anyone to get without maiming that person, saying, 'Excuse me,' as he did. Then he sat in the closest available seat to Victor and began playing a game on a phone. Everything the man did was wrong for a shadow, choosing to board near the mark when other doors were available, then speaking to the mark, sitting closer than necessary and drawing avoidable attention to himself by playing the game.

Which left the woman.

She did everything right: she chose the furthest door from Victor, entering behind the old couple, and sitting a good distance from him.

Victor absorbed every detail of the shadow, searching for where weapons might be concealed or weaknesses that he could exploit. At this moment, he didn't know her motives – whether only to follow, or to engage. The other guys he'd seen had been there to observe, but orders could change or this woman was the designated trigger-person.

But now she had lost the advantage of surprise. If she made a move, Victor would be ready.

It was at the next stop that he realised he had made a mistake.

The overweight guy alighted and a trio of young women boarded through the middle doors. They wore smart business attire, but were dishevelled from boozy lunch drinks. They stood near the doors, hanging and swaying from the support bars. They were as loud and they were attractive, laughing and joking with one another. Everyone in the car glanced their way at least once, whether amused by them or annoyed. Every man looked several times.

Every man except Victor and the man playing a game on his phone.

Victor noticed this in his peripheral vision and realised he had been wrong to dismiss the man in favour of the woman sitting further away.

The man playing the game was bold. He did everything against the book. He had boarded at the closest door, spoken to Victor, and had sat nearby, attracting attention with the game. That behaviour had been all wrong, and in acting that way he had removed himself from suspicion. Victor was impressed. The shadow was good. But he wasn't exceptional because he had not looked at the three young women because it was all he could handle playing the game and keeping watch on Victor at the same time.

The three young women alighted at the next stop and the car became quiet again.

Victor looked at the man, now assessing the threat. The man had no height or bulk of note, but speed and technique were more dangerous. He wore hiking boots and loose cargo trousers. His cheap nylon jacket had the zip unfastened. The vest beneath was tight. Good attire for combat: boots, to provide support for the ankles and deliver extra force through kicks and stomps, hiking boots for grip; loose cargo trousers for manoeuvrability. The nylon jacket was light and unrestrictive, unzipped so it could be taken off with speed, whether before a fight or slipped out of it clutched by an opponent. Cheap, so it would rip without much effort if an enemy grabbed it and the wearer could not slip out of it. The tight vest would be difficult to grab hold of too, whilst not restricting movements as much as a tight T-shirt would.

So he wasn't just a watcher.

He had no gun, else Victor would have noticed, but a small knife could be hidden on his person in any number of places.

Victor made no disguise of his evaluating look. The man detected it fast. He tried to ignore it, hoping he was mistaken, but then it became pointless. They both knew.

The man quit the game and slid the phone in a pocket of his cargo trousers. He ignored the pockets of his jacket because there was a good chance it would come off, one way or another.

'What was my mistake?' he asked, not looking at Victor – at least not making eye contact.

Victor saw no harm in answering. 'You ignored the three women.'

The man paused, recycling through events. 'I could be gay for all you knew.'

'Then you wouldn't have ignored me.'

His lips tightened and he nodded.

Victor said, 'Take comfort in knowing you did everything else right. I would not have made you otherwise.'

The man thought about this, then shrugged. 'A failure is still a failure, however close.'

Victor said nothing. He had no intention of placating the man any further.

'What now?' the man asked, meeting Victor's eyes.

'That depends.'

'On?'

'Whether you're a better fighter than you are a shadow.'

They stared at one another.

'I'm good,' the man said.

Victor nodded. 'I believe you. You're a good shadow too.'

'But you still made me.'

Victor nodded again.

'Then,' the man said after a long moment, 'maybe I'll stay sitting here when you get off.'

'That sounds like the best idea you've ever had,' Victor said. 'Do you know what your second best idea will be?'

'To tell you everything I know?'

Victor said, 'Right first time. Who sent you?'

'Halleck.'

'I figured as much. Why?'

The man said, 'To keep you under observation.'

'Termination too?'

'No.'

Victor was surprised to find he believed the man. 'How many of you guys are there?'

'Twenty.'

Victor raised an eyebrow. 'Twenty?'

'Well, twenty-one including me.'

'Three seven-man teams on eight-hour rotations?'

The man shrugged. 'I don't know anything about the others.'

'Then what are you doing exactly?'

'Keeping an eye on you. Reporting back. That kind of thing.'

'But not interfering.'

The man said, 'Surveillance only.'

'You're ex-military, right? Not intelligence.'

'Ranger,' the man clarified.

The train slowed as it neared the next station.

'This is me,' Victor said as the doors opened.

The man said, 'Thanks for the lesson.'

'You're welcome.'

'And thank you for not killing me.'

'Don't thank me for that just yet. I still might before I leave town.'

The man nodded to himself. 'I'll tell them you gave me the slip.'

Victor said, 'Tell them whatever you want to. But know that if you're put back in circulation and I see you again—'

'You'll *never* see me again,' the man interrupted.

'Ah,' Victor said. 'Now that is the best idea you've ever had.'

He disembarked and the train rolled away. Victor, alone on the platform, watched it disappear into the tunnel.

THIRTY-ONE

The Metropolitan Museum of Art stood on Fifth Avenue in the Upper East Side. Victor arrived on foot, having taken the subway to 86th on Lexington Avenue, followed by a meandering route around the local area to lose possible surveillance. The neighbourhood was overflowing with other museums and galleries, grand apartment buildings, and upmarket stores and boutiques. It smelled of money and culture.

It was a good area for counter surveillance too. Watchers and shadows tended to wear casual clothes to blend into the widest variety of environments. Here, the populace fell into two distinct categories: residents and tourists. The residents wore stylish and expensive attire whereas the tourists were even more casual in appearance than the typical watcher.

He saw no one that registered on his threat radar, but the area was so busy with foot and vehicle traffic it would be impossible to be sure no set of eyes watched him.

He approached the museum from the north, walking alongside Central Park behind a crowd of German tourists. He didn't look like them. Neither was he dressed as they were. But their numbers were of use to him.

When they reached the museum, the Germans hung around on the wide stone steps outside near an American flag fluttering in the breeze. They were waiting for one of their number to join them. Victor overheard something about someone oversleeping. He left them – waiting around only increased his exposure – and climbed the steps up to the entrance framed by enormous pillars.

There were lots of tourists outside the entrance, milling about and taking photographs. He saw signs for exhibitions, noting the ones he was most interested in seeing while at the same time working out which ones would be best for drawing out shadows while he looked for Raven.

The building was huge and spectacular; a sprawling Gothic giant that housed seventeen acres of galleries – the largest in the United States. The museum spanned almost a quarter of a mile from the south corner to the north. The façade was a stunning example of neoclassical style with high, arched windows, deep cornices and elaborate sculptural decoration. Victor, well used to beautiful architecture, was impressed. The museum occupied over two million square feet and contained some of the greatest examples of art in the world. Victor had longed to visit for many years, but he stayed away from the United States for anything less than vital visits.

Locating Raven in a building of this size was going to be a challenge. If he was still being shadowed without his knowledge, he would have a better chance of identifying shadows in an interior environment where he could control the situation and set them up to reveal themselves.

He passed through the entrance and into the Great Hall, a huge cavernous space where visitors stood in awe, necks straining to look up at the beautiful domed ceiling above. Others paid for admission or checked the maps of the museum and collected information on exhibitions, tours and lectures.

Victor waited his turn and paid the suggested donation for admission. He wanted to pay more – he loved museums – but he had to remain inconspicuous at all times. Generosity now, even that which he felt was just, would make him memorable. The English woman behind him donated a dollar.

The main entrance hall was no good for trying to identify watchers. There were too many people passing through or hanging around, too many ways in and out, and overlooking balconies. And Halleck's team had the advantage of knowing what he looked like. Victor had only seen five of twenty-one.

He headed into the gift shop. An uncommon first choice for a visitor, and a far smaller space with fewer people than the entrance hall. It also had two entrances/exits, so shadows either had to follow him inside or divide forces to watch both. He loitered for five minutes, memorising anyone who came in after him. As he left, he did the same with anyone in a good position to watch the exit he passed through.

He browsed information leaflets and purchased an audio

tour guide of the museum, in German, while his gaze swept the area for women matching Raven's description.

As expected, he saw no woman that could be Raven in the hall itself. He had no idea where she might be located, so he did the same as the other visitors tended to do. He walked straight ahead towards the Grand Staircase on the far side of the hall, which led up to the European galleries.

He felt guilty for not taking the proper time to walk around and marvel at the masterpieces displayed, but he wasn't here to sightsee. He was here to end a threat on his life. Maybe when he had a new face and enough downtime between jobs he would return and spend a week exploring all the museum had to offer. He wanted to absorb everything. He wanted to miss nothing. He glimpsed Jackson Pollock's *Autumn Rhythm*. It reminded him of wallpaper in the corridor of a Parisian hotel.

Another time, he promised himself. It was nearing half past three in the afternoon. If Raven was as careful as Victor, which he believed from what he had witnessed and learned, then she would be here already to perform her own counter surveillance. He imagined she was meeting a client or broker or contact of some kind.

He perused the Greek and Roman galleries next. They were teeming with people. No Raven among the tourists staring at the various statues and artefacts from ancient times. He stood aside to let a guided tour walk by. As a participant in such a tour he would have the advantage of anonymity, but the rigid structure of the route around the museum would make looking out for Raven, and any potential threats, all the more difficult.

Paintings and drawings, sculptures and furnishings, arms and instruments from throughout thousands of years of human history all competed for his attention as he passed through the museum. There was so much to see, so much to distract him, it was almost a challenge to remain focused on his objective. But a lifetime of discipline and adhering to protocol meant any distraction lasted but an instant.

In the sunlit atrium that housed the Temple of Dendur he detected a potential problem. He stood with the other visitors as they admired the great sandstone blocks that formed the Egyptian place of worship to the goddess Isis. A pool of water set within the hall reflected the sky above the atrium and those that stood nearby. Victor's own reflection danced on the surface.

So did that of a man in a blue suit. He was tall and slim, about thirty, with pale skin and receding brown hair cut clipper short. There was nothing remarkable about him. He did not pay Victor any attention or do anything to suggest he was trying not to pay Victor attention, but he felt wrong.

It was impossible to qualify why. Maybe Victor had seen him somewhere else, whether on the subway, on the streets of the city, or perhaps even elsewhere inside the museum itself. He did not recognise the man, he could not place when or where he might have seen him, but that did not mean he had not and was now remembering.

He didn't seem like one of Halleck's guys. That was obvious by his dress, build and manner. Victor moved on, curious to see what the man in the blue suit would do as a result.

In the hallway leading to the next gallery, Victor stopped

and thumbed through one of the leaflets he had picked up from the information desk inside the Great Hall. He skimmed over text and photographs relating to a new, temporary exhibition while he waited to see if the man in the blue suit followed.

He did not.

Victor continued on his way.

THIRTY-TWO

Victor saw no more of the man in the blue suit while he scouted through the rest of the museum, but he had only identified a fraction of the watchers. Twenty-one men formed a huge crew. To shadow one man it seemed beyond excessive, but after Victor had managed to steal Halleck away from eleven men it made a certain sense. Halleck was taking no chances. As eleven hadn't been enough, he had almost doubled the number of men. But the eleven in Ireland had been there to protect him. The twenty-one in New York were here to keep track of Victor. That didn't make sense.

The watcher on the train wouldn't know the overall objective. If he had, he would have told Victor. He had been too intimidated to withhold any information. And he knew Victor wouldn't let him walk away a second time, so however the watcher managed it, he would find a way to get out of his duty – pretending to be sick or injured or perhaps even going AWOL. Whatever the excuse, Victor had taken the total number of Halleck's men down to twenty. Still a huge opposition. Although, at least for now, they were just a nuisance.

It was a task made more difficult whilst trying to hunt down Raven without her knowledge. He kept moving. He didn't know how long she would be in the museum. There was a chance that if Raven was in motion too, he might fail to see her as they both passed along their separate routes, never crossing through the same place at the same time. It was a risk he had to take. This was the only lead he had. With federal agents on to her safe house, Raven might never return to it, and Victor might not get another opportunity to take her by surprise.

Then, he might only see Raven again in the second before she killed him.

The museum housed a number of cafés and bars where visitors and staff alike took breaks for refreshment and reflection. He checked them all out because if Raven was meeting someone here one of these locations seemed an obvious place. He drank a bottle of water to stay hydrated, but did not linger in any one place. He had to be fast. He was running out of time.

In the Ming-style scholar's garden of Astor Court he saw a woman from behind who was an equal for Raven's height and physique, but on closer inspection she proved to be a negative match.

He headed for the Modern Art wing and ascended to the museum's roof and its outdoor sculpture gallery and garden. The roof garden would be a good place for a meeting – no through traffic of tourists; fewer opportunities to be observed and overheard. It was ten to four. The cool air was refreshing and now the rain had ceased the autumn sunshine felt warm on his face. Visitors stood, mouths open, awed by the magnificent views of Central Park.

He wandered around the roof garden, his gaze passing over tourists and art lovers, looking out for slim women over five foot nine or the man in the blue suit.

The sculptures were comprised of installations by contemporary and twentieth-century artists, changed each year. Victor had little time for modern art, but the arrangement of the sculpture garden, its position on the roof, and the sweeping backdrop of the park to the west of the city made it a pleasurable space. The sculptures were almost unnecessary. The panoramic view of Manhattan alone was worth the trip up to the roof. The sun was low and the skyline to the west was a silhouette of black against blazing red and orange.

He saw a woman in a grey dress standing by the wall and hedge on the roof garden's southern edge. She had her back to him as she gazed out. At what, he didn't know. He judged her to be five-nine, made almost six feet by heels. She had dark hair tied up in a bun. The height and physique were right. She was alone. If she was here to meet someone they hadn't arrived or had already gone.

As he neared he adjusted his trajectory, wandering close to sculptures he did not understand to disguise his intentions. He looked around. The whole area was busy with people engrossed in the sculptures, the views or one another.

This would not be a clean kill. There would be witnesses.

It might even be captured as an image or video recording by the numerous cameras and cell phones that were everywhere.

He wanted to end the threat now. He didn't know when, or if, he would get another opportunity to strike.

But the risk of exposure was too high. He would follow her instead and wait for a better opportunity.

He became aware of someone standing next to him a second before Raven said, 'Do you have a light?'

THIRTY-THREE

Victor turned and took a step back to create distance, but did not raise his hands to strike or defend for the same reason he had decided against attacking the woman in the grey dress he had thought to be Raven. The rooftop was too exposed. If it was not, Raven could have killed him. He hadn't seen her. His focus had been on the woman in the heels. Raven had a cigarette in between her right fore and index fingers.

Raven said, 'Why don't you quit staring at her and ask for her number? You look like a creep.'

She had red hair and wore tortoiseshell-rimmed glasses. She was wearing a well-tailored business suit, black with a pinstripe. A smart black bag hung from one shoulder. Her manicured hands were free of weapons, but unencumbered save for the cigarette, which was no encumbrance at all.

'So, about that light?' she asked.

Victor said, 'You can't smoke here.'

She sighed, as if a genuine sadness had come over her. 'Next you'll be telling me that I shouldn't be smoking at all.'

'It's bad for your health.'

She held his gaze. His eyes were so dark they were almost black. Hers were even darker.

She said, 'It'll kill me?'

He stared back, right into his own reflection. 'No, smoking isn't going to kill you. That's one thing you can be certain of.'

She put the cigarette away into a silver case. It snapped shut and she dropped it into her bag.

'I take it you want to make sure my demise is sooner, rather than later.'

Victor nodded. 'How did you guess?'

She looked away and out over Central Park. 'Do you even know why?'

'I'm not irrational, if that's what you're asking.'

She looked back at him. 'Because I took a few shots at you?'

'You did more than that.'

'So you're after revenge?'

He said, 'Revenge is never part of my actions,' thinking about the single time it had been.

She regarded him as if she could see both the truth and the lie at the same time. 'Then why?'

'Self-preservation,' he answered. 'That's the only reason I kill anyone I'm not paid to.'

Her eyebrows moved closer together. 'So no one paid you to come after me?'

'I'm paying myself. Pro bono.'

She smirked at that. 'I like you.'

'The feeling isn't mutual.'

'Give it time. You'll end up quite besotted.'

'Nothing is going to stop me from killing you.'

'Then why don't you kill me now? I'm standing right here next to you. I'm unarmed. Vulnerable. Just a weak little woman against a big strong man.'

'You're not weak,' he said. 'And you're not vulnerable.'

'So you're chicken?'

He smiled to acknowledge the joke. 'Two reasons: one ...' He glanced around at the numerous witnesses. 'And two: I want information first.'

She seemed surprised. Which in turned surprised him. 'About what?'

'About who sent you after me. I want everything you know about them.'

The surprise mellowed into curiosity. 'Why would you think anyone sent me?'

'You're a hired gun, like me. Who hired you?'

A corner of her mouth turned up a fraction. 'Is it completely outside the realm of comprehension that I might be working for no one, that I might be my own client? The same as you're telling yourself that you are now.'

'It is outside the realm of comprehension,' Victor said. 'We've never crossed paths before now. People try to kill me all the time, and it's never by accident. There's always a client or a broker behind it. There's always a good reason. I always deserve it. But not this time. I didn't even know you existed before you tried to kill me.'

'And that means you can't be my enemy?'

He studied her. 'Did I kill your husband or brother or father?'

'No, no, and no,' she said. 'At least as far as I know.'

'Exactly. Who paid you? Who are you meeting here? If it's your client or broker, maybe you can survive this after all.'

'You're so close to the truth and you don't even realise, do you?'

'One way or the other, I'll find out.'

'I have no doubts you will. You've got this far, after all.'

He detected sarcasm in her voice but didn't respond. He said nothing more for the moment. Neither did Raven. Around them people young and old, male and female talked and laughed and admired the views and the art. They took photographs of the installations and themselves and of themselves with the installations. They sipped coffee and cocktails and ate expensive snacks in the roof garden's café and martini bar.

'I love this place,' Raven said. 'It was created through arrogance. The founders wanted to build somewhere to rival the great museums of Europe.'

'I'd say they succeeded.'

'First time here?'

He looked at her. 'And last.'

She understood what he meant. 'That's a shame. For both of us, I mean. But it doesn't have to be like that.'

'Yes, it does. You know that.'

A look of sadness passed over her face. 'I suppose we should get this over with. But as you said, it's too public up here. Why don't we go somewhere with some privacy? No need to upset these nice people, is there?'

It was a trap, he knew. But he also wanted to leave the roof and all the witnesses.

He nodded as she stared into his eyes. 'Some privacy would be good.'

THIRTY-FOUR

They walked across the roof to the elevator. She headed that way and he let her. He kept her close – but not too close – and in his peripheral vision at all times. She did the same. They waited to allow a chubby family out and stepped inside. They faced each other from across the car. No one else was inside. Victor didn't blink as she extended her arm to knuckle the button for the ground floor.

Her fingers were long and slender but he could see the strength in her wrists and exposed forearms. The wrist flexors were defined and the brachioradialis had uncommon prominence.

She saw him looking and made a fist to greater emphasise the muscles. 'Would you like to arm wrestle?'

'You should wear long sleeves.'

'I tell people I climb.'

'I tell people the same,' he said. 'But I do climb.'

'Sure you want to go through with this?' she asked.

He said, 'I haven't survived this long by ignoring threats.'

'I'm no threat to you.'

'You tried to kill me.'

'What's the significant part of that statement?'

He studied her face. Her skin was smooth, and freckled over the cheekbones. 'Are you saying you no longer want to kill me?'

'I never *wanted* to kill you.'

'Games don't work on me, Constance,' Victor said. 'You can't manipulate me. Playing sweet and innocent is a waste of your time. You can't appeal to my humanity. I have none left. I traded the last of it in a long time ago. I'm here to kill you before you kill me. There's nothing more to it than that.'

Her eyebrows raised at the use of her name. 'You know a lot about me then.'

'Of course.'

'Of course,' she repeated. 'It's not sexy, is it? Constance. Sounds so old-fashioned. My parents were hippies. My American mother and Indian father wanted to celebrate their uncommon bond. At least, it was uncommon back then. They wanted a name for their first child that encapsulated the bringing together of East and West. Have you ever heard anything so corny?'

'Constance for Constantinople, where Europe and Asia meet.'

'I guess they couldn't make a name from Istanbul.'

'I like Constance,' he admitted. 'I like names that have meaning.'

'I guess I'm used to it by now. But I feel at a disadvantage,'

Raven began. 'If you know my name then you know everything about me. I, on the other hand, know nothing about you.'

'Which is the way I prefer it.'

She said, 'What's your name?'

'I don't have one.'

'Everyone has a name.'

'Not me.'

'Fine. Be like that. But what happened to sportsmanship?'

'Do I look like I play by a set of rules to you?'

She examined him, a groove between her eyebrows. 'Actually, you do. You look like a gentleman. You look like someone who believes in fairness.'

'Then I'm a better actor than I thought.'

'When we act,' she countered, 'there is always a part of ourselves in the role we play.'

Victor remained silent.

'Don't you agree?' Raven said.

'I didn't come here to chitchat,' he replied. 'And I'm getting bored of this now.'

A small smile played on her lips. 'No, you're not.'

The elevator doors opened on the subterranean parking garage.

'After you,' she said.

Victor smirked and stepped out backwards. The ceiling was low, only four inches above his head. Raven followed him.

'How do you want to do this?' she asked.

'I'd prefer to keep that to myself for now.'

She said, 'What I mean is: should I start running yet?'

'I'm not fooled by your passivity, Constance. We both know you're not going to let me kill you. You'll fight to the very end.'

'And how do you know that?'

'Because that's what I'd do,' Victor said. 'You're just like me.'

She frowned. 'I'm not sure if that's an insult or a compliment.'

'It's neither.'

'I think it was a compliment,' she said with a teasing smile. 'I think you like me.'

'Then you have an inflated opinion of yourself. And you're stalling for time. Don't think I don't know that. What are you waiting for? Your employer? Backup? Is that who you had arranged to meet at four p.m.?'

'I'm not meeting anyone,' she said. 'Besides you.'

'Why bother pretending?' Victor asked. 'I tracked you here, didn't I? How do you think I did that?'

She smiled at him, incredulous. 'You tracked me?'

He looked at her lips and eyes, open with surprise and mirth and disbelief.

He regarded her for a moment. Her expression looked genuine. He thought about the book and the code and how he had come here thinking he was following a lead when maybe it had been nothing more than bait. He had realised in Prague she could predict his actions as he could hers. He should have remembered that lesson.

Victor said, 'You left the book for me?'

'What are you talking about?' She frowned. 'What book?'

He stopped himself answering. He reminded himself that

manipulation was as powerful a weapon as any gun. He saw she was regarding him as he had regarded her.

Then her expression hardened as she looked over his shoulder. Victor didn't look too. He wasn't about to fall for such an obvious trick.

'Did you come here alone?' Raven asked.

'I work alone.'

She absorbed this, then said, 'Could anyone have shadowed you? Don't look back.'

'I'm not going to look back. You're going to have to try a lot harder than that to take me by surprise.'

'It's not a trick.'

Something in her voice made him believe the enquiry could be sincere. His mind flashed back to the man he'd seen reflected in the pool in the Temple of Dendur. But she could still be lying, hoping to convince him to look away and give her the window to draw a knife from her bag and slip it between ribs and into his heart.

Victor said, 'If he's tall and slim. About thirty. Balding. And wearing a black suit, then yes.'

'No,' she said. 'Blue suit.'

Victor's back straightened. 'That's him. But if he is interested in me he's nothing more than a watcher. I've already crossed paths with some of his teammates. He won't get in the way of our business. In fact, he might even offer to help me.'

'He's no watcher. He's a hitter.'

'That makes no sense. What does he want?'

'What do you think? He doesn't like me very much. Well, the people he works for don't. I'm not very popular.'

'Then he and I are on the same side,' Victor said.

'That's where you couldn't be more wrong,' she replied. 'He's after me, not you. But now we're together he's after us both. Just by talking to you, I'm afraid I've marked you for death.'

Victor shrugged. 'Perhaps, if you're telling the truth. But even if that is the case, it's two to one against him.'

She shook her head, but was smiling, acting as if she were lost in a happy memory. 'He's brought friends.'

THIRTY-FIVE

The parking garage was well lit and quiet apart from the sound of nearing footsteps. He could see neither the approaching men nor any visitors. There were parked vehicles everywhere in neat rows interspaced with pillars and shining under fluorescent lights.

Victor said, 'How many of them are there?'

'Four,' Raven said. 'Including blue suit.'

'Assessment?'

'They're a clean-up crew. And they're not amateurs. Someone must have seen us together in the roof garden. They think we're working together, or you know what I know.'

'They've spotted us?'

She nodded, still smiling and looking carefree. 'Not yet. But they will. They're spreading out and they're coming this way. They know we came down in the elevator. It's only a matter of time.'

Victor resisted the urge to turn and look. Whatever Raven said, he wasn't prepared to turn his back to her. Besides, he still needed more information.

'Who do these guys work for?'

'I don't have time to explain everything. All that matters for now is that they want me dead. And though they're after me and not you, you're here. That means you're a witness or a threat. They won't take any chances.'

'I know how these things work.'

'How do you want to do this?'

A line appeared between his eyebrows. 'What are you talking about? We're not on the same team here.'

'They don't know that. We need to work together.'

'There is no "we", Constance. We're not allies.'

'But they don't know that, so either we work together or they'll take us down one by one.'

'No,' Victor said. 'I operate alone.'

'Then we're both dead. These guys are serious operators.'

'I'm harder to kill than I look.'

Her face softened, but this time he saw it was real. 'I'm not.'

She looked at him as though he were the most important person in the world, because right then that's what she needed him to be. And she was right: two guns were better than one, especially if these guys were as good as she made out.

'Weapon?' Victor said.

She shook her head. 'I don't carry one, usually. Too much of a risk.'

'I'm the same. What about them?'

He saw her peering over his shoulder. 'I can't see any bulging on their suit jackets, so only handguns in the worst-case scenario.'

'Is there a best-case scenario? They're not going to be unarmed like we are.'

She cocked her head to one side. 'Who said we're unarmed?'

Raven reached into her bag.

Victor said, 'Careful, Constance.'

She withdrew a small handgun and Victor couldn't help but tense. She held the grip out to him. He looked at it, surprised and suspicious.

'Take it,' she said.

He did, expecting a trap or trick or for the gun to explode in his hand. But it was genuine. He could tell just by the weight of it.

'You really don't want to kill me,' he found himself saying.

'I've been trying to tell you that.'

Victor turned to see the four men, including the man he had seen earlier, as Raven had noted. They were all wearing suits. None young. None old. Raven was correct to say they didn't look like amateurs. They were not here for surveillance. They had spread out and were approaching as they swept the area. All four of the men had their suit jackets unbuttoned.

'But what about Prague?' he asked.

She said, 'That was then. This is now.'

'I need a lot more information than that.'

'And you can have it,' she said. 'But we don't have time

now. Meet me at the apartment in the Bronx in two hours. Don't be a second late.'

'Where are you going?'

'These four won't be the only ones here for me. There'll be others nearby. If we stay together they'll box us in. We need to split up.'

Victor said, 'You can't run from me.'

She looked at him like he was an idiot. 'I gave you my gun.' And for a moment he felt like one.

One by one the strip lights flickered and went out.

The parking garage was enveloped in a blanket of utter blackness. It lasted only a second because the lights came back on, albeit dimmer – backup power from the museum's own generator, necessary to protect the priceless exhibits. Which meant this wasn't someone taking out the lights but shutting down the primary power to the entire building.

'It's started,' Raven said, but to herself. 'Damn it, I'm too late.'

Victor pointed the gun at her face.

'It wasn't me,' she was quick to say. 'Not this time.'

'What's started?' he asked.

'There's no time to explain. Later.'

He said, 'We can't go back to the apartment. It's blown.'

'Good,' she said, nodding. 'That's what we need. We need to draw them out into the open.'

'Who are they? What are you talking about?'

She said, 'Later.'

He shook his head. 'I'm not going back there. I was there earlier. Homeland Security know about you. They're watching your safe house.'

'Homeland Security isn't after me.'

'Two agents kicked the door down. I saw their IDs. They were genuine.'

'Their bona fides might be legit, but they're not. Whoever you met may have had real Homeland Security badges, but they weren't there on legitimate business. Trust me on that.'

'I don't trust anything you've said.'

'Thirty seconds until they see us,' she said, looking over his shoulder. 'Here we go.'

He ignored her. 'Why?' he asked, staring into her eyes. 'Why are you certain the two I met weren't really Homeland Security agents?'

'Because,' she answered, 'I didn't leave any book there. That isn't my safe house.'

THIRTY-SIX

There was no time left to question her further because the four-man team was approaching. She backed away from him, turned, and walked away. He watched her go. It would have been simple enough to shoot her in the back and finish what he came here to do, but he had a bad feeling she was telling the truth.

That isn't my safe house.

In seconds she had rounded a corner and was out of sight. He tucked the handgun she had given him into the front of his waistband, where it would be hidden by his suit jacket, and stepped out of cover.

The four men saw him and stopped. They had the look of professionals: serious expressions but no attempt to intimidate. All four wore suits that gave them an air of respectability and authority. Their ties were clip-ons, impossible to distinguish from the real thing except for the fact a true professional expecting trouble would never wear a ready-made noose around his neck.

None of the men were taller than Victor and none had broader shoulders or thicker arms. They were lean and fit and dangerous. They knew speed and stamina were more often more valuable than strength and bulk.

Raven was right: these were no mere watchers.

The guy in the blue suit said, 'Where is she?'

'Who?' Victor said.

'You were seen with her.'

Victor remained silent.

Several seconds passed as they looked at one another, evaluating and seeking strengths as well as weaknesses. Neither showed any fear or made any rash movements.

'You're coming with us,' the guy in the blue suit said.

'I really don't think so.'

They were spread out, but had stopped because he had. They didn't know his intentions, but now he knew theirs. *You're coming with us.* They wanted to take him – maybe they wanted to interrogate him about Raven; maybe they wanted to kill him somewhere without witnesses or CCTV.

The guy in the blue suit stared at Victor. He seemed experienced enough to come to accurate conclusions about him as Victor was about them. But the guy in the blue suit was smiling because Victor had his chin pointed down in a tell of submission and therefore fear. He knew they would pick up on such subtle clues and their evaluation of him would be inaccurate.

Then the guy in the blue suit gestured and the three others began to move closer. They converged on him well, not heading to where he was now, but where he would head to if he made a break for it. He glanced at each in turn to identify the weak link, but found none. All three looked tough and fast, confident in their ability to take him.

He saw what they were doing while the opportunity to act was still there, but they were smart to come at him several metres apart so the three trapped him in a triangle formation. To act against one would mean leaving his back facing the other two.

Good operators. Pros.

When he sidestepped between two cars, the one ahead of him moved to the open space at the end of the row, cutting him off. Victor slowed as if to give himself time to determine the man's intentions, which gave the two behind him time to catch up while his attention was elsewhere.

They were already committed to making their move, so he had nothing to gain by pretending he wasn't going to make one himself.

He continued for the exit and the one blocking it. He pictured snapping out a jab, fingers extended for the eyes, to blind or at least distract, buying him a split second to close that last distance, breaking the nearest knee with a stomp kick or the nose with an elbow that would become a lock, then choke; turning the man round and shoving him at the two others.

The two behind increased their pace, sensing he was intending to fight his way through.

The man blocking the exit put his left foot forward, turning side on and bringing up his hands in a fighting stance, reacting as Victor strode towards him, violence in his eyes.

The two behind him could not see Victor's eyes, but they could see the man's reaction. Victor heard their pace increase again, breaking into a jog. He pictured them rushing closer between the parked vehicles and then coming out into the open, converging on him.

Which was what he wanted them to do.

Victor stopped, spun round to face them, now no longer two points of a wide-based triangle, but close to one another.

He exploded into action, leaping at the first, swinging a roundhouse kick that connected his shin with the side of the man's knee.

It folded inward with a crack and the man dropped, wailing.

The other man reacted fast, drawing a suppressed Ruger pistol that was batted from his hand, and then attacking with an open-handed strike. Victor blocked it on a forearm, grabbed the wrist before it could recoil and the triceps for an arm bar, but the man's reactions were too quick and he curled his arm to prevent the arm bar, so Victor went with the man's movements and instead locked the arm behind the man's back.

He twisted him round one hundred and eighty degrees, so he took the pistol-whip meant for the back of Victor's head, thrown by the third man.

Teeth and blood splattered on a nearby windscreen.

Victor shoved his captive into the third man. They both collapsed, the closest concussed from the pistol-strike to the face and trapping the other guy beneath him.

The one in the blue suit had his own weapon drawn and was lining up a shot while speaking into a wrist mike.

Victor read *We need backup now* on the guy's lips before dashing into the cover of parked cars.

He drew Raven's handgun and kept low and out of sight and snaked his way between vehicles, trying to put as much distance between him and the guys in suits. He'd disabled two, but that still left two, with backup arriving at any second.

A suppressed shot sounded, loud and close by, but it was impossible to pinpoint its source in the echoing underground parking garage. He dropped low, out of sight behind a wheel, while more shots came his way. Bullets punched neat holes in the bodywork of surrounding vehicles and took chunks from nearby support columns.

He stayed down and waited until he heard footsteps, hurrying closer, nowhere near as loud and echoing and easier to determine the origin as a result.

He popped up to fire in the direction of the footsteps, spotting the approaching shooter – a man in his thirties, tall and wearing a leather jacket with the collar up and cream scarf tucked inside, but the tall man – ready, aiming – shot first.

The incoming rounds distracting Victor from acquiring the target and lining up the pistol's iron sights. The gunman's bullets pinged close by. Victor's missed.

The tall man in the leather jacket shot again, this time striking even closer, bullet cracking windscreen glass as Victor shuffled along the car to get a better angle for his own.

The gunman, seeing he was exposed, sidestepped as he shot twice more, seeking cover while putting rounds Victor's way. Victor crouched low behind the protection of the car and returned fire, tracking the guy as he sidestepped, aiming not at him, but ahead, because even a bullet travelling at six hundred miles per hour took a thirtieth of a second to cover the ten-metre distance. The man, sidestepping at four miles per hour, moved forty-six centimetres in that same time. A shot aimed at his head would miss every single time.

So Victor aimed ahead and for centre mass for the best chance of hitting and the second squeeze of the trigger resulted in a round striking the man high up on the right shoulder.

He twisted and cried out, losing his grip on the gun, which flew from his hand. He threw himself down into cover before the third shot could finish him off.

Victor moved closer. He was cautious, staying close to cover in case the man had a backup and could still shoot.

The echo of squealing tyres and revving engines alerted him to new threats, coming fast.

THIRTY-SEVEN

He turned side on and smashed the driver's window of the closest car with an elbow. Glass shattered into hundreds of pebbles that scattered across the car's interior. The intruder alarm sounded, loud and shrill. He ignored it and pulled open the door before he tore away the housing from the steering column, separated out the correct cables, exposed the copper wires and crossed them.

The starter motor whined into life and the engine rumbled.

White smoke from the spinning tyres mixed with exhaust vapour and Victor shot out from the parking space.

A black Audi sped towards him. In his rear-view mirror he saw the silhouette of the passenger lean out of the open window.

A muted flash of yellow flared in the darkness and glass cracked in the rear windscreen, ruining his line of sight via the rear-view mirror.

Victor ducked down as far as he could while still being able to see where he was going. More bullets struck the car, punching holes in glass and bodywork. But they were subsonic rounds; the damage was superficial.

A white minivan screeched to a stop ahead of him, blocking the route out. The sliding panel door opened to reveal a man in a dark jacket and woollen hat.

He had a UMP sub-machine gun clutched in both hands, muzzle swinging Victor's way.

He released the accelerator, hit the brakes and swung the steering wheel, sliding the car to a stop so the passenger side faced the gunman, putting as much space and metal between Victor and the automatic weapon as possible.

He threw open the driver's door and was diving out into the haze of tyre smoke as the shooting started.

The UMP was a fierce weapon and heavy .45 calibre rounds thumped into the car, which continued to slide, leaving crazed lines of burnt rubber on the smooth floor, before it spun and veered into a parked SUV.

Victor slid as well, rolled and scrambled to his feet, then ran as the gunman saw him and changed his aim, fire spitting from the UMP's muzzle as the weapon tracked Victor's run.

Fat holes appeared in nearby cars and fragments blew from exploding window glass as he reached the exit and darted through the door into the stairwell beyond.

Victor made it outside, coming on to Fifth Avenue to a chorus of horns. Traffic was gridlocked as far as he could see. He saw no accident or other incident to explain it until he noticed the traffic lights were neither green, amber nor red. The power was out here too.

A huge inconvenience to all those stuck in unmoving traffic, but a benefit to him because he was on foot and his enemies could not follow him out of the parking garage in vehicles. He saw worried civilians looking in his direction or hurrying away from the entrance. Word of gunshots had spread fast. A cop was talking into a radio and heading his way.

I see him, Victor read on the cop's lips.

It was too fast for his description to have filtered from witnesses or CCTV to an operator and been passed to a dispatcher and then to officers on patrol. Something else was going on.

He glanced around. He could see no lights at all from any building. Daylight was fading but the electricity seemed to be cut as far as the eye could see. Maybe the whole city had lost power.

He dashed out into the street and between the stationary cars. On the opposite pavement a woman wearing a bright blue tunic and hat tried to stop him to talk about the charity she volunteered for. She laughed as he took her by the shoulders when she held open her arms in a comic bid to block his path. She stopped laughing when he pushed her out of the way.

He headed across a small plaza where tourists took photographs of one another by statues, and business people drank coffee and toyed with their phones. He maintained pace, resisting the instinct to break into a run. They had vehicles. He could not outrun them. His best chance was to hide and wait and slip away unnoticed.

He headed deeper into the crowd. The more people, the

more chance of going unnoticed. His gaze scanned in a continuous back-and-forth manner, searching for threats, whether cops looking for perpetrators of a gunfight in a parking garage or enemies with lethal intent.

Victor walked fast, but no faster than anyone around him. He needed speed to take him away from his enemies, but too much speed would tell them his route by way of the annoyed or staring pedestrians he had knocked or elbowed out of his path or those curious enough to watch the hurrying man. He stayed on the boulevard, eyes moving but head remaining still. He had anonymity in the crowd but only as long as he blended into those around him.

He slipped off his jacket as he walked, again taking his time so as not to draw attention to himself. He folded it in half and rested it over his left forearm, as if to carry, but he let it fall into the next rubbish bin he came across.

An intersection lay ahead. Traffic was gridlocked. The streets were dense with New Yorkers and tourists. Keeping east was the quickest way of creating distance, but also the most obvious. Pursuers expected prey to flee, not double back.

He cut into an alleyway that opened up next to him, rounding the corner at a measured pace as might someone following a pre-planned route. He did not look back to see if the action had been noted. If it had, he would find out soon enough. If not, the action of looking back for confirmation might alert them.

Europe was Victor's primary area of operation. He knew the cities there far better than he knew those that lay to the west of the Atlantic. He knew how to use the piazzas of

Bologna to lose shadows and draw out enemies. He knew which streets in London were most saturated with CCTV cameras. He knew how to use the back alleys of Paris to ambush targets out of sight and sound.

He was no stranger to New York City, but its layout and idiosyncrasies had not ingrained in his memory the same way. But he was far from lost. Manhattan's organised and planned layout was easier to navigate than a European city that had grown and developed in an organic sprawl over a millennium or more. Before he had reached the age of eighteen the importance of navigation had been instilled into him, so that knowing which way north and south lay came as naturally as knowing his left from right. Combined with Manhattan's layout of regular city blocks and numeric street names, that sense was as good as any memorised map or satnav.

The alleyway opened up into a market, teeming with browsers and buyers and stalls packed together. He had no choice but to press on, squeezing and pushing and shoving through the crowd until he had made it out on the far side.

His pursuers were quicker through the market, following his path and using their greater numbers to barge through.

He dashed across a street, weaving through the passing traffic and the chorus of horns and abuse. He dodged a braking cab, but not fast enough to stop the bumper clipping his thigh and knocking him off balance.

Victor rolled and broke the fall to avoid injury, but it took a couple of seconds before he was back on his feet and his enemies had made it halfway across the street by then.

He turned into a narrow arcade lined with fashion boutiques and tailors'. He heard sirens growing louder. He saw police cruisers rush past the far opening of the arcade, on their way to some call. Not coming for him. At least for now.

Had his lead been greater he would have entered one of the boutiques, convinced or bribed or threatened the owner or clerk inside to let him out through the back. But there was no time. He pushed on.

He hurried down stairs, footsteps echoing throughout the confines of the stairwell. He reached the bottom, moving fast, using a palm to stop himself colliding with the opposite wall.

Victor reached the end of the alleyway and paused, looking behind for pursuers. He could see all the way to the other end some fifty metres away. No one. He'd lost them.

He exited the alleyway, hearing someone shouting, '*Move, move*,' and saw a couple of cops pushing their way through the crowded street. They hadn't seen him.

He fled into a shopping mall, rushing down steps, pushing people out of the way. In Europe he might have received abuse for doing so, but Americans had far less tolerance for rudeness and shoved him and cursed and threatened him.

Inside the mall entrance he stopped. He stood as if he was waiting, drawing no attention as he watched through the plate glass for anyone following. A cop ran past, glancing Victor's way, but moving too fast to see him. No other police followed, nor did any of the kill team.

Victor released a breath. For the moment, he had lost both sets of enemies. But it was far from over yet. He was far from safe. It would be foolish to think otherwise. While he was in the city, he was trapped. He had to get out of Manhattan, but he could not leave without understanding his enemies. He had come here to eliminate one threat, and in doing so had embroiled himself in another. If he left, he still had two problems: Raven and Halleck's kill team.

THIRTY-EIGHT

The blackout made it harder to slip away, yet also gave him an advantage, but it was only temporary. At some point the power would come back on, and with it street lights and CCTV cameras and facial recognition and more efficient communication between police officers. There would be less chaos to hide within.

He asked to move past a couple arguing, switching his accent to sound like an American – a generic Midwestern lilt, like Muir's, indistinct and commonplace. It was not hard to change his voice. He was good at languages and dialects and colloquialisms because he had to be. He had to be because he worked all over the world. He had to blend into and disappear within all manner of places and situations. He maintained his language skills in the same way he maintained his strength and endurance – with consistency and the continued dedication only possible when existence might rely on the result.

Everywhere he walked he saw people were using their phones, their faces up-lit by glowing screens, trying to make calls or to find out information via networks that were down because of the blackout or struggling to cope with the demand because everyone was doing the same thing at the same time. He carried no phone himself unless in specific circumstances. They were too easy to track. They presented too much of a risk. Now, he felt exposed without one. He stood out from the crowd because he was not staring at a little screen.

He saw no cops, but did not allow himself to relax. They were still looking for him, but the blackout was hindering their efforts. With the electricity down, emergency services were overstretched dealing with people trapped in elevators or on the subway system or in any number of problematic situations. Police switchboards would be jammed with calls. Dispatchers would be overwhelmed. Even slick and well-funded organisations as the NYPD, FBI and Homeland Security would be disorganised. They had not yet been able to coordinate their efforts to track him down, least of all with one another.

He kept to the ground floor of the shopping mall, seeking the far exit. Going up would mean trapping himself in the building. Some instinct buried deep told humans that higher ground was safe. In most natural instances, it was. But not in the artificial urban wilderness. Even if he made it to the roof unfollowed and unnoticed, there was nowhere to go from there. No other building would be close enough to leap to. He would be hidden from eyes below him, but trapped, and exposed to aerial surveillance that could relay his whereabouts to forces on the ground.

Hiding was never as good as escape, least of all when trapped on an island swarming with security services and hired guns.

His gaze, sweeping over the crowd, fell across a man with a moustache and wearing a uniform.

A rent-a-cop security guard was looking his way.

There was no ambiguity. The guard was looking straight at him, but he wasn't yet acting. He must have received some information about a fugitive with a vague description that matched Victor's, but he wouldn't have access to anything more.

Victor did nothing. He maintained his composure. It required no effort because he needed to and was used to staying calm when others panicked. He had to fight the same physiological responses as the next man or use them to his advantage, but his mental reaction to danger was that of a problem solver, detached and emotionless.

When that very first bullet, years before, had zipped past his head he had remained in position because he knew his cover was good despite the incoming rounds, and had kept his head up as more shots came his way while his teammates had dropped to the ground, scared and overwhelmed. He had kept his head up to look for muzzle flashes so he could return fire, because he had known to survive the ambush meant fighting out of it.

He had known then that what he possessed was not normal, but he had known long before that he was different, that there was something inside him others did not have.

Victor did not jerk his eyes away or turn or stare at the

security guard, but held the man's gaze for a brief quizzical second, before blinking and continuing on his way as would anyone with nothing to hide but curious as to why they were being looked at.

The rent-a-cop's gaze passed over him, searching the crowd for a more obvious suspected fugitive.

Men and women and children bottlenecked at the mall's exit. Victor followed the masses, allowing himself to be shoved and guided along in the crowd until he was outside again.

There was a police presence outside, but far too many people spilling out on to the street for them to have any hope of detecting him. He headed in the same direction as the majority of the expelled shoppers. The crowd thinned out the longer he walked as they headed in different directions.

More cops lay ahead across the intersection at the end of the block. Flashing light bars lit the street to his left. He headed right.

Within a minute he had lost the guaranteed protection of other pedestrians. He felt alone and exposed. He maintained a casual pace regardless. Running would only draw attention.

A police motorcycle was cutting through the stationary traffic ahead. For an instant it seemed it was on its way somewhere else, but then it veered in a sharp line straight for him. The rider's face was obscured by the darkness but Victor knew he had been spotted.

He ran.

The motorcycle siren blared into life. Light flashed. The

600cc engine revved and whined as it accelerated for him. He leapt over a bench and slid over the bonnet of a stationary coupe and carried on running.

More sirens from police cruisers sounded from behind in a chaotic chorus, piercing and violent.

He fled from them, his shadow propelled before him by chasing headlights.

THIRTY-NINE

Victor turned through a plaza near to the shopping mall, knowing only the motorcycle could follow him, not the nearing cruisers. The place was almost deserted and his running footsteps echoed, loud and fast.

On the street on the far side of the plaza, he saw a massive crowd, dense and sprawling, outside the entrance to a subway station. Commuters and tourists were angry and confused, eager to get home or to work or to the next sight on their itinerary. Station staff were trying their best to explain the situation, but the crowd was too big and too noisy for the staffs' voices to carry far. People jostled and shoved to get closer.

He hurried into the crowd. A few seconds later, the police motorcyclist exited the plaza and skidded on to the street behind. The rider looked around, but could not see him. There were too many people, too many faces. Victor looked away.

The pedestrians were not paying attention to him. They were too preoccupied with the blackout and their over-loaded cell phone providers to care about some guy hurrying through them. They were getting used to the sound of sirens by now. It took a lot for city dwellers to pay attention to such things.

Victor had his chin down as he pushed on. He heard cop cars nearby but didn't turn to look and risk his face being seen. He sidestepped through the crowd, putting more and more obstacles between him and the motorcycle cop, further reducing the chances of being spotted. He decelerated to a brisk walk to better blend in. Now, his best chance was to hide from his pursuers, not run from them.

He glimpsed more police officers up ahead on the periphery of the crowd. The motorcycle cop behind him might have called for backup or the ones ahead had been out searching for him regardless or just helping with the black-out. The two ahead hadn't seen him yet. They were straining their necks trying to pick him out of the crowd. Neither was tall.

He walked towards them, reminding himself to act casual, to behave like those around him. While he did that, the cops had their work cut out trying to identify him. He was no more than an anonymous face within an ever-shifting mass of hundreds of faces. A sudden change of direction would make him stand out. He kept walking towards them, the risk of being noticed increasing with every step, but they didn't see him because they were looking for someone fleeing the cops, not approaching them.

They looked away and moved to search another section of the crowd. It was too big to cover from one place.

Victor stepped out of the crowd where the cops had been standing. They didn't notice.

He walked away at the same pace as a young woman in a pink beanie hat and transparent umbrella who had had enough of trying to get on to the subway. She chewed gum while Victor walked a little behind her and to the side, not close enough to make her concerned about his proximity, but if the cops turned this way, they would see a couple walking together, not a lone man on the run.

He passed tenements with painted cast-iron façades. The thrum of rotor blades above alerted him to an incoming helicopter. It could be an NYPD chopper or one owned by a television network. He didn't look up to check because no one else did. New Yorkers were used to their buzzing presence in the sky above their city. If it was operated by the NYPD then it would have infra-red capabilities and he would glow white on a screen above, but so would everyone else on the street. While he acted like them the infrared camera was useless.

Victor turned on to a street locked with stationary traffic. The sound of intermittent horns disguised the mechanical whine of the helicopter. One driver, immobile behind his wheel, was making the most of the bad situation by thumping out a beat with his horn while he rapped freestyle about the blackout and being stuck in traffic. He wasn't bad.

'Hey, man, you got the time?' asked a passer-by in a baggy T-shirt and baseball cap. 'My phone is out of juice.'

Victor shrugged and shook his head.

'I'm just asking for the damn time, asshole.'

He increased his pace because he saw no cops to pay attention to it and heard no helicopter above to see him, hurrying past plate-glass storefronts glistening with raindrops, the wares on display unlit and lost in shadow.

He saw a roadblock up ahead at the end of the block. The traffic sat unmoving before it. The roadblocks were meant to trap him, but they helped him. The already stilted flow of traffic in the area was now at a standstill. The cops could not use the road at all now. They had taken away their best advantage.

Victor passed an electrical store with a display of blank TV screens. His reflection jumped from black screen to black screen.

He rounded a corner, slowing his pace to blend with the pedestrians because a watchful cop across the road had half-climbed a street lamp to get a better view.

The cop jumped down from the street lamp, shouting into his radio for backup as he ran in pursuit.

Victor sprinted.

A chain coffee shop with its own generator had a sign glowing further along the street. Victor rushed towards it. The queue of people eager for a hot drink or snack snaked outside on to the street. He moved past the waiting men and women, smiling and patient despite the circumstances, and squeezed past a man in the doorway as he assured him he wasn't trying to jump the queue.

Inside, the harried staff were working hard to deal with the amount of customers eager for something hot to fight the chill. Every seat was taken. Some people were even perched on the tables. The air was warm and humid. Despite the situation, most patrons were in good spirits.

There was a queue for the restroom, but he ignored it, and the protests, to push ahead and kick open the door.

A short Russian in sportswear was urinating and almost fell over with shock. He was too surprised and scared to speak. Victor didn't enter. There was no point. No windows.

When he turned, a dozen or more faces were staring at him, almost as shocked as the poor Russian and just as silent. He ignored them and headed to a doorway marked Staff Only that was locked with a punch-button system. Such a system was hard to get past, but the doorframe was no stronger than the one to the restroom had been.

It flew open, rebounding off the interior wall on the other side and back into Victor's raised arm as he hurried through the doorway.

One of the members of staff – maybe the manager – was shouting at him, but no one was brave or stupid enough to chase after someone as crazy or desperate or dangerous.

At the end of a short corridor with beige walls, stairs led up. Not ideal, but there was nowhere else to go. There were no doors leading off to the rest of the ground floor.

The stairs creaked and groaned as he leapt up them three at a time. They took him to the floor above the coffee shop. Doors led off here to storerooms or offices or a kitchen or staff bathroom. He didn't try any of them. He wanted a way out, not a way to trap himself.

He heard a voice below shouting, '*Which way did he go? Which way?*'

Victor looked around, finding a window and heaving it open.

He dropped down into the alleyway behind, exploding open a bag of refuse and slipping on food waste as he rushed away.

The alleyway opened out on to a wide street almost devoid of traffic.

He saw the entrance to a park up ahead, but ignored its lure. Cop cars couldn't follow, but they could box him inside. He needed to maximise his ability to manoeuvre to his advantage if he was going to stay ahead them.

A staccato yelp of tyres alerted him to braking vehicles. As headlights washed over him, he squinted and turned away. He powered on, rushing past a parked delivery van, knowing it would block his pursuers' line of sight for a second or two, providing him with a window to slip down another alleyway.

It stank of rotting food and worse. Halfway along it, a slim young man in a cook's apron and with long black hair bunched up in a nylon net leaned against a wall by an open doorway, smoking a cigarette. Victor slowed to the quick walk of a man in a hurry, not hunted. The guy in the hairnet stared at Victor until he had gone out of sight.

At the end of the alleyway, he paused to look both ways along the adjoining street. He saw no police presence, but sirens were growing louder from the east, so he went west. He walked at the same speed as the other people on foot so as not to draw undue attention to himself. He mimicked their body language.

It did no good.

He heard the approaching cruiser's wheels shriek on the wet asphalt surface as the brakes went on, sudden and hard.

The cop car angled after him. He snaked as he ran, trying to throw it the wrong way, but the driver knew what he was doing. The cruiser stayed with him, but the tyres lost traction on the slick road surface and skidded and the car mounted a kerb, swerving back on to the road before it collided with stunned pedestrians.

Victor risked a glance over his shoulder, seeing the cop car was pulling up behind him, the passenger staring his way while he shouted updates into his radio.

Victor was sprinting before the two officers were out of their car and chasing.

FORTY

He ran. Sweat and rain made his shirt stick to his back. People and cars and buildings blurred in his peripheral vision. He looked ahead and ahead only. He knew they were chasing. Losing speed by looking back would not help him escape.

The cops were laden with heavy belts of equipment and weapons. Even without, they couldn't run as fast as Victor. Few could. He turned a corner, extending his lead on them. He could outrun these two, but not every cop and federal agent in the city.

A market up ahead offered sanctuary. Traders were doing big business, taking cash, no shutdown electronic registers denying customers. The market was busy, so packed with people it was difficult to squeeze through. Tempers were frayed and Victor received pushes and elbows as he fought his way through.

A man shouted, 'Watch where you're going, dick,' and shoved Victor in the shoulder blades with both hands.

He fell against a stall, knocking merchandise over and on to the ground. The owner yelled abuse at him as he stumbled away. He lost his balance, falling to his hands and knees, taking a couple of teenagers to the ground with him.

He was up and moving again before they had finished cursing at him.

Any moment now the cops would follow. He pushed on, picturing them debating which way he had gone having lost sight of him, but having the sense to know he would have headed for the cover provided by the market instead of remaining exposed and visible on the streets where he could be intercepted by backup.

He headed to a trader selling hats, fighting his way through the crowd. He grabbed one at random – then stopped and spent precious seconds picking a more suitable garment – and shoved bills into the trader's hands, over-paying by several times to the man's delight. Victor pulled the cap down over his head. He had no idea whether the motif was for a baseball team, a band or just a logo. He didn't care. He cared only that the cap was a dark colour and the motif had been the plainest on offer.

He moved on, the brim of the cap pulled down low to help hide his face, but not so low it affected his vision. Disguising himself was no good if he couldn't see threats coming his way.

The cap would make it harder for the cops to spot him, and even harder for the ones still looking for a man in a suit. Taking off the jacket had proved useful, but he realised he should be wearing a vest. That way he could remove his dress shirt when he was again identified. The scars on his arms would make him memorable, as would his muscle tone, but only at close range. From a distance, a man in an undershirt and baseball cap looked a lot different to a man in a suit.

He told himself if he got out of this situation, he was going to start wearing one.

He changed direction to avoid knocking over an old man, elbowed between two big guys in construction gear and saw a set of stairs leading down. He shoved and pushed and fought his way towards them, leaping over the railing to save a handful of seconds that could be the difference between death or capture at a later point.

He almost collided with a woman coming up them, but she flattened herself out of the way as he rushed past her.

He heard shouting voices nearby, incomprehensible against the background of sirens and the chatter of trade in the market, but he sensed they were police officers, maybe shouting directions or updates at one another or ordering civilians out of the way. Either way, they were near.

They didn't know if he was carrying a gun but they would know he was dangerous. They would be scared and pumped up and all had handguns at the least or shotguns taken from their cruisers. Even a grazing bullet could end him here. Ripped clothes and blood would make it impossible for him to blend in.

And if they thought he was a terrorist, if they believed he planned an attack – or even if they weren't thinking straight – they could shoot him on sight.

He collided into a squat cop coming round a corner.

Victor raised his arms, fast, ready to strike and break and

maim and kill if necessary to facilitate his escape, but the cop was shouting:

'*Clear the way*.'

Victor did as instructed and watched in silent disbelief as the cop rushed away from him while yelling into his radio that he was joining the hunt. The cap and lack of jacket had paid off.

'Get out of here,' the cop yelled to Victor without looking back. 'Shit is going down.'

'I saw a guy in a suit running towards the river,' Victor called after him.

The cop raised high a meaty thumb so Victor could see, while he shouted into his radio. 'Perp was seen heading to the river. Repeat: perp is heading to river.'

FORTY-ONE

A block away Victor found a car he liked the look of. The streets were a lottery in terms of gridlock, but the cops were looking for a suspect on foot. He wrapped his belt around his elbow and smashed the passenger window. He cleared away some stubborn shards and reached inside to the door release. With a knee on the passenger seat, he leaned across to unlock the driver's door. He then went round to climb behind the wheel and sit on a seat not covered in glass.

The car's interior was a mess even before he had smashed the windows. Dust was embedded in the grooves of the dashboard and the footwells were full of rubbish. The exterior hadn't been any better. The bodywork was smeared with grime and spotted with rust.

He tore the panel out from under the steering wheel and hot-wired it blind, knowing from long experience where to find the correct wires and how to cross them.

The car vibrated as the engine woke from its slumber. A

sweep of the mirrors and quick look around told him no one had entered the area. For now, he was as safe as he could expect to be. A temporary respite, but he was glad of it all the same.

He eased the car out of the space, still cautious, still expecting an ambush.

His reflection looked back at him, tired but energised, hunted but focused.

In his rear-view, he saw a vehicle turn on to the street behind him. It skidded, spraying rainwater, because it had gone into the corner fast, and was now accelerating hard out of it, back end fishtailing. It was a dark blue Ford sedan. Anonymous, except for the antenna protruding from the roof.

A government vehicle, but not a cop car. Two silhouettes the other side of the windscreen had to be federal agents.

He gripped the wheel tight, arms rigid. Ahead, red tail lights glowed through the rain.

He floored it as he approached the intersection, trusting to speed as he shot across and through the slow-moving traffic. Headlights flashed around him. Horns sounded. He glimpsed vehicles braking and skidding and swerving to avoid him, creating unpredictable obstacles that hampered his pursuers.

The car clipped a parked sedan, sheering off metal. Its alarm sounded as Victor rebounded away. He controlled the steering wheel, avoiding a crossing pedestrian, tyres splashing through puddles, spraying up tall fountains of water. He punched the horn to warn the vehicles passing up ahead he was hurtling towards them.

Two cars heading in opposite directions heeded the warning and missed him as he shot between them, but caught each other as they swerved out of the way. Steel buckled and was torn away. Glass shattered. A bumper tumbled through the air. Shrieking tyres sent up clouds of smoke and misting rainwater. Debris scattered across the intersection.

The dark blue Ford hurtled along the street behind him.

Victor shifted into drive and accelerated away, rubber hissing and screeching, the car shaking and swerving. The Ford grew larger in his rear-view, the two silhouettes forming into two men, the passenger black, the driver white. Both suited. Both serious and determined.

He slid into a hard right and the Ford charged, but missed his rear bumper by inches. He worked the wheel and saw the guy driving the Ford doing the same, crossing over his hands as he fought to keep the car under control, going at speed on a slick surface. It clipped the kerb before he managed to control the Ford's lateral movement.

By that time Victor was already fifty metres along the road, residential buildings flashing by.

Cold air rushing through the smashed-out passenger's window made his eyes water. The rain soaked his hair and shirt. Pedestrians were blurred smudges of colour in his peripheral vision.

A stationary bus blocked the lane, the driver and passengers having long since abandoned it. Victor swerved around its left side. He jerked as the front wheel jumped the kerb for a second before dropping back down on to the road, hitting a puddle and splashing up a wall of dirty rainwater.

He saw no pursuing vehicle in his rear-view. No head-lights sparkled through raindrops on the rear windscreen. He doubted he had lost it with such ease. He wasn't prepared to fool himself into thinking so. It was still out there. Still close. Where?

The question was answered as he shot across an intersection and the Ford appeared at his side, swerving from the bisecting road.

Horns sounded as they rounded other cars moving at slow speeds, cautious and sensible drivers taking no risks with the lack of street lights and traffic lights.

The Ford nudged into the passenger side, denting bodywork and forcing Victor to fight the wheel to stay straight. The driver threw him a look of satisfaction that said *you're mine*.

The engine roared as he pushed the car for all it had. The Ford stayed with him, the newer vehicle having the advantage in horsepower and torque. He wasn't going to lose it in a straight-line race.

He yanked the steering wheel, careering into the Ford as it had done to him. Steel buckled. The driver hadn't expecting Victor to fight back, only to run. Rending metal shrieked. The impact took the Ford driver by surprise and he reacted too hard, fighting the wheel too much. Tyres skidded and screeched on the wet road. The Ford swayed in a lateral back and forth rhythm. The driver, panicking, fought harder to control it. The wrong thing to do.

He lost control. The Ford spun. Black smoke from burnt tyre rubber mixed with the mist of rainwater.

In his rear-view, Victor saw the Ford crash side-on into a parked taxi.

For now, he'd escaped. But the car was a dented, broken wreck. Still drivable, but its plate and description no doubt already gone out to every cop and federal agent in the city. A mile away, he brought the car to a juddering halt and ditched it on a quiet street beneath an overpass.

The air by the river was cold and refreshing. Victor drew in big lungfuls. Looking at the river made him aware of his thirst. His mouth and throat were both dry. He was hungry.

The blackout was helping him in several ways. Without street lights many roads were blocked by traffic or clogged with pedestrians, making the NYPD's job more difficult. They were struggling to get enough manpower into the area, even if their resources weren't already strained dealing with an overload of emergency calls. Otherwise there might be forty or more cops in the area by now, sealing it off and searching for him.

He walked away from the car. Even if they weren't here yet, more agents or cops would be on the way.

FORTY-TWO

Victor headed south. He allowed himself to slow down to a walk. The chase had elevated his body temperature and he was sweating in an attempt to cool down. That would be a problem if not for the rain coming down hard disguising his body's attempt to regulate itself.

He was fit and as well conditioned as a professional athlete, but fatigue was beginning to take hold. His limbs were feeling heavy. His mouth was open. His heart raced.

Two cop cars formed a loose barricade ahead. He could get around it easy enough, but not the four cops who stood guarding it. He backtracked through the crowd, only to see more NYPD were setting up another barricade at the other end of the street.

He was forced east with the crowd, taking long strides to reduce his height a little. He saw two cops in his peripheral vision cross the road and head towards him.

Accelerating tyres squealed on the wet asphalt. He looked

back to see the white minivan coming after him. He ran, veering across the road and heading west.

A blue-and-white cruiser appeared ahead.

He doubled back and hurried north, the only way left. He heard the helicopter again, or maybe it was another. He felt the net tightening around him. No escape from capture or death.

The sound of sirens, rotor blades and revving engines filled his ears. Nowhere left to go. Nowhere to hide.

Stealing a vehicle was no good. The streets here were too gridlocked to escape behind a wheel. He would only trap himself.

But that gave him an idea.

He headed on to the road and pulled open the back door of a yellow taxi stood still in a line of unmoving traffic.

'We ain't goin' nowhere,' the driver told him before he had sat down. 'Power's down across the whole city. No lights. It's gonna take a damn week just to get off this street.'

Victor shut the door. 'That's fine by me.'

The driver turned round in his seat, disbelief further creasing his worn face. 'What you say?'

The man appeared to be in his late thirties, with a face worn down by hard experiences. His head was shaved but he had several days' worth of stubble on his face. His neck was covered in tattoos.

'I'm happy to sit here.'

'Are you nuts? What do you think this taxi is, a damn park bench? Take a hike.' He gestured.

Victor took out a hundred and held it up for the driver to see. 'Park benches are free though, are they not?'

The taxi driver's eyes were wide as he took the bill. 'True that.' He shoved the bill into his pocket. The firm wouldn't be taking their cut because the meter wasn't running. He turned back.

They sat in silence until the driver said, 'Say, you wanna listen to some tunes while you sit?'

'Sure. Do you happen to have any Brahms?'

His gaze met Victor's in the rear-view mirror 'Any *what*?'

'Silence will be fine.'

'Suit yourself, brother. It's your park bench.'

He tapped his fingers on the steering wheel in a practised rhythm, supplying a beat to the silent melody his head was moving back and forth to.

Running footsteps made the driver stop and check his wing mirror. Three cops ran by on the pavement and disappeared into the distance. Then four more did the same.

None of the cops so much as looked at the line of traffic, let alone who was sitting in the back of any taxi. They were pursuing a man on foot, at least that's what they thought.

The driver sat still for a long beat, thinking, deciding, then made eye contact in the mirror and said, 'Are they . . . ?'

'Yes.'

It would have been pointless to pretend otherwise. Victor held the driver's gaze in the rear-view.

The driver burst out laughing. 'Man, that is some funny shit.' He slapped a palm on the steering wheel. 'Now, I knew you were crazy when you climbed into my ride. But I had no mind that you were *that* crazy. You must have balls as big as balloons to pull off a stunt like this.'

'I don't like to brag.'

The driver laughed louder, and Victor managed to smile in the rare moment of calm and humour, sitting in the back of a stationary taxi while a legion of cops hunted for him nearby.

The driver stopped laughing and frowned. 'Say, you're not some kind of terrorist or some such shit, are ya?'

'Do I look like a terrorist to you?'

'I don't know,' the driver said. 'I'm not sure how a terrorist is rightly supposed to look. You wearing one of those suicide vests under that shirt? Nah, I guess I could tell.'

Victor thought of a time in Italy. 'Not necessarily.'

He unfastened a few buttons so the driver could see a section of chest.

The driver smirked and waved a hand. 'Put that shit away, bro. I don't need to be seeing that. I guess you're no terrorist.'

Victor refastened the buttons. 'I'm glad we can agree on that.'

'But if you ain't no terrorist looking to blow yoself up, what the hell are you to be on the run from Five-0?'

'How long do you have?' Victor asked.

'I got as long as you sit there, don't I?'

Victor risked looking over his shoulder to check the street. No more cops had appeared. The sound of sirens had faded as the search headed away.

He said, 'I think we'll have to save it for next time, I'm afraid.'

The driver looked too. 'Coast clear now, is it?'

Victor nodded. 'Looks like it.'

The driver grinned. 'All part of the service. Tell your

friends I'm the best damn cab driver in this town.' He used a thumb to point at himself. 'I'm Leo.'

Victor said, 'Now, you're not going to tell anyone about me, are you?'

'Do I look like a snitch to you?'

'No,' Victor said. 'You don't look like a snitch to me.'

'Damn straight I ain't. I know the rules. I know how shit works on the street. I didn't always drive a cab, you know?'

'That's good, Leo,' Victor said, 'because I really didn't want to have to kill you.'

The driver didn't laugh or smirk. He looked at him, intrigued, like he believed Victor hadn't been joking and in that fact saw far more about his passenger.

He said, 'Next time I see you I'll buy you a beer and you can tell how you ended up hiding in the back of my ride. I got a feelin' that story is worth listenin' to.'

'Some things are best left unsaid.' Victor reached for the door handle. 'Thank you for this.'

'No problem, amigo.'

'I owe you one,' Victor said. 'I really mean that. If we ever cross paths again then you can cash it in.'

The driver nodded, thoughtful, then said, 'Hey, don't you go nowhere without telling me your name, brother,' as Victor began to climb out. 'Not after I saved yo ass.'

For fun, Victor told him.

FORTY-THREE

Three blocks from the cab he bought food and a soda at a taco truck unaffected by the blackout with its own generator. He ate while sheltering from the rain in a doorway with two other taco eaters. They made eye contact with him and each other but no one spoke. They communicated only with grins of contentment, enjoying their meal in silence, but for Victor it was all about the calories. He would have devoured anything with the same relish. His blood needed sugar and his muscles needed glycogen.

One guy went back to the stand for a second taco. Victor followed suit.

Once again they shared a moment's silent camaraderie as Victor allowed himself to relax. In this brief instance he had no problems nor was in any more danger than the man next to him. A temporary respite, because it was far from over. He needed to be refuelled and ready when they next came for him.

Which they would. The only question was who would find him first: cops or killers.

On another street, he passed a homeless guy in an old, dirty army jacket and beanie hat.

Victor said, 'I'll give you a hundred bucks for the jacket.'

He waited while the homeless guy weighed up the offer. He saw Victor's urgency, and with it, the strength of his own negotiating position.

'Two hundred.'

'Deal,' Victor said. 'But for that I want the hat too.'

A minute later, he stank of urine, but the green army jacket and hat transformed his appearance. Anyone who looked at him was quick to look away. Everyone noticed him, but no one wanted to. He was as visible and invisible as he had ever been as he set off north towards the Bronx.

The street looked the same as it had earlier. The blackout had made no difference. It had been as dirty and rundown and neglected under a bright afternoon sun as it was in unlit twilight. He saw no government vehicles or midnight-blue panel vans or white minivans or any other vehicle he had seen before. If any of his enemies were nearby, he couldn't see them. Dressed like a tramp, he hoped they wouldn't see him either.

It was nearing six p.m. Raven had said to be here in two hours just over two hours ago. Victor hadn't wanted to be on time or early for once. He didn't want to wait any longer than he had to. He hadn't wanted to come back here at all even before he was a fugitive.

He used the alleyway behind the building to break in. The interior was dark and gloomy. He made it to Raven's front door without seeing another person.

He waited, listening. He could hear no one moving around on the other side. He stood to one side of the door and used the back of his hand to push it open hard enough to surprise someone on the other side, but not hard enough so it would bang against the wall.

No gunshots, so no one had been waiting in the dark to shoot at whoever came through.

Inside, he had walked forward, gun in hand, with slow, careful steps along the hallway before he heard someone further inside the apartment. Maybe Raven. Maybe Guerrero or Wallinger. Maybe cops or residents or Halleck's people or anyone else.

He kept Raven's gun low and pointed at the floor because it was dark, and if it wasn't an enemy waiting for him, he didn't want someone else to see the gun raised. He didn't want to get killed by a trigger-happy resident investigating a break-in or the like.

Ahead, the lounge area was better lit than the hallway because someone had opened the blackout blinds and what remained of the sunlight illuminated the open space. He stepped into it to see a man in a suit, wearing a tan raincoat. He was trying to get his cell phone to work.

Wallinger.

'Hands where I can see them,' Victor said.

Wallinger turned to face him, surprised at the sound of Victor's voice, but not shocked; not scared. Wallinger's gaze fell to the gun in Victor's hands.

'Why does a credit enforcement agent need a piece?'

Victor said, 'It's a jungle out there.'

'A jungle gone dark,' Wallinger replied. He held up his phone. 'Cell towers must be down too or the networks are overloaded.'

'Everyone's calling home or trying to find out how to get home.'

Wallinger nodded. He dropped the phone into a pocket of his raincoat. 'Why don't you put that gun away?'

He gestured with an outstretched hand while the other hovered near his waistband, fingers making small movements as if playing the keys of an invisible piano.

Victor looked from the moving fingers to the coat that hung open centimetres away.

'What?' Wallinger asked.

'What's under your jacket?'

'Nothing,' he was quick to answer. Too quick.

'Move your hand away from your gun.'

Wallinger looked down and seemed surprised to find the hand hovering at his waistband. The fingers stopped moving, the hand clenching into a fist that remained in place. His gaze rose to meet Victor's.

'Why?' Wallinger said.

'You know why.'

The man said nothing.

'You have two choices,' Victor said. 'We don't need to go into details, but it's in your best interests to pick the second one. So do it.'

'You can't tell me what to do. I'm a federal agent. I think you're forgetting your place here.'

'I'm not telling you what to do,' Victor explained. 'I'm advising you on what you should do.'

Wallinger's jaw clenched as he thought.

'Take your time,' Victor said.

Wallinger raised his hands. 'You're making a mistake.'

Victor nodded. 'I've been making a lot of those recently. Another isn't going to make much difference. I want to see your identification.'

'You've already seen it.'

Victor gestured with the gun. 'I have short-term memory issues.'

Wallinger smirked and moved his right hand towards his chest.

'Use your left instead.'

Wallinger frowned. 'My badge is in my left inside pocket.'

'I'm in no hurry.'

It took a little effort for Wallinger to work the ID out of the pocket, but he managed the awkward manoeuvre better than most would.

'Now what?' he asked.

'Throw it to me,' Victor said.

Wallinger did. Victor caught it in his left palm while his gaze remained on Wallinger.

'Put both hands on the top of your head.'

Wallinger sighed. 'You've got to be fucking joking.'

'Do it,' Victor ordered. 'And watch your language.'

With obvious indignity Wallinger did as he was told. Victor flipped open the badge booklet. It was the same as before. Genuine, or a fake as good as genuine.

Victor said, 'Where's Guerrero?'

Wallinger didn't answer, but Guerrero said, 'I'm behind you. Drop the gun.'

FORTY-FOUR

Victor heard the soft click of a hammer being cocked behind him, so he did as he was told. When he turned round he saw why he hadn't heard her enter. She had no shoes on her feet.

'You're not very smart,' Guerrero said. 'Are you?'

'Try not to judge me on my recent actions. I'm usually a lot better at this.'

Wallinger said, 'At debt collecting?' and drew his own gun.

He didn't cock it, Victor noted, so he knew they weren't planning on killing him. At least, not yet.

Guerrero stepped into the lounge and gestured for Victor to back up. He did, until he was equidistant between them. He glanced around at the Spartan furnishings. There was nothing he could use as an improvised weapon or even as a distraction.

'I'd like my badge back,' Wallinger said.

Victor tossed it to him. He caught it in his left hand as effortlessly as Victor had.

'Who are you?' Guerrero asked. 'And why do you look like shit?'

'You know who I am,' Victor said.

'Sure we do.'

Wallinger said, 'I'd like to see your ID again.'

'I lost it.'

'Sure you did,' Guerrero said. 'What happened to your clothes?'

'I traded them.'

'With who, a bum?' Guerrero asked.

'I'm a humanitarian.'

Wallinger said, 'Quit with the bullshit, pal. You're fooling no one.'

Victor remained silent. He didn't know what they knew. He didn't know who they were. He didn't know what they wanted. Until he did, he couldn't afford to tell them anything.

'You want to find Angelica Margolis, yes?'

He didn't answer.

Wallinger said, 'We know you do. You told us so. You're in her apartment for the second time in one day. There's no use choosing to play dumb with us now. One way or another you're gonna talk.'

Guerrero added, 'We know you're not really a debt collector. Why don't you tell us what Miss Margolis has done to you and we can help each other out?'

He looked at both of them in turn, still not knowing whether they were who they claimed to be.

She continued: 'Do you know that's not her real name? Do you know she's an enemy of state? She's a terrorist. Do you know what that means? She's way more dangerous than you could possibly know. You may think you're something of a badass enforcer, but you're punching way above your weight with this one. Whatever she's done to you or whoever you work for, you want to back out. We can help you do that. Trust us.'

Trust ...

'How?' he asked.

Guerrero glanced at Wallinger. They thought they were making progress. Guerrero even lowered her gun to make herself seem less threatening; more trustworthy.

'Do you know where she is?' Wallinger asked.

'No,' Victor said.

Wallinger said, 'But you know where she's going to be, don't you? She's coming back here, isn't she? That's why you're here.'

Victor nodded and pretended not to see the glimmer in Wallinger's eye.

'When?' he asked.

'Thirty minutes,' Victor answered. 'Give or take. Probably closer to an hour, given the blackout.'

Guerrero said, 'And you know this how?'

'I have my sources.'

Wallinger took out his phone and tried to make a call. He growled in frustration and looked at Guerrero. 'We're on our own here.'

She shrugged. 'Doesn't matter.'

'What has Raven done?' Victor asked.

Guerrero's head couldn't twist his way fast enough. Wallinger didn't blink.

'How do you know that code name?' Guerrero asked.

'*Code* name?' Victor said with eyebrows raised. 'I thought it was merely a *nick*name.'

Guerrero relaxed. 'You don't need to know the full details. She's a very bad person. That's all you need to remember. Be grateful you haven't actually found her yet.'

Victor glanced at Wallinger. He hadn't moved a muscle since Victor had said the word *Raven*.

Tension in Wallinger's forehead pushed his eyebrows close together and created two creases that followed the vertical lines of his nose, making it appear longer and sharper. His skin was thin and seemed older than the thirty-four years his ID stated he'd been alive. Fine lines spread out from the eyes and corners of the mouth. Veins in his temples were prominent beneath the skin.

Wallinger said, 'Who are you, really? Agency, right?'

Victor remained silent.

Wallinger said, 'You'd better not be. You know you CIA guys aren't allowed to operate on US soil. That's our job.'

'I didn't say I was CIA.'

'Freelance operator then. Same thing.'

Victor ignored him and said to Guerrero, 'Mind if I clean up?'

'Forget it,' Wallinger said. 'You're coming with us.'

'Happy to,' Victor replied. 'But let me clean up first. Unless you want your car to stink like me for a week.'

The two agents looked at one another, communicating without words, then Guerrero said, 'Fine, go de-stink.'

'But you're still coming with us as soon as you have,' Wallinger answered. 'We have a lot of questions for you.'

'Which I'll be more than happy to answer.'

Guerrero pursed her lips, then said, 'You know there's no fire escape in reach of the bathroom window, don't you?'

Victor raised an eyebrow. 'Don't worry, Agent Guerrero. I'm scared of heights.'

FORTY-FIVE

Victor stepped inside the bathroom and closed the door behind him. The hinges made a quiet squeal of resistance. Twilight filtered through the blinds covering a small window on the wall to his right, perpendicular to the door, and illuminated a space just long enough to fit a bath along the wall opposite the window, and a pedestal washbasin and toilet opposite the light switch. A bare bulb coated with dust hung from the ceiling was useless in the blackout. The walls were about the same size as each other, but were not at exact right angles, creating a skewed cube twice as tall as it was wide. The wall tiles were white, but dulled with neglect. Black mould had sprung up along the silicone sealant where the bath met the wall. Dusty cobwebs hung above the window, their creators long since departed or deceased. A faded circular mat lay in the approximate centre of the room. Maybe it had once been white. The air felt moist and smelled unpleasant – stagnant water and mould.

On the wall across from Victor, a mirror smeared with water marks hung above the sink. Victor's reflection looked back at him, his features hardened by the twilight and deep shadows.

He turned a brass catch to lock the door. He gripped it hard and turned it harder. The noise it made was loud and distinctive. *Clunk*.

A cheap plastic shower curtain was suspended above the bathtub by plastic hooks. The curtain's swirling pattern was obscured in places by mildew. The hooks rattled as Victor drew the curtain back; a long, flexible stainless-steel pipe was attached to the back of the taps and the showerhead supported high above it.

He turned the shower dial, rotating it all the way to the hottest setting. The pelting of water on the cast-iron bathtub was loud enough so that when Victor eased the catch to unlock the door the *clunk* sound was almost inaudible.

He raised the closed toilet lid, then removed the homeless guy's jacket and hat and dropped them across the toilet bowl. He stood with his back against the wall to the side of the door next to the handle, thinking. Waiting.

The water coming out of the shower was hot because the boiler had heated it before the blackout had cut the electricity supply. The air inside the bathroom grew warm and humid. Steam began to darken the mirror above the small sink. Victor watched his reflection fade away.

Forty seconds, he decided. Maybe fifty. If he was wrong he lost nothing. If he was right . . .

He raised his left forearm so it was horizontal before

his face, palm facing inwards. When his count reached forty-seven, bullets punched through the door.

Wood splinters, paint flakes and dust burst out into the air. The steaming mirror above the taps cracked. Glass shards rained down into the sink. Wall tiles shattered, exploding fragments of ceramic around the bathroom. Victor's forearm shielded his eyes from the storm cloud of debris.

Bullet holes appeared in the wall either side of the destroyed mirror as the shooter on the other side of the bathroom door spread out the rounds, then walked them to Victor's left, aiming at the shower. Bullets sliced through the plastic shower curtain. He heard tiles shattering and the curtain rippled and swayed as it was peppered by shrapnel.

He counted eleven shots from a single shooter by the time the firing ceased. The 9mm SIGs carried by Wallinger and Guerrero held fifteen rounds in the magazine.

Victor waited a second and then stretched out a foot to toe the toilet lid and seat. They fell together, banging shut against the toilet bowl. Nothing like the sound of a dead or dying man falling over, but muted and made more organic by the homeless guy's jacket enough to convince the shooter to kick the door open and charge into the bathroom.

The door flew open with a bang, crashing into the wall on the other side from where Victor stood, and the shooter stumbled forward, off balance. Stumbling because the door had been kicked hard enough to break the lock that they heard engaged but not disengaged.

The remaining glass of the small mirror was steamed over, preventing the agent from seeing Victor's reflection, and reacting he slammed a forearm against the extended right wrist to knock the suppressed SIG from the agent's grasp. It clattered on the floor and was knocked into a corner as the agent twisted round to respond.

It was Guerrero, not Wallinger as Victor had expected.

There was no time to consider how he'd been wrong, because the bathroom was small. There was nowhere to move to; no room to dodge; no space to manoeuvre; no opportunity to create range or openings. Tactics meant nothing here. Ferocity meant everything.

Guerrero was small but knew how to fight. She parried Victor's next attack and they exchanged blows – short punches and elbow strikes. Some were blocked. Others scored glancing hits. One elbow caught him on the jaw and he tasted blood. He was a lot bigger and stronger, but she was quicker and her shorter arms were better suited to the close confines. She hammered his ribs with hooks and elbows he wasn't fast enough to defend.

He feinted a similar body blow to lower her defences and struck Guerrero with a palm heel to the side of the face. She collapsed into the sink then rebounded away and to the floor as Victor swept out her load-bearing leg.

She knocked the door shut again as she went down, before scrambling for the gun in the corner, but Victor kicked her in the ribs and she let out a gasp of ejected air. He went to kick again – this time to the face – but she grabbed the mat he was standing on and tugged it out from under him.

With only one foot planted for balance, Victor fell backwards into the bath, tearing the shower curtain from the hooks as he did and passing through the shower spray.

The middle of his back took the force of the impact on the curved shelf of the bath, but spared his skull smacking against the wall tiles. Hot shower water rained down on to him.

He blinked to clear his eyes and struggled to shrug away the shower curtain that fell over him and gain purchase enough to stand, while Guerrero grabbed her disarmed SIG from the corner and stood.

Victor snatched the flexible shower pipe in his left hand, and with a hard pull, wrenched the shower head free from its perch. It fell and he caught it in the same hand, then launched it as she turned to shoot.

The showerhead struck Guerrero in the chest and sent her reeling backwards, slipping and losing balance on the now-slick floor tiles. The unsecured showerhead fell and hung over the side of the bath, pipe snaking back and forth, and spraying water throughout the small room.

Victor ripped the shower curtain aside and threw himself up and into Guerrero as she recovered her balance.

They collided into the closest wall, Guerrero taking the brunt of the impact against her face, dropping the gun once more, and not having the strength to stop Victor grabbing her jacket and pulling her away from the wall and throwing her down to the floor.

She hit the wet tiles with force, but on her hands and knees. She tried to push herself upright, but Victor grabbed the showerhead and looped the flexible metal pipe around her neck. Water sprayed everywhere.

As soon as the metal touched the skin of her throat Guerrero went wild, reacting fast, and flipping over on to her back to face Victor before he could get a secure hold.

She wedged four fingers between the cord and her neck before the noose was complete, preventing Victor from strangling her, but sacrificing one of her hands in the process.

Victor grabbed Guerrero's free wrist in his own free hand as she went to strike, rendering her defenceless.

But Victor still had one hand to employ, holding the showerhead.

He used it as a club to batter against the side of Guerrero's head as she turned to protect her face. Two hits was enough to stun her but also half-wreck the showerhead so Victor pressed it against Guerrero's face, pinning her head against the side of the bath and sending the pressurised spray of water into her mouth and up her nose. She gurgled and thrashed as the showerhead forced hot water down her throat faster than she could gag it away, until her stomach filled with water, and then when her stomach was full the water entered her lungs. She tried to fight with her free hand but Victor had his arm locked out so no matter how fierce her attempts, her strength was negated.

She coughed and retched and vomited but Victor kept the showerhead in place until Guerrero had stopped moving and the bathroom floor was flooded under an inch of water, pink with swirling blood and dark with an oil-slick of spreading vomit.

FORTY-SIX

Victor released the showerhead when he was sure Guerrero was not going to get up again, and recovered the SIG and shook the water from it as best he could. He wasn't sure if it would fire or not with water in the barrel and chamber and magazine, but it would dry out soon enough.

He stepped out of the bathroom, fast and smooth, gun up, but saw that Wallinger was not going to bother him so he tucked the weapon into his waistband and reached past Guerrero's corpse to twist the taps and turn off the shower. He was soaked. There was no towel in the bathroom so he had to make do with swiping the excess water from his hair and face.

He swallowed the blood that had drained into his mouth from the cut on the inside of his cheek. The instinct was to spit it out, but that would leave his DNA and blood type behind. Swallowing blood wasn't pleasant, but it was better than spending the rest of his life behind bars. He wiped the smear of blood from his lips with the back of a hand and pushed his cheek against his upper jaw to apply pressure to the cut.

He went through pockets, taking Guerrero's wallet and identification and car keys and smartphone and spare magazines.

Victor left the bathroom and approached Wallinger, who was stationary in the lounge, slumped against a wall, his white dress shirt stained with blood where he had been stabbed multiple times in the abdomen and chest – a surprise attack, swift and savage. The knife that killed him was still buried in his chest, pinning his blue tie in place, an inch of bare blade protruding perpendicular from the dead man's breastbone. It looked as if Guerrero had tried to remove it but the blade had stuck in the sternum. The fight in the bathroom might have had a different outcome had she been able to pull the weapon free and employ it after Victor had disarmed her of the SIG.

Had their roles been reversed, Victor would have had the knife to use in the bathroom because he would never stab a man through the solid bone of the sternum, and only in the chest with the blade on the same horizontal plane as the ribs, so it would slide between the bones and not become stuck. The corpse in the bathroom had never learned to do this or had been too rushed or sloppy to employ her knowledge.

Victor went through Wallinger's pockets and compared his credentials to Guerrero's. They looked as official and genuine as each other.

Wallinger was a little shorter than Victor and a little

broader. Regardless, the suit jacket, trousers, socks and shoes fitted well enough for his needs. He was not going to turn heads dressed in another-sized man's clothes, but that was fine by Victor. He left on his own shirt, given that it was not soaked all over and was less attention-drawing than a shirt marked with holes and bloodstains. Victor bundled his wet clothes and shoes into a plastic bag he found under the kitchen sink. He used a dishcloth to soak up some of the water from his hair and used his fingers to comb it until it looked respectable again.

When Victor went back into the lounge area, Raven was waiting for him.

He pointed Guerrero's SIG at her face and said, 'I want answers.'

Raven sat on the folding camp chair opposite Wallinger's corpse. The red wig was gone and her own black hair was held back by a band. Her clothes were different too: jeans and a sweater replaced the suit. She looked relaxed and comfortable, but he saw from her pose she had not let her guard down. She was sitting on the edge of the chair, feet planted and square with her knees, and her head was over her hips. If required, she could launch up with speed. However casual she acted around Victor, she did not put herself at needless risk. He paid her the same compliment by keeping his distance and never letting her out of his peripheral vision.

'Such a mess,' she said and frowned at the body between them. Then she looked up at him and said, 'Do you always leave a trail of corpses wherever you go?'

He shrugged. 'It's not uncommon. But two separate

entities have tried to end my life on the same day. Even for me, that's a little on the high side. So start talking.'

'Killing everyone who gets in your way is hardly the best way of staying unnoticed, is it?'

'Something tells me these two aren't going to notice me again.'

She smirked. 'Surely better for them to not notice you in the first place than leave corpses behind for others of their ilk to notice?'

'It's a vicious circle,' he admitted.

She looked at the gun in his hand, still aimed at her. 'If you're not going to shoot me, could you point that thing somewhere else?'

He tucked it into his waistband.

'Thank you. Did you have to steal his clothes? Are you really struggling for cash that badly?'

He ignored her.

She studied him, annoyed he wouldn't take the bait, and then her expression became more serious. She glanced at Wallinger's corpse. 'Who were these guys?'

He tossed her the two IDs. She scrutinised them, running a thumb over each one in turn, as if she could measure their veracity by touch alone.

'It's a genuine ID and genuine badge,' Victor said.

'I don't know either of these two,' Raven said. 'But it's really not smart to kill federal agents. Whatever their temporary risk to you, you've done yourself far more harm than good. Do you know how many cops and government agents are in this city? Or in this country? Do you have any idea the lengths they'll go to to get justice for these guys?

You should have run. You should have done anything you could to avoid capture and get away, but you never should have killed them.'

Victor said, 'You told me before they weren't real agents.'

'No, I told you they weren't on genuine Homeland Security business. You've made things a lot worse for both of us by killing these two.'

'Look at the knife,' Victor said. 'Tell me what's wrong with it?'

She looked confused, as if trying to work out what trick he was attempting before deciding he was, to her surprise, being genuine. She leaned forward for a closer look. It only took her a second to see what he meant. He hadn't expected her to take any longer.

'Why did you stab him through the sternum?'

'I should have gone for the ribs, right?'

'Obviously, but with the blade thrusting on a horizontal axis so it wouldn't have become trapped on bone. I would have thought you would know better than that.'

'Exactly,' he said. 'I do know better.'

Her eyes rose to meet his own. 'You're saying you didn't kill these two?'

Victor said, 'I'm saying I didn't kill this particular one, but I did take his clothes. He won't need them again. The dead woman in the bathroom is my own work. She stabbed this guy here, and then tried to kill me. I was acting in self-defence. I haven't stayed alive this long by killing those who I don't need to, especially people who will be missed who have powerful friends.'

'Why did this Guerrero try to kill you? And why did she kill her partner?'

'She tried to kill me because I said your code name. He wanted to take me in. She couldn't let that happen.'

'Why would you use my code name?'

'To test a theory,' he answered. 'And to find out if you were telling me the truth before.'

'I'm offended.'

He shook his head. 'No, you're not.'

'True, but this would all have gone a lot smoother if you would just trust what I tell you.'

'I trust no one. Least of all the word of people who have tried to kill me.'

She rolled her eyes. 'You're not going to let that go, are you? It's not healthy to hold on to grudges. Forgive and forget, as they say.'

'What are you doing here, Constance? Why didn't you get out of the city while you had the chance? I might not have found you again.'

She frowned. 'I really wish you wouldn't call me that.'

'What are you doing here? What am I doing here?'

'Apparently, I'm helping you see the obvious.'

'Which is?' Victor asked.

'Halleck set you up.'

'Of course he did. But I still don't know why. He told me he didn't send you after me. I believed him.'

'That's because he was telling the truth. He didn't send me after you, it was the other way round.'

'No,' he said. 'I was after a Saudi prince.'

She was shaking her head before he'd finished talking.

'He orchestrated it so I came after you, but his intention wasn't for me to kill you. It was for you to kill me. So, technically, he was telling the truth. He must have thought you, being historically so effective at taking out threats, would be more than a match for me.'

'Then he overestimated my abilities.'

'More like he underestimated mine. But it's irrelevant, because we both walked away from that encounter. Which gave him a problem: I was still breathing.'

'Why does he want you dead so badly?'

Raven said, 'Because I'm trying to stop him.'

'Trying to stop him from doing what?'

'Committing a terrorist attack on US soil.'

FORTY-SEVEN

'The blackout?' Victor asked.

'We shouldn't talk about it here,' Raven said. 'Not with two dead federal agents.'

'I'm not going anywhere without answers. We're okay for a few minutes. Even if someone were to walk in, what are they going to do? Send a carrier pigeon to notify the police?'

Raven frowned, then said, 'The blackout is the first stage of it, yes. Not the whole thing. This city has had blackouts before. It's no big deal and certainly not what you'd call a terrorist attack.'

'Then what happens in the second stage?'

'Now that, I'm afraid, I don't know exactly. It'll be a bomb though, for certain. Halleck's people acquired two tons of black-market C4 earlier this year. A Turkish banker named Caglayan brokered the deal.'

'So he was the true target in Prague,' Victor said. 'Halleck wanted me to sever the connection.'

Raven shook her head. 'No, Caglayan was my target. Halleck knew I would go after him, that's why he sent you after the prince, to make sure our paths crossed. I knew he would send someone after me, so I killed Caglayan and waited for Halleck's assassin to arrive.'

He nodded, thinking that Halleck would have known about the prince's activities from dealing with Caglayan and gone to Muir under the guise of the prince being a legitimate target, which he was.

'And Halleck couldn't have hired me to go after you directly,' Victor said. 'He had to trick my CIA broker as well as me. He couldn't risk them knowing your name, because like me you'll be on a list, and that could expose him. He even said he wanted to keep my broker in the loop. But I said no.'

'Because you didn't want anyone other than Halleck to know what you were doing,' Raven added. 'Which he would have predicted.'

Victor said, 'So it was you who I was communicating with then in Prague.'

She said, 'I was pretending to be Caglayan while you were pretending to be the prince's accountant.'

'You're good,' he said. 'You almost killed me.'

'Almost,' she echoed. 'As you can imagine, that two tons of plastique will make some serious mess in an urban environment.'

He said, 'A bomb doesn't first require a blackout.'

'That depends where the bomb is planted, doesn't it? No power means no CCTV to record them placing it, overstretched emergency services, no cell towers, no—'

'I understand how electricity works.'

She nodded in apology. 'Whatever Halleck plans to blow up, the blackout is necessary to make it happen. I don't know any more about the attack than that, but what I do know is that this blackout is only going to be active for twelve hours. Well, under twelve now. So whatever it is Halleck is planning, it has to be occurring very soon. Sometime tonight.'

'Under the museum you said, "It's started." How do you know how long the blackout is going to last for? You also told me when the lights went out that it wasn't you this time. Explain.'

'I didn't activate it,' she explained, 'but I caused it. I made sure the virus got into the system.'

'I assume you mean a computer virus.'

'A computer virus, yes. A pathogen, we called it. We stole the idea from the Israelis. Mossad used one to knock out an Iranian nuclear reactor by making the turbines run too fast. Set Tehran's enrichment plans back several years. They released the virus into the world and sat back and waited while it infected computer after computer, doing no damage but spreading exponentially until it naturally found its way on to a USB stick that someone took to the nuclear power plant. Obviously, the computers that run such things aren't linked up to the web. It worked brilliantly. They were a bit more sophisticated than us. I broke into the house of one of the guys who works at a power plant upstate and infected his home computer with our virus to make sure it got into the power plant's system on the right timescale. The Israelis were a lot more patient than Halleck.'

'I don't understand,' Victor said. 'Halleck works for the government. Why is he going to commit a terrorist attack in the US? He's no terrorist.'

She stood and stepped towards a window, giving him her back. 'One man's terrorist is another man's freedom fighter.'

'I don't buy it.'

'I bought it at first,' Raven explained, turning to face him again. 'When he first had me killing people I couldn't rationalise as bad guys. I believed his bullshit about sacrifice and the greater good and all of those clichés. But eventually I figured out that he works for whoever pays him the most. More often than not that's the government. But not always.'

'Halleck said you lost a teammate in Yemen. A lover. He said you blamed him and were going after his people in revenge.'

She looked sad for a moment and avoided eye contact. 'I did lose a man I cared about in Yemen. But it was no one's fault. The intelligence was bad.'

The intelligence was bad. Halleck had used the exact same words. The man was a skilful manipulator, hiding the lies within truths to convince Victor of his veracity.

'And who is paying Halleck this time?' Victor asked.

'*They* are.'

'And who exactly are you talking about?'

'The one per cent. The old white men. The guys who run the world.'

Victor said, 'I don't do conspiracy theories. Who?'

'The man who Halleck has been answering to this time was a lobbyist for the arms industry.'

'Ah,' he said, understanding. 'Cause a false flag attack

and blame it on ... let me guess: some hotspot in the Middle East?'

She nodded. 'Cue increased defence spending and billions more to the share values of the corporations who manufacture the bombs and bullets. Like I said: the old white men who run the world. Do you know why they call it a false flag attack? It dates back centuries, from naval warfare, when ships used cannons and sailors fought each other with swords and hatchets. It was a ruse, flying the flag of your enemies to deceive the target ship, allowing you to sail close enough to strike. But the ship flying the false flag would raise its own before engaging in battle. It would admit the deception before the fight began.'

'I don't imagine Halleck will show the same kind of honour.'

'Of course he won't,' Raven agreed. 'Governments have been doing this, and getting away with it, forever. In 1962 a plan was drawn up to justify the invasion of Cuba to overthrow Castro. The Department of Defense put together Operation Northwoods to sink ships and shoot down planes and blame it on Cuba. It was never put into action, but it wasn't the first and it won't be the last.

Victor said, 'This lobbyist will know who he's working for.'

Raven shook her head. 'Don't be naïve. He's only a middleman. Besides, there isn't someone in charge of this. There isn't even a conspiracy. It's just the way it works. It's like a consensus. In fact that's what I call them: The Consensus.'

'The Consensus,' he repeated.

'The old white men who keep the wheels turning for their

benefit, and those who support them. In this case it's all about peacetime, which is bad for business. The US spends over a trillion dollars a year on defence, most of it going to US arms manufactures. That has to be justified. There has to be war to keep that bankroll. The problem is there's been too much of it recently. The politicians need to be able to justify those wars. They need to get public backing. No better way to do that than have something blow up.'

'I'd like the name of the lobbyist all the same.'

She said, 'His name is Alan Beaumont. Or, to be more precise, it was his name.'

Victor said, 'You killed him,' and she nodded.

'I've been doing what I do best, trying to stop Halleck.'

'But Halleck's going forward anyway?'

Raven said, 'I was too late getting to Beaumont. He'd already transferred the money to Halleck. Now, the vested interests are expecting their fireworks. Halleck's got a job to do or he's going to make some extremely powerful enemies.'

'Okay,' Victor said. 'Then it's time to leave the city. I have no desire to be a casualty of Halleck's attack.'

'Good luck with that.'

He said, 'I don't believe in luck,' and headed towards the door.

'Well, whatever you do believe in, you'll need its help.'

Something in her tone made him turn round. 'Why do you say that?'

'Because you're going to be Halleck's patsy. By coming here you've set yourself up to take the blame for the attack.'

FORTY-EIGHT

He was silent for a long time. He thought about the book and the safe house and the coded message and believing he had tracked Raven to the museum. A trail left by Halleck's people to take him to a certain place at a certain time.

You're coming with us, the guy in the blue suit had said. At that moment Victor had thought the team had wanted to take Victor into their custody because of his association with Raven. Now, he realised that must have always been part of Halleck's plan.

'It doesn't make sense,' Victor said. 'Halleck couldn't have known for sure I would want to meet him; he couldn't have known I would come after you nor how I would go about it. I found one of your Dominican cigarette stubs in Prague. It led me to Marte.'

'I always knew Jean Claud would sell me out,' Raven said. 'But I could never bring myself to kill him merely as a precaution. I guess scaring someone only works for so long. He gave you my aliases?'

'Yes, and then—'

He stopped himself because he knew the rest. He had passed the information on to Halleck, who had told Victor about the apartment.

He shook his head, annoyed at himself. 'He gave me this address and I didn't question it. I came straight here. You were right, I did set myself up.'

'Don't be too harsh on yourself,' Raven said. 'Halleck is a master at this kind of thing. He fooled me for years.'

'I should have known better. I do know better.'

'Life is one long lesson. We never know how much we learned until we're facing the end.'

He considered this, then said, 'But I could have killed you in Prague. He *wanted* me to kill you in Prague. If I had, I would never have been here now.'

She looked at him with some sympathy. He never liked such looks. She said, 'Then he wouldn't have used you. He would have used someone else. Maybe one of his own men even. But, he didn't need to, did he? He had you. You made it easy for him by trying to find me. You gave yourself to him. You gave him a perfect patsy: a professional killer coming to New York of his own accord.'

'I told Guerrero and Wallinger not to judge me on my recent actions. I told them I was usually a lot better at this. Maybe I'm not. Maybe I've simply been lucky until now. And I don't even believe in luck.'

Raven stood up from the folding chair and retrieved the paperback novel from the floor. She thumbed through it.

'He didn't make it easy for you. That's why you fell for it. If at any stage it didn't feel right; if it felt easy, you would have smelled a rat. Put that down to Halleck's competence, not any incompetence of your own.'

He shook his head again. 'It still doesn't make sense. Even giving me this address he couldn't guarantee I would be in the city for the day of the blackout.'

She looked at him like he was missing something obvious, which he realised he was.

'Ah,' Victor said. 'The blackout happened today *because* I'm in New York.' She nodded. 'And the museum ... Another good trick. It's a good location for a clandestine meeting. I didn't even suspect a trap.'

'I told you: Halleck knows exactly what he's doing. He's been operating for a long time.'

'If you hadn't been there to warn me I might be dead by now.' He paused. 'I guess I should thank you.'

'Only if you want to.'

He swallowed and said, 'Thank you.'

She bowed her head a little. 'You're welcome.' She looked around the apartment. 'We should make a move. Even with the NYPD overloaded, we've probably outstayed our welcome.'

Victor looked around the apartment too and nodded. 'I thought the camping gear was here because you liked to keep your safe house free of anything identifiable, but it serves his narrative, doesn't it? He's had a huge crew following me around the city. Just to observe, one of them told me. But also to record, no doubt. Someone will have photographed me entering this building. After the attack, this will be *my* apartment where I planned it.' He glanced at Wallinger's corpse. 'And these two told me they were looking for you. They said you were a terrorist. But they were here to add to the deception. They could have testified after the fact to my presence. When I came back here, Guerrero must have known the plan to grab me at the museum had failed so she tried to take care of things herself. Wallinger was obviously not part of Halleck's network. He thought he was just doing his job.'

Raven shook her head. 'That's not how Halleck operates. Guerrero wouldn't have known what was going down. Only a few key people will be in the know. I was one of them.'

Victor ran through the two conversations he'd had with the two Homeland Security agents, especially the second one before Guerrero attacked him. 'Then it was because I said your code name. She didn't know about the museum. She didn't know about Halleck's crew following me. But she did know about you. That I did too marked me for death and made her partner collateral damage.'

'I did say I'm not very popular. If you'd have trusted me and not said my name to test your theories then your shirt would be dry and we wouldn't have two dead federal agents here. Even if we stop the attack, you're still fucked.'

He frowned. 'I don't like profanity.'

She laughed. 'But killing people is okay?'

'I never said I was consistent. And there is no *we*. I appreciate your assistance at the museum, but you're on your own. I'm no fan of bombs and the carnage they cause but I'm not staying in this city a second longer. The authorities were on to me within moments of leaving that museum. I almost didn't escape. Every cop and federal agent in the city will be looking for me.'

'They were on to you so fast because Halleck gave you up to them.'

'Of course,' Victor said. 'Which is why I need to get out of here.'

'If you run and I don't stop it on my own then you'll be a fugitive with half the Western world looking for you.'

Victor said, 'That's pretty much my life right now.'

'Even a mercenary like you cares about taking the blame for an act of terrorism. And however much you're a wanted man now, that's only going to rise exponentially afterwards.'

'Of course,' he said again. 'On both counts.'

'How are you going to keep working when your face is plastered on every news bulletin?'

He didn't answer.

'And how are you going to avoid all those enemies of yours when you're the world's most wanted man?'

'Okay,' he said. 'You make a compelling pitch. What are you proposing? That we work together to stop Halleck setting me up?'

'That's a somewhat selfish way of looking at it,' Raven said. 'I like to think of it as we work together to stop a major act of terrorism.'

'Semantics. How do we stop Halleck? All we know is that he's going to set off a bomb and the blackout is helping him do that. We don't know where it is or where he is.'

She said, 'The cops are looking for us, right? Especially

you. We make sure you come to the attention of New York's finest. It'll be called in. Cell phone towers are down, but cop radios will still work. Halleck's people will be piggybacking on the airwaves or they'll be informed by one of his people on the inside. He'll know where you are five seconds after the cops do. We don't need to find Halleck. We just have to make sure his people find us.'

'Then what?'

'Isn't it obvious? We take one alive. By now they'll have to know more. They'll know where Halleck is or where the bomb is. If we're lucky, that'll be the same place.'

'That sounds too much like guesswork to me.'

She shrugged. 'What choice do we have?'

'You mean the choice beyond putting ourselves on the radar of the NYPD, the FBI and Halleck's people at the same time?'

She nodded.

'If we use ourselves as bait when the whole city is look-ing for us then it's more than likely we're going to get into a situation we can't control. The cops outnumber us by a factor of five thousand. They have helicopters. They have SWAT teams. And that's without FBI and Homeland Security and Halleck's people. It's too much of a risk. It can't be done.'

Raven gave him a look and held up Wallinger's car keys.

Victor raised an eyebrow. 'It's so ridiculous it might actu-ally work.'

FORTY-NINE

They found Wallinger and Guerrero's vehicle on the east side of the block. It was an anonymous Ford Crown Victoria. An older model, parked in the mouth of an alleyway. Walking distance from the tenement building, but also hidden from passers-by. Raven used the key fob to unlock the car and she climbed behind the wheel.

There was a radio positioned in the console.

She lifted up the receiver and said, 'Do you want to, or shall I?'

Victor took it from her. 'I heard them both speak. You didn't.'

She shrugged and settled back into the driver's seat.

He cleared his throat and thumbed the send button. 'This is Agent Wallinger. I have a possible sighting on the Met museum suspect.'

He released the send button and a dispatcher said, 'Go, Agent Wallinger.'

'I have a witness claiming they saw a six-foot-two male, dark hair and wearing a suit, acting suspiciously inside Joyce Kilmer Park within the last five minutes. He may or may not be in the company of a female. I'm stuck in gridlock. I can't get there.'

The dispatcher said, 'I'll pass it on. You stay safe out there, Clarence.'

Victor said, 'You can be certain of that,' and replaced the receiver on to its hook.

Joyce Kilmer Park was one block north and one east. It was a short walk through the dark streets. They didn't want to risk taking Guerrero and Wallinger's vehicle. The last of the twilight had gone and a pale moon glowed through thin clouds above them. Without light pollution, stars could be seen too.

Even with some roads gridlocked and an overstretched emergency service they figured the NYPD would get to the park fast. Halleck's people would take longer. They were a big crew but spread over the city there might not be anyone nearby if they were searching for them on an even spread. But Victor doubted that would be the case. The mock safe house was a known location, and even if Halleck didn't know that Victor and Raven had arranged to meet there, it would be smart to have people check it out in case either one returned.

'We can't wait there though,' Raven had insisted. 'If the cops catch us in the vicinity of dead Homeland Security agents, we're done.'

Victor had agreed. It would be more problematic to take a captive in an enclosed space. If they knew – or even

282

believed – Victor or Raven was in the building they would send in every man they had. On the streets, they could be divided.

Joyce Kilmer Park was long and thin, occupying three blocks north to south and one wide, surrounded by road on all four sides. It was crisscrossed with walkways cutting through the grassland. Trees lined most of the walkways. With the moon above, the open spaces were lit well enough to see the scattering of people sitting on benches or walking or drinking or smoking or looking at the stars.

Raven said, 'Halleck's people are already here.'

Victor turned to face her and put his hands on her waist as though they were a couple conversing. He waited for more information.

'One guy on his own,' she explained. 'Dressed in a dark sports jacket. Short blond hair. Thirties. He's by a bench. Ten metres to your seven o'clock.'

He didn't look. She took a step left, hands on his shoulders, positioning herself so Victor blocked her line of sight, and the blond man's in return.

'He made it here fast.'

She nodded. 'He was probably on his way to the apartment when we made the call. We must have missed him by minutes.'

He nodded too. 'At least we don't have to hang around in the rain.'

'I thought you were a pessimist. How do you want to do this?'

'That depends if he plans to shoot us on sight.'

She said, 'So give me the options.'

'You peel off and hang back,' Victor explained. 'I'll make sure he sees me and I'll lead him out of the park. Either he'll follow me to see where I'm going or he'll shoot me between the shoulder blades as soon as we're alone. Thanks to the blackout there are plenty of dark streets and darker corners. You follow behind him and make sure he doesn't. Either way, we'll be alone with him.'

Raven said, 'It won't work.'

'Why not?'

'Because he's not alone. There's another one. Dark-skinned with a dark beard, at your three o'clock. And he's seen us.'

This time Victor looked, because there was nothing to lose.

Raven was right. The dark-skinned man had seen them and he was speaking to his left wrist. He was wearing a sports jacket too.

Got 'em, Victor read on his lips.

He led Raven away, towards the closest exit, knowing the two guys behind would converge and follow without having to look. There was no danger of being shot in the back while still inside the park boundaries. No matter how loyal these two were to Halleck, they were not going to gun down Victor and Raven with so many witnesses. They would wait for a better opportunity and maybe even for backup to arrive. Either of which gave Victor and Raven time to lure them to a place of their choosing.

They left through one of the east exits and crossed the many lanes of Grand Concourse. They headed between H-shaped tenements, walking in darkness where the moonlight failed to reach. Victor heard the footsteps of their pursuers nearing.

They walked round a corner. Where the pathway between buildings met the road a cop car was parked. Two NYPD officers were talking with concerned locals – explaining and reassuring and answering questions as best they could.

Victor slowed to back off and find another route, but Raven shook her head and walked towards the cops. Victor hesitated until he understood what she was doing, then did the same.

The two guys in sports jackets appeared soon after, saw him and Raven walking and tasted success, but only for an instant. They saw what he was doing, saw the cops, and slowed down to look casual, hands retreating away from holstered guns and zipping up their jackets to hide them.

Victor and Raven stood with the group of locals as though they were paying attention to what the cops had to say, keeping their two pursuers in sight all the while.

They reached the crowd. They didn't know what to do but they were not going to start shooting in front of the NYPD.

Their eyes were locked on to Victor and Raven, full of anger at being so close but neutered. Victor gave them a measured smile of triumph, knowing it would only anger them further, knowing that anger in turn would lead them to make a mistake.

They held their nerve though. For the moment, at least, they kept their cool. They were not amateurs. Then they started thinking and communicating with looks and facial expressions.

The one with short blond hair pushed his way to the flank, boxing Victor and Raven into the crowd with nowhere to go. It was a smart, if predictable move. One Victor had expected.

And wanted.

He edged towards the other guy, the one with the beard and dark skin. The man was confused but tense and ready for Victor to make a run for it, not—

For Victor to strike him in the solar plexus.

The man collapsed straight down to his knees, clutching his chest, trying without success to suck air into lungs with a paralysed diaphragm.

'*Hey, help,*' Raven called to the cops. 'Something's wrong. This guy just . . .'

'Stand aside, stand aside,' one of the cops yelled as he moved closer.

He waved his partner over while the man with the beard wheezed, breathless and desperate.

'I think he's having a heart attack,' Raven said.

'Give the man some room, yeah?' the cop said and ushered people back. 'Don't crowd him.'

Victor and Raven walked away as a cop unzipped the guy's jacket, snapping out his Glock from the holster on his belt when he saw the man's suppressed pistol in the shoulder rig.

'*Hands in the fucking sky, asshole,*' the other cop shouted, drawing his own gun.

The man with the beard gasped and tried to splutter a

protest. He didn't have the strength to raise his hands. The second man glanced between Victor and Raven and then his team mate, then headed after Victor and Raven.

Again, a predictable move. Again, one that Victor had wanted.

He waited until he was nearing a corner and ran round it, only to stop as soon as he was out of sight.

The man with the blond hair bolted round the corner four seconds later.

Victor whipped the blade of his forearm into the guy's face, the force multiplied by the guy's own speed.

His feet carried on forward while his head stayed put and he folded and dropped, landing hard on his right shoulder. He went slack, conscious but dazed, blood from his face smeared on the pavement.

Victor glanced around and spotted a building he liked the look of. 'There,' he said and dragged the man to the doorway.

It took Raven a matter of seconds to pick the lock and they hurried inside.

FIFTY

On the other side of the door was a dark room full of cardboard boxes and piled junk. A dim glow of moonlight shone through a window. The man with blond hair moaned as Victor dragged him by his ankles through the doorway and deposited him in an unceremonious heap while Raven performed a quick recon.

Victor searched through the man's pockets while he breathed with a high-pitched wheeze because his nose was crushed flat. He found a wallet, spare ammunition, a radio, a cell phone and the suppressed Ruger in black leather shoulder rigging. Victor took everything and dropped it on the floor out of the man's reach.

He held up the wallet for the man to see. 'Personal effects? That's such a basic error. I guess you must be part of the B team, Mr Sean Pachulski.'

The man's eyes began to focus as his senses returned. His gaze flicked between Victor and Raven. Despite the obvious pain and his captive status he was angry and defiant beyond bravado. This was a warrior.

'*Fuck you*,' Pachulski shouted.

He was somewhere in his forties, face aged further by sun, alcohol and tobacco. Gold glinted at his neck and around his left ring finger. Tattoos and scars covered his thick arms. He had a Bronx accent.

Victor brought a finger to his lips. 'Shh.'

The man growled, 'I'm gonna kill you.'

'Of course you are.'

He tried to stand to deliver on his promise, but his right shoulder was useless – dislocated or suffering from a torn rotator cuff. He couldn't get himself upright with only one arm. The more he tried, the more he cried out in pain.

'Have you finished?' Victor asked.

Pachulski stared, nostrils flaring in rage and frustration.

Raven returned and said, 'It's clear. We're alone.'

Victor nodded and looked down at the warrior. 'Did you hear that?'

The man said nothing.

'Do you understand what that means for you?'

'I'm gonna fucking kill you,' Pachulski hissed.

He rolled back on to his front and tried to stand. For all his determination, he had neither the strength nor coordination to do so with only the use of a single arm.

'I respect your will,' Victor said, 'if not your distorted sense of reality. You couldn't kill me with two hands, a gun and backup. Now you can't even stand.'

'You're a dead man.'

'Empirical evidence states otherwise.'

The rage became acceptance. He stared. 'Shut up and kill me, you fuck.'

Victor said, 'All in good time.'

Raven gestured for him to hurry. Victor gestured to say that he had it under control.

'Your shoulder looks painful,' Victor said.

'I've had paper cuts that hurt more,' Pachulski growled. 'You're a pussy.'

'I need some answers.'

'Go fuck yourself.'

Victor said, 'I'm not a vindictive type but try not to swear and I assure you this will go a lot easier.'

The man sneered. 'You think you can torture me and I'll talk? Fuck you. Fuck you. *FUCK. YOU.*'

There was no false confidence, but defiance and self-belief wrapped up in fury. A powerful combination. This was a man who would not be broken without considerable effort. Any pain would fuel that anger and solidify the defiance. It might be hours before his will cracked. Victor considered for a moment.

'I believe you when you say that, Mr Pachulski. I don't think pain is going to make you tell me what I need to know.'

'You'd better fucking believe it.'

Victor said, 'But pain can be an emotional as well as a physical response. What other emotions are there? Fear? That's no good; I can't scare you. Love? What do you love most in this world?'

The man named Pachulski hesitated, not knowing how to answer; confused or wary of some trap or manipulation attempt.

'I said: what do you love most in this world?'

Still, the man gave no answer. His eyes narrowed, suspicious and growing nervous.

'It's not a trick question,' Victor assured.

Victor held open the wallet so Pachulski could see the contents, in particular a photograph behind clear plastic.

The man stared. Swallowed.

Victor said, 'Is this what you love most in this world?'

Pachulski said nothing. He didn't blink.

Victor said, 'You have a beautiful family, Sean. May I call you Sean?' He didn't wait for an answer. 'Your two girls look just like their mother.'

Anger and pain left the man's face, replaced by fear.

'You're a bit broader now than in this picture. A couple of years old, is it? That would make your girls ... Seven and eight? Something like that. The little one looks like she's trouble. I can see the mischief in her grin.'

The man tried, but failed, to stop his eyes welling.

Victor took out a credit card, examined it for a second, then held it up for the man to see. Victor did the same with the driver's licence. He tapped the printed address.

'This is exactly why you don't take personal effects with you on a job, Sean. And this is exactly why I have no one in my life. Are you going to tell me what I need to know?'

Tears streamed from Pachulski's eyes, flowing over his temples and into his hair.

'You don't live that far from here,' Victor said. 'In fact I was close to your address earlier today. I think I can be there in about twenty minutes.' He looked to Raven. 'What do you think?'

She said, 'The roads will be clearer now, so maybe fifteen.'

Pachulski's eyes were as red as his bloody nose.

'I can have your two girls on the radio within half an hour,' Victor continued, 'begging Daddy to save them. Will you be brave enough to tell them you can't?'

The man wailed.

'Tell me everything I need to know and when I walk out of here I won't make a detour.'

Finally, Pachulski spoke between sobs: 'How do I know you'll keep your word?'

Victor said, 'The only thing you can know for certain, whether or not you tell me what I want to know, is that I will kill you. There's nothing you can do to stop that happening. It's not personal, Sean, but you work for people trying to kill me. I haven't stayed alive this long by showing my enemies mercy. ' Raven glanced at him. 'So, you're dead. Like I said, a certainty. But if you don't tell me who sent you then I won't kill you until after I've made that detour we talked about.'

Pachulski blinked the tears from his eyes, swallowed, and said, 'I'll talk. I'll talk.'

'Good,' Victor said.

Raven said, 'Where's Halleck?'

Pachulski said, 'I don't know, I swear.'

'Then where are you guys based? Where's your HQ?'

'Brooklyn,' Pachulski answered. 'Floyd Bennett Field.'

'What's that?' Victor asked.

'It's a disused airfield,' Raven explained. 'I know where it is.'

Victor said, 'How many of you are there?'

'We had twenty-four,' the man said. 'I'm not sure how many are left now. I'm sorry, I—'

Raven said, 'Where's the bomb? Where's the C4?'

His mouth hovered open. 'What bomb? I don't know anything about a bomb.'

'Why did Halleck base you guys at an airfield?'

'Waiting for a delivery,' Pachulski said.

'Details,' Raven demanded.

His words came out fast and frantic: 'That's all I know, I swear. Halleck is having something delivered. I don't know what. I'm a foot soldier, that's all. I don't know anything else. If I did I would tell you. *I swear*.'

'I believe you,' Victor said. 'Relax.'

'So you won't hurt my family now?'

Victor said, 'I don't need to any more, do I?' and broke Pachulski's neck.

FIFTY-ONE

The street was empty when they left. The rain fell in a light but steady drizzle. The breeze was intermittent and cold. The moon pierced through the clouds above. The city beneath was dark and quiet – a rare instant of peacefulness in an otherwise chaotic metropolis.

Raven said, 'Floyd Bennett Field is at least twenty miles away. It's right on the bottom of Brooklyn. That's a hell of a lot of ground to cover as fugitives.'

'What choice do we have?'

They kept their eyes moving as they walked, looking out for cops or Halleck's men.

'Would you have done it?' Raven asked.

'Done what?'

She frowned. 'Don't play dumb. You know what I mean. The stuff about the kid. The daughter. Was it a threat or would you have followed through if he hadn't talked?'

Victor said, 'We'll never know, will we?'

She was quiet for a moment. 'I wouldn't have let you, had it come to it.'

Victor didn't respond.

Raven said, 'Maybe you only want me to think there's no line you won't cross. Maybe that's why you won't tell me.'

'Believe whatever you wish.'

No one gave either of them a second glance as they threaded their way through a crowd of citizens out to pick up supplies of perishable goods being sold cheap by a local supermarket looking to offload them before they spoiled. He paid for a loaf of sliced white bread and ate three slices as he walked to get some simple carbohydrates into his system. Raven took a slice for herself. Victor gave the rest of the loaf to the next person he passed.

He felt a little light-headed from the fight with Guerrero. Not concussed, but hard blows to the head made the brain rattle inside the skull. He could have some swelling, or in an extreme case an aneurysm. If it was the latter, it didn't matter about the people after him because he would be dead soon regardless. If it was only the former the light-headedness might progress to feeling faint or dizzy or nauseous. Neither of which would help him get out of this situation. He needed his mind sharp and fast, not dulled and slow.

They passed a man in an astrakhan fur hat who stood sheltering in the doorway of a closed store. The man was laughing to himself. About what, they would never know.

They walked south for almost an hour, back into Manhattan until all around Victor tall buildings rose high into the night sky, but whereas their façades should glow from lit interiors and glimmer with the infinite lights of the city at night, they were dark and featureless. Moonlight shone off their glass windows and the windscreens of abandoned cars. Traffic lights suspended on long beams hung useless. A homeless guy lay next to a bin on the pavement, buried under a deep pile of blankets, lost in the slumber of alcohol, unaware of the blackout and its effect on the city.

Something was wrong.

Victor did not see or hear anything that alarmed him, but he sensed it regardless. He noticed the change within himself. He felt the physiological adjustment to danger. His subconscious had detected some threat and had responded by sending out messages to release hormones, which in turn resulted in the elevation of his heart rate and a heightened state of alertness.

He didn't yet know why, but the organism wherein his consciousness existed knew all it needed to prepare him for fight or flight.

This was the innate feeling of something being wrong – the inexplicable bad feeling – that modern humans sometimes experienced but often ignored. For Victor, his life often depended on heeding its message.

He saw no other people. He heard no one approaching.

He moved anyway. Raven detected it also, or saw his reaction to it, and followed his lead. Victor did not know where the threat would come from, but standing still and waiting for it to manifest was not his style. That would be idiocy. He picked his own battlefields. He had not survived this long by being reactive.

A few metres along the street, he understood. On a store-front up ahead were pinpricks of floating red light, growing larger and further apart.

Vehicle tail lights were red, but if these were tail lights they would grow smaller and closer as the car moved further away, not larger and further apart as they drew closer. Which only left one type of red light they could belong to.

They were the lights of a police cruiser approaching, maybe a block away, light bars glowing but siren silent not to alert him.

His subconscious, always alert and processing data, had noticed anyway, many seconds before his conscious mind was aware of those pin dots of red light and had worked out what they meant.

Now, they were both heading straight towards the threat.

Raven saw it too and they backtracked, turned, walking fast. They took a set of steps leading down to get off the road, heading into an alleyway, narrow and stinking, and louder with the ambient sound of the city, trapped and intensified.

The cop car approached, out of sight behind them and up the steps, but he heard the rumble of its exhaust becoming louder despite the attempt at stealth. Glancing over his shoulder, he saw the cruiser drive past the mouth of the alleyway. He glimpsed two cops inside. The red glow of the light bars played over the concrete steps, casting shadows where once had been darkness.

They waited, wrapped in shadows and leaning against a damp wall, until the rumble of the exhaust had faded into the background murmur of the rain.

For now, they had avoided the cops, but those inside the cruiser would not give up so soon. The car would circle the area searching for them and only leaving again if they were sure the sighting they were responding to proved to be false. Or maybe they wouldn't go at all, convinced of their presence, or they might call in reinforcements to join the hunt. There was nothing for it but to keep moving.

Active, not reactive.

They passed under a bridge. The rain struck riveted steel in a jarring patter. Junk burning in a charred barrel sent yellow and orange flames licking beyond the blackened barrel rim. The smell was abhorrent. Three homeless men stood around it, forming the corners of an equilateral triangle, warming their hands. Their faces were empty and thin, worn down to masks of skin and hardship. Firelight flickered on empty wine bottles around them. Glowing embers floated skyward.

Victor and Raven walked past the men, knowing they stared the whole way, but he kept his focus ahead. He had seen from their body language that they were not going to bother them. This was no more than a curiosity to them. The homeless men might speculate why they were down here with the lowest of the low, but the vagrants were not any kind of threat. These men had bigger problems to deal with, like staying alive for one more night.

They emerged from under the bridge and back into the rain. They took a set of concrete stairs back up to street level. He did not want to end up trapped with the river on one side of them and cops on the other. They would become hypothermic long before they reached the other side, even if they were fortunate enough not to be struck by some barge or ferry. Victor had no desire to die, and even less so in a river, freezing and drowning, body washed out to sea, maybe never found, remains eaten by sharks.

He pushed on, crossing a metal footbridge over a road, his steps more like shuffles, splashing water from puddles up his legs. The noise of the traffic below was a loud roar of engines and exhausts, echoing under the bridge.

Sirens sounded behind them, growing louder with each passing second. Maybe the one from before, or a new arrival. He straightened his back and focused on his gait to appear not as a man fleeing but as a pedestrian walking. Raven did the same. A couple not worth investigating.

In the darkness and rain, the deception worked. The cruiser sped past. It didn't even slow.

Not the one that had been looking for them before, but another. Maybe responding to some other emergency.

They waited until it had gone and walked fast – a couple in a hurry, stressed and harried, but not chased. They had to find somewhere to hold up, and soon. No one they passed paid them any attention. Civilians were more concerned with the rain and the blackout or so used to keeping themselves to themselves it made no difference how fast he and Raven walked or how suspicious they acted.

The rain was falling harder as Victor and Raven entered a plaza. He began to shiver as he weaved past people, avoiding the umbrellas that seemed determined to find his eyes. People still struggled in fruitless attempts to get their phones to work through the downed networks. The collective glow from the screens up-lit their faces, disembodied in the otherwise darkness.

Raven said, 'We've got company.'

FIFTY-TWO

It took him an extra few seconds to identify them. He identified them because they used neither umbrellas nor phones and by their clothes, their postures and their actions. They were looking for him and Raven, and looking hard, drawn to the area by the police presence. Maybe they had access to police radios or scanners or were just receiving updates by cooperating agencies.

The specifics did not matter for the time being. What mattered was avoiding them.

He hadn't seen these guys before. But that wasn't surprising given the numbers Halleck had access too. These guys looked new. They looked and acted like a competent team brought in at short notice and asked to do a difficult job in difficult circumstances.

One guy with black-framed glasses neared him, gaze sweeping back and forth, intense and thorough. The suppressed Ruger in the guy's shoulder rig made the canvas jacket bulge. Victor lowered himself to one knee and retied his shoelaces until the man had passed by. Raven drifted away a little so they did not look like they were together.

The team was all male, all fit and in shape, all wearing casual civilian attire. They were working in pairs, three mini-teams converging on their location from different directions.

Whichever direction Victor and Raven headed, they would risk crossing one of the teams' line of sight. Halleck's men had been effective at spreading out across the plaza and implementing a sweeping pattern that offered few avenues to chance. But to wait would mean getting trapped between all six and a guarantee of eventual discovery. They had no choice but to go.

Victor timed his move, approaching an arcade on the plaza's west side using cover provided by a cute young couple with matching umbrellas. He passed behind one of the two-man teams, close enough to hear one say:

'. . . we better get double for this . . .'

As Victor and Raven drew near to the arcade entrance he had to veer away from the cute couple, but saw he had made it far enough in cover that he was going to get through unobserved by the six men. But another problem was waiting for them. Standing to one side of the entrance, in the shelter of an awning, was a squat cop with a huge stomach and neat moustache, who had removed the plastic lid from his waxed takeaway cup and was blowing on the surface of the hot coffee it contained.

Don't look up, Victor willed as he neared.

The cop's eyes were focused on the coffee. He lips were wet and pursed. Steam rose into the air.

When Victor and Raven were less than ten metres away the cop raised the cup and sipped. He grimaced, the coffee too hot despite his attempts to cool it, and glanced up.

Right at Victor.

The cop blinked and looked away in an idle sweep of his surroundings while he waited for the coffee to cool. Victor and Raven continued towards the arcade, now only five metres from the cop.

Who glanced back, a line of curiosity forming between his eyebrows as he searched his memory banks for why Victor looked familiar.

When he was two metres from passing out of the cop's line of sight, it seemed as if he wouldn't be recognised, but as he entered the arcade Victor saw, via the reflection in the plate glass of a storefront, the cop leaning over to place his coffee cup on the ground, and follow.

The cop followed them into the arcade.

The cop had not reached for his radio. He had not yet called it in. No backup was on the way. He was not sure about Victor. The curiosity had yet to become recognition. The squat cop had no wish to report a false sighting. He wanted to find out more before acting one way or the other.

For that, he needed to get close.

Victor went to one knee as if to tie his shoelaces again. Raven kept walking. Victor left his laces alone while he listened to the footsteps approaching, using the loudening sound to picture the cop at four metres, then three, before stopping two metres behind him.

'Excuse me, sir . . .'

Had he been closer, Victor could have sprung up as the

cop's shadow fell over him, driving a fist into the cop's abdomen and a palm strike into the cop's jaw, taking him out of action fast and clean and maybe before anyone else saw what was happening. But the cop had stopped a tactical distance away. He was not sure about Victor's identity, but he was not stupid either.

'Excuse me, sir,' the cop said again. 'Can you turn around and show me some ID, please?'

Victor did not turn round, because he wanted the cop to only see his face when he was standing and ready to act. He rose, nice and slow so as not to scare the cop and draw an unnecessary reaction.

He turned.

The cop's gaze met his own. The cop recognised him.

There was no mistaking the reaction, which gave Victor a split second to act as the cop went for the pistol holstered on his belt.

Victor launched forward, driving an elbow into the cop's jaw.

His teeth cracked together and his head snapped back and he tipped over backwards, unconscious before he knew he had been hit.

Victor caught him so he didn't slam the back of his head on the ground. A hit like that on an unconscious brain could kill.

He lowered the cop down and into a recovery position as if he were nothing more than a good Samaritan, glad no one seemed to have seen the attack and not too surprised by this. City folk more often than not went out of their way not to see trouble.

As he stood again, he heard a cry. A child, closer to the ground and not jaded by city life, saw the unconscious cop and the blood pooling out of his mouth. The child burst into tears.

The mother looked to see what had upset her child, and gasped.

Other people reacted and turned and stared at the cop, and in doing so at Victor.

He didn't speak. There was nothing he could say to change the fact he was standing over a knocked-out police officer. *He fell* wasn't going to cut it. No explanation was going to convince anyone they weren't seeing what was right before their eyes.

He ignored the accusing stares and hurried away to where Raven waited for him. A teenager turned his phone in Victor's direction to take a picture or record or whatever else kids did. Victor snatched it from the teen's hand and hurled it at the closest wall. It smashed into pieces.

'*HEY, MAN. What the*—'

Victor ran.

He didn't have to look back to know someone from the team in the nearby plaza would have seen or heard the commotion and if not pursuing right now would be in moments.

He followed Raven, vaulting over a barrier at the end of the arcade and on to the road. They weaved through the slow-moving traffic to the other side of the street.

Victor heard the roar of revving engines and ahead of him two black Audi sedans turned a corner on to the street, bright xenon headlights sweeping over him. The cars roared closer, then swerved to pull over, tyres sounding a squelch of temporary resistance on the wet asphalt. Doors were open before the cars had stopped. More men in dark clothes spilled out. Four – two from each Audi.

Victor and Raven took a sharp change of direction, crossing the street, heading east.

The men followed, jogging while signalling commands and relaying updates via wrist-mikes to the team in the plaza. At least he hoped that was the case and there were not even more out there to cut him off.

The street sloped at maybe fifteen degrees. Buildings dark with grime and pollution, made darker by the blackout, lined the road. Vehicles were parked nose-to-tail along the kerbs.

Victor increased his pace to a run. Raven did the same. The team had seen them. They were following. There was no point trying to remain inconspicuous. He dashed across the street. On the far side the slogan on the huge billboard stretching wide above a bank was unreadable.

The men sprinted. He heard the clatter of their shoes on the asphalt behind. They were fit and fast and determined to catch them or kill them and succeed and receive praise and glory and promotion. But his determination was to survive and remain free, and no other potential reward could equal that most basic of motivations. Raven had to have the same desire, else her need to stop Halleck was as strong.

They ran under signs, once illuminated, hanging dull and lifeless. They passed through the warm yellow glow spilled out from a bar's windows; inside hundreds of candles had been lit to keep the business running. The front door had been wedged open to let the cold air in to counteract the heat of all the flickering flames.

Behind them, the men shoved people aside who were too slow to move or too wrapped up in their own existence to notice what was going on. A coffee cup was knocked from a woman's hand.

Victor leaped over a pushchair and skidded round a corner. A guy walking his Rhodesian ridgeback almost collided with Raven and hurled four-letter words as they ran past.

The dog barked as their pursuers rushed by a few seconds later.

He ran fast, breathing hard, breath clouding in the cold.

He felt himself pulling away from them. He had a sprinter's pace and a marathon runner's endurance fuelled by the unparalleled will to survive. He could outrun the men, but not their bullets if they opted to shoot him down on the street. The two Audis were out there as well, unseen for now, but closing in. It was only a matter of time before they became trapped between the Audis and the men pursuing them on foot.

On the next street, when they had created enough distance, Raven hailed a cab and it pulled over in front of them. She gestured to the driver – a nonsense hand movement, but enough to distract – and approached the driver's window, mouth open as if struggling to find the words or with a language barrier.

The window descended so the driver could better hear. He was a skinny Indian guy in a string vest, arms and shoulders covered in dark hair, teeth bright and crooked.

Still gesturing with one hand, Raven wrenched open the door with the other. The driver, distracted, was too slow to react and stop it from happening. By the time he understood his predicament, Raven was dragging him from his seat and throwing him to the road surface.

She ignored the man's cries of protest and climbed behind the wheel. She slammed the door shut. Victor jumped into the passenger seat.

Flashing lights alerted him to the approaching cop car.

FIFTY-THREE

The blue-and-white cruiser skidded to a lateral stop in front of the taxi before Raven had a chance to pull away, blocking the road with no space to accelerate around it.

Two cops exited, fast and smooth, rushing towards them with guns drawn and cocked, leaving the driver and passenger doors open in their hurry. They shouted at Victor and Raven in two voices of overlapping contradictory commands to freeze and put their hands in the air and get out of the vehicle and stay where they fucking were and not to do anything at all.

Victor waited, acting scared, with Raven performing a similar routine of passivity, as the cop from the far side of the cruiser circled around the bonnet to join his partner.

As one, they came forward.

Raven ducked low and put the transmission into reverse and stamped the accelerator.

The front wheels spun and shrieked. A plume of tyre

smoke and rainwater mist clouded in front of the taxi, spraying and blinding the two nearby cops for an instant, so when they fired their handguns the bullets went high. One cracked a hole through the raised sign on the roof, scattering fragments of glass and plastic over the bonnet.

When the taxi had reached fifteen miles per hour Raven pulled the handbrake and swung the wheel, spinning tyres flaring up rainwater, before changing up to drive and accelerating. By the time the taxi finished its tyre-screeching one-eighty, she was speeding away. Glass and plastic fragments from the bonnet scattered on the asphalt behind them.

The two cops dashed back to their cruiser.

The road surface was slick with rainwater. The cab's tyres threw up huge sprays of it while the wipers worked hard to keep the windscreen clear. They sped past the team in pursuit on foot. The four men from the two Audis stood impotent on the pavement, shouting at each other and into their wrist microphones. But with cops nearby no one drew a weapon to shoot.

Ahead, another cruiser was rushing towards them, racing fast and weaving between the cars in the opposite lane.

Raven took a hard right, the oncoming cruiser following seconds later. An orange Mazda coupe appeared at the intersection ahead. She veered around it, deft and assured, but the cop car clipped the Mazda on the rear end, shearing off its chrome bumper and sending it cartwheeling along the street.

A white four-door sedan swerved to avoid the bumper, and in doing so collided into the back of the Mazda. Brakelight glass exploded into a cloud of glittering red. Tyre smoke swirled. The boot shot open, dented and distorted. A detached alloy hub cab spun end over end.

The driver of an oncoming delivery van managed to swerve around the crash as the coupe was sent into a spin.

Raven accelerated down a side street, a second NYPD blue-and-white now in pursuit. Another nearby patrol car called in to assist. The two cops who had taken shots at them would have little chance of catching up now, but others like this one could be on the way. She veered to the left, slipping into a bisecting road, speeding past townhouses and tenements and trees that lined the road.

Up ahead, vehicles were slowing and pulling over in reaction to the nearing cop car and the flashing lights and blaring sirens. Brown leaves scattered and swirled as they shot by in the taxi.

The driver of the nearest cruiser was caught off guard and went shooting past the turning. The second car, further behind and with more time for the driver to react, braked as it neared and slid into the corner, wheels spinning and tyres smoking, but losing ground on them.

Screeching rubber alerted Raven an instant before a panel van collided into the passenger side of the taxi as she sped across a four-way intersection.

The van caught the cab on the rear fender, crumpling the metal siding and sending the vehicle into a spin. A passenger window exploded and the rear windscreen popped out and flipped end over end until it hit the asphalt and disintegrated.

Victor tensed against the force trying to throw him around as Raven controlled the wheel and accelerated out of the spin, leaving the van driver staring aghast at her from out of a lowered window.

The spin had given the cops time to catch up and Raven manoeuvred at speed round the slow-moving traffic. Horns sounded and drivers yelled at her. The impact with the van had canted a rear wheel and Victor felt the immediate loss of power and control. The damage caused the rear tyres to lose traction on the slick road and she had to fight the wheel and ease off the accelerator to prevent the swerves becoming a spin.

Raven braked and changed down to slip through denser traffic, tyres protesting against the erratic back and forth movements. She sent the car into the opposite lane, making the oncoming vehicles swerve and brake to avoid her as they raced towards them.

The two cruisers followed, close behind. Headlights and brake lights reflected off the water misting behind the taxi. Raven swerved to avoid a truck. In the rear-view, their pursuers did likewise, one cruiser going to the right of the truck as Raven had, the second going around the left.

But the cops going left didn't have the room they thought and the cruiser's nose, crushed between the truck and a parked car, came to a sudden, juddering halt.

One cruiser remaining.

Raven took a hard left, clipping a parked sedan as she did, shearing off a wing mirror as the taxi rebounded away, tyres smoking, into the oncoming lane. A Lincoln Town Car braked in time to miss the speeding taxi, but an SUV coming up behind crashed into the back of the Lincoln, crumpling the car's rear end and knocking it forward so it clipped the taxi on the passenger side. Victor jolted in his seat. The front bumper was ripped away. Headlight glass and fragments of metal and plastic sparkled as they passed in spinning patterns through the headlights.

The taxi spun away while the Lincoln careered up the kerb and into a trash can, sending it skyward. Pedestrians ran out of the way as the can came crashing back to earth.

Raven wrestled with the controls and against the force of the spin. Rubber squealed against wet asphalt, painting wild black patterns before she had regained control enough to stop the vehicle colliding with a parked removal van.

The police cruiser was right on them now, no more than half a car length behind. Sirens wailed. Victor glanced back to see the cop in the passenger seat shouting into a radio.

A motorcyclist, weaving fast around the traffic, saw the taxi too late and turned too hard to avoid it. The bike tipped on to its side and grinded along the road, the rider sliding and rolling behind it amid a trail of sparks.

Alarms and horns were sounding all around them as Raven accelerated away, avoiding the rider who lay alive but groaning near the crashed Town Car. A confetti of glass covered the road surface, glinting and sparkling in the wash of headlights.

The cop driving the chasing cruiser didn't see the rider until he was almost hitting him. Smoke billowed from screeching tyres, but braking wasn't going to be enough to avoid running the man over. The driver wrenched the wheel and the cruiser missed the rider by inches, jumping the kerb and ploughing into a fire hydrant, knocking it over, sending a jet of pressurised water skyward.

Within seconds the cruiser was a dot in the taxi's rear-view.

A truck passed over the intersection ahead, blocking the way. Raven slammed the brakes and slid the taxi into the mouth of an alleyway, losing the remaining wing mirror as she did.

In the narrow confines of the alleyway, the cab's exhaust roared loud and fierce. Metal screeched against brickwork. Sparks brightened the darkness.

They emerged out of the other side, skidding into the line of traffic.

Two oncoming cars swerved and braked as the taxi appeared ahead of them, shunting into each other with a scrape and crunch of denting metal. Crossing pedestrians fled from the careering vehicle, some throwing themselves to the pavement to avoid being hit.

Slow-moving traffic hampered their route. To get caught up in gridlock meant certain death or capture, but there was nowhere to turn. Besides, the taxi was a wreck. It couldn't take much more punishment.

Raven said, 'We need to switch.'

'Do it.'

She switched lanes and slowed until they were three metres behind a silver Chrysler, tough and powerful, as if she had chosen to push on through the jam, and put the cab into neutral.

It collided with the Chrysler's rear bumper hard enough to cause a dent, but not moving fast enough to do any serious damage to either vehicle.

Victor heard the Chrysler's driver scream in rage and he

jumped out of his vehicle. Victor and Raven climbed out too.

The driver was big with weight training and steroids, his good suit tight and straining to contain the swollen musculature.

'What the holy fuck?'

He reached out to shove Raven, who was closer. She grabbed the hand and twisted it into a goose-neck wrist-lock.

The Chrysler driver yelled through gritted teeth as she put him to the ground.

'Stay down,' she said, then to Victor: 'Would you like to drive?'

The man did as he was told, cradling his damaged wrist, as Victor jumped behind the wheel of the Chrysler and Raven climbed into the passenger seat. Putting the transmission in reverse, Victor pushed back the taxi in neutral gear until there was room to manoeuvre out of the line of traffic. He cut between the gridlocked cars in the other lane.

Ahead of him were two black Audi sedans.

FIFTY-FOUR

Their xenon headlights gave them away even before Victor could make out their distinctive shape and manufacturer's badge on the grille. He worked the gear shift and accelerated away, the big eight-cylinder engine of the Chrysler working hard and doing what it was designed to do. The difference in acceleration to the taxi was monumental. He sped between the Audis, which had to brake hard and swing U-turns to give chase, one driver handling it better than the other and losing only seconds.

Even with a head start, the lead Audi was catching fast. It was almost as powerful as the Chrysler, but much lighter – a far better power-to-weight ratio and more grip from four-wheel drive resulting in better acceleration.

Victor shot under an overpass, turning when he came out the other side, heavy back end sliding out but under control. The black Audi followed, just as controlled, but much faster because it was four-wheel drive.

Victor accelerated past a slow-moving SUV on the outside, then cut inside to avoid a taxi. He saw the black sedan close behind, impossible to shake. In a straight line the Chrysler would pull away with its bigger engine, but on city streets the more manoeuvrable Audi had the considerable advantage.

'Gun,' Raven warned.

Victor saw the man in the passenger seat was readying his pistol.

They raced down a sloping road, out of the black city and towards the bay. Victor braked and swerved to avoid a cyclist and the Audi caught up the last of the gap, coming alongside him on the near side.

The passenger – a man with a shaved head and small, sunken eyes – took aim with his Ruger and squeezed the trigger.

Raven was already down, and Victor dropped low in the seat as shattered glass scattered over him. More shots thudded into metal and smashed small holes in glass.

A stamp of the brakes sent the Audi shooting past him. Victor swung the wheel, taking the Chrysler into the closest street, knocking over trash cans on the corner and almost hitting a lamp post as two wheels went up the kerb.

The black sedan swerved on to the street behind him, faster, smoother.

The second Audi appeared, having headed him off, guided by the guys in the first car. It swerved into him from the side, forcing him towards the centre of the road and the oncoming traffic. Victor worked the steering wheel and pulled the silver Chrysler ahead of the Audi, which then charged him from behind.

Gunshots popped behind him. The rear bumper came loose at one end, dragging along the road, and Victor jolted in his seat, for a second losing control as the car fishtailed back and forth. Raven shot out a palm to brace against the dashboard.

Another charge, this time into the driver's side rear fender.

The collision knocked the air from Victor's lungs and hit the right spot to send the Chrysler spinning. He grimaced, g-force flattening him against the seat as the tyres squealed and smoked and fragments of destroyed bodywork and bumper clattered on the asphalt. Pebbles of windscreen glass rained down over the car in a brief storm.

The Chrysler ended up perpendicular to the Audi, which collided with the car yet again and propelled it along the road in a T-shape of moving metal.

More shots came Victor and Raven's way, but with better accuracy now they were an almost stationary target. A .22 calibre bullet took a chunk out of the steering wheel. Another tore a hole through the driver's seat. Victor smelled the melted and burned foam.

He ducked and changed into reverse and scraped away from the Audi, metal shrieking against metal, which knocked the Chrysler's nose straight again as it sped past. A brake light exploded.

Victor slammed the brakes, changed back to drive, turned the wheel and accelerated towards the Audi as it braked as well to perform a U-turn, and headed his way. A panel van swerved to avoid the oncoming black sedan and tipped on to its side, blocking the lane.

'This is going to hurt,' Victor said to Raven, who nodded.

The Audi driver realised Victor's intention too late as both Victor and Raven turned their heads ninety degrees, and had no time to get out of the way before Victor rammed the Audi head-on.

On impact, the Chrysler's driver airbag exploded out of the steering wheel and slammed into the side of Victor's head with enough force to have broken his nose. The strong, heavy build of the Chrysler did what it was designed to and protected Victor and Raven while demolishing the front of the Audi and pushing it back and into a half-spin of its own.

He reversed away while the two men inside were still dazed, and spun the Chrysler into a one-eighty, because the other Audi had appeared in his rear-view.

He accelerated away, taking the next available inter-section, the rear bumper only half attached and scraping along the road surface. Horns blared and tyres screeched. Brake dust, rainwater and smoke swirled together in the cold air.

Rundown storefronts flashed by. Citizen volunteers directing traffic fled out of the way as he raced towards them, the black Audi sedan in pursuit.

A police cruiser rushed towards Victor and Raven, but made no effort to block or engage. It raced past them, on its way to some other violation. Maybe in pursuit of a stolen yellow taxi.

The Chrysler struggled on, damaged and dented in many places, but still drivable. He followed a ramp down into a tunnel. Without lights it was black save only for the headlights of the vehicles within, travelling even slower than usual because of the poor visibility.

They were easier to swerve around as a result, for Victor and their pursuers. The horns sounding in their wake were louder down here, piercing and incessant. The Audi hurtled closer and closer.

They exited the tunnel, the rain and puckered windscreen obscuring the road ahead. Victor gripped hard on the steering wheel as he struggled to see through the downpour, accelerating fast, vehicles and buildings blurring by. He tensed to stop sliding in his seat as the Chrysler's wheels lost traction on the wet road surface. The tyres screeched, rainwater misting in huge clouds.

He stayed with the wet street as it veered deeper into the industrial neighbourhood.

The Audi shunted him from behind. Bullets exploded through the rear windscreen. Sheets of cracked glass disintegrated and fell away. The Chrysler lost both wing mirrors at the same time as he squeezed it between a Jeep and a bus. Orange sparks flared as metal grinded and screeched against metal.

Horns and the screech of tyres filled his ears. He weaved the car through tight turns, roaring exhaust alerting pedestrians ahead to get out of the way.

Reverberations told him the car was taking more rounds, this time to the chassis. One passed through the interior and tore away a chunk of dashboard plastic. Raven used an arm to shield her face from the shrapnel. Another took out the odometer. The driver's side window fell apart.

Rainwater came through the destroyed window, splashing his face and getting into his eyes. He used a sleeve to wipe them clear.

A bullet had damaged the Chrysler's wiper controls and they ceased swinging back and forth. In seconds the windscreen was covered in rainwater, reducing visibility even further. He strained to see through it. Sooner or later he would crash into something.

He pulled a ninety-degree turn at speed. The rear wheels lost grip and slipped away, tyres skidding across the asphalt. The Audi followed through the tyre smoke and spray, its own turn wider, but more controlled. It dented and scraped against parked cars as it accelerated in chase.

Victor wrenched the wheel from side to side to keep the Chrysler moving and a harder target for the gunman in the passenger seat of the Audi. The faster, more manoeuvrable vehicle charged past other cars, clipping bumpers and fenders and causing them to skid and crash.

Muzzle flashes brightened the Chrysler's rear-view mirror and Victor ducked low as rounds punched holes in the safety glass of the windscreen before him. He repositioned himself to see through them. The passenger window was hit and fragmented, cascading glass across the road.

Ahead the street fell away at a sharp gradient.

Raven said, 'Speed up.'

He glanced at her.

'Then brake,' she explained.

Victor hesitated, then realised what she meant and stamped the accelerator before braking hard a second before they reached the drop.

The Chrysler flew over the crest of the slope, all four wheels leaving the road surface. For a second the vehicle gained altitude, leaving a comet trail of sparkling glass pebbles, misting rainwater and tyre smoke, before gravity tipped the nose forward and pulled the front bumper down and crashing into the asphalt. It cracked and distorted, falling clear as the tyres then hit the road an instant later and the suspension bounced the nose back up. The rear tyres found the ground and the whole car shook and skidded.

Victor hung on to the steering wheel, in part to control the car and in part to prevent himself flailing around.

The passenger's side rear tyre peeled away. The Chrysler swerved and skidded on the wet street, losing control, splashing up rainwater, tipping on to two tyres while swaying and zigzagging off the road and on to the pavement and then back again. The Chrysler tipped over from two wheels and flipped on to the roof, momentum carrying it back over on to four wheels again, groaning and shuddering to a stop. Pebbles of glass scattered across the road surface as the vehicle rocked from side to side against its suspension.

The pursuing Audi followed over the slope's crest, faster and lighter, the driver not braking as Victor had done – not seeing the coming slope in time – gaining more altitude and flying over a longer arc. The vehicle then had further to fall and with more force. The nose tipped forward past sixty degrees, almost to ninety, almost dropping straight down on to the road. The bumper crushed and the headlights exploded. Fenders crumpled along with the bonnet, flames flaring from the crushed engine.

The car skidded forward on its nose for a split second

before tipping over on to the roof, metal whining, and glass smashing. Upside down, it slid along the sloping road surface, sparks trailing behind in a glowing shower.

The upturned Audi came to a slow stop. Glass and dust and debris filled the air. Steam and smoke billowed from the engine. Flames hissed in the rain. Three wheels spun useless, trying to grip nothing but air. The fourth had come off and arched away, landing on and denting the roof of an approaching minivan.

The two guys in the Audi hung upside down, suspended by seat belts. Blood smeared the passenger's shaved head. Neither man was moving much.

Victor squinted away the pain and checked for injuries. His neck ached from the whiplash and he was sore where the seat belt had dug into his shoulder and chest, but there was nothing worse to be concerned about.

'Are you okay?' he asked.

Raven nodded, grimacing. 'Never better.'

He turned the ignition key. The starter motor whined, weak and fading. Not surprised, Victor gave up but remained in the Chrysler while he looked around for other enemies. They were exposed while stationary, but the dense bodywork, heavy chassis, big engine block, and even the thick chairs, all offered significant protection from the low-powered .22 calibre rounds their hunters were using. If more gunmen were near he would prefer to be shot at while inside the vehicle than while on the coverless street.

When he was as sure as he could be that there were no immediate threats, he tried the door release but the door wouldn't open. It was stuck fast. The frame had buckled, steel warped and unyielding to his strength. The windows were too small to crawl through with any kind of speed so he used a palm to punch out the remains of the windscreen, and twisted and pulled himself through the resulting gap. Raven did the same.

Onlookers stood aghast. No one was yet brave enough to approach. Some took out phones to take pictures or video recordings. Victor kept his face turned away.

He stood, a little unsteady, and walked backwards away from the wrecked vehicle, watching the street for more pursuers. He turned when he saw none, and hurried to the upturned Audi.

He pulled open the closest door and squatted to retrieve the passenger's Ruger from where it lay on the inside of the roof. He went through their pockets, but aside from a radio transmitter these guys were operating sterile. The passenger groaned and wheezed, one eye filled with blood but one open and staring at Victor.

Help me, the man mouthed. *Please*.

Victor mouthed, *No*.

He pushed the radio into a pocket and tucked the Ruger into his waistband and under his shirt and hurried away along the pavement past a grand office building while a couple of young guys approached the crash, looking for people to help or perhaps wanting a better view of any bodies.

Raven said, 'We need to go. Now.'

At the corner of the block Victor glanced over his shoulder to see the Audi he had rammed earlier reaching the crash site. The passenger was jumping out for a closer look at the wrecked Chrysler. He saw Victor was not inside and rushed back to the Audi, shaking his head. He had no interest in the upside-down vehicle or the fate of the two guys inside.

Victor watched from the shadows until the Audi had disappeared into the night.

FIFTY-FIVE

They left Manhattan on the Staten Island ferry. The ferries were still running and packed to capacity with otherwise stranded commuters unable to take other forms of public transport or use their cars on closed roads and bridges. The police presence felt heavy at the South Street terminal but the overworked cops seemed more interested in keeping the dense crowds under control than looking out for fugitives.

The East River ferry would have taken them straight to Brooklyn, but if Halleck's crew were watching any route, that would be the one.

Victor and Raven stood outside on the top deck because it was almost impossible to get inside with so many people competing for space. Raven positioned herself to Victor's left. To his right a frail woman with bone-white hair clutched a handbag-sized dog. A teacup chihuahua, the woman told him, named Teddy.

'They don't allow pets on the ferry,' she explained. 'So I normally take the Q to Coney Island.'

To be polite, Victor asked, 'How did you get Teddy onboard?'

'I said to them, "If you don't let me take him with me then I'll have to swim instead."' She grinned, mischievous. 'I turned on the waterworks.'

'A shrewd tactic.'

She nodded. 'A lady must use all weapons in her arsenal.'

Raven said, 'I couldn't agree more.'

The woman stroked Teddy and asked Victor, 'How long have you two been together?'

He hesitated, but Raven said, 'Not long. But it's something of a whirlwind romance.'

The woman said to Raven, 'The best kind, dear,' and then to Victor, 'You're a lucky man. I hope you treat her right.'

Victor remained silent.

'If I were you,' the woman said to Raven with a wink, 'I'd make the most of him before he gets fat. Because they all do.'

Raven laughed and said, 'Oh, I intend to.'

The woman excused herself to find a toilet for Teddy to use. Victor didn't enquire as to how Teddy might use facilities designed for humans or even how she knew the dog needed to.

They arrived at the St George terminal a few minutes after nine p.m. The power was running on Staten Island, and they could see the same was the case across the bay in Brooklyn. A bus took them over the bridge and south to

Coney Island. It was nearing ten when they stood on the sea wall, facing east, and looked out across the water to their objective, some two kilometres away.

Floyd Bennett Field was little more than wide empty space on the map. It was located on Barren Island, a spur of artificial land, filled and claimed from the sea on the southeast coast of Brooklyn, surrounded by water on three sides. To the east lay Jamaica Bay; west was the Lower Bay. To the south across the narrow strip of water between the two lay the Queens Peninsula, which marked the last stretch of dry land before the Atlantic Ocean. It had been built as New York's first municipal airport in 1931, but these days it was only in service during air shows. The area was now managed by the National Park Service and was used for camping, motorsport events and other leisure activities.

But not in the middle of the night. Now, the disused airfield would be unoccupied save for Halleck's team.

'If I'm right, there are four bridges that lead to the island,' Raven said. 'Two at the north, one at the west and one south.'

Victor could see the Marine Parkway Bridge in the distance, stretching over the water from the Queens Peninsula.

'Halleck has a large crew, but it's not big enough to keep watch over the entire island. He has enough men to watch the bridges though.'

'I'm hoping you don't suggest we swim,' Raven said.

'I didn't bring my shorts.'

She gestured with her chin to where sailboats and pleasure boats and small yachts were moored on a nearby jetty. 'No one is out on the water at this time of night.'

He nodded.

She said, 'I don't know how to sail.'

'Neither do I.'

'Outboard motors are noisy. They'll hear us coming a mile away.'

He said, 'What's your upper-body strength like?'

She turned to follow his gaze to where an inflatable lifeboat was moored behind one of the larger yachts.

'I can bench twice my bodyweight,' she said. 'Can you?'

He didn't answer. 'Any idea what Halleck is having delivered?'

She shook her head. 'Your guess is as good as mine. But I think it's safe to say it will be related to the attack.'

'Will Halleck be there to collect it?'

She regarded him, close and searching. 'Halleck doesn't die until I know what he's planning and where the bomb is. Are we clear on that?'

'I understand what your motivations are, yes.'

'That's not what I said. Remember: if that bomb goes off, the person who is going to take the fall for it is you, so it's in your own best interests that it doesn't go bang.'

Victor said nothing.

For a minute they watched the moonlight dance on the water and listened to the lapping of waves.

'What now?' she asked.

'We eat.'

They found places still open easy enough, but they ignored the busy restaurants and bars, settling instead on a quiet diner with only one other patron. They sat in a booth along the far wall where they could both see the door. The waitress who took their order had the tired eyes of someone who was at the end of a double shift and didn't disguise her annoyance at having another table to serve. Victor reminded himself to leave a good tip.

He ordered coffee and the all-day breakfast. Raven only wanted coffee.

'Never go into battle on an empty stomach,' he told her after the waitress had gone.

'You do it your way,' Raven said in return. 'I'll do it my way.'

The diner had a television mounted high in one corner. The sound was off and even without reading the anchor's lips, Victor knew what was being discussed and what was not.

He said, 'They're saying the blackout was caused by a computer fault.'

Raven shrugged. 'That's true, kind of.'

'And the power will be back on by morning. No mention of it being deliberate. Certainly not an act of terrorism.'

She nodded. 'Even if they know what caused it, there's no point alarming people. It's like we have a collective consciousness to maintain the lie that everything is fine, even when it's not.'

They said nothing more until the waitress had returned with the coffee flask and gone again.

Victor said, 'If you were Halleck, what would you do? Would you have your guys out looking for us, or would you pull them back to protect the delivery?'

She didn't have to consider the options. 'Protect the delivery. His guys have failed twice while they've been spread out, and the authorities are looking for us anyway. Plus, even if he doesn't know we've found out about the airfield, he needs to consider the possibility. Especially if I'm Halleck and I'm there too, or will be. He's a warrior and he's no coward, but he's not stupid.'

Victor nodded. 'I agree. Pachulski said there were twenty-four guys. The guy I spoke to earlier today said twenty-one.'

'That's Halleck not keeping his people in the know. It could be either or it could be less or it could be even be more.'

'Let's go with twenty-four. Anything else is optimism or wild speculation. I don't do either.'

'We took out two who came after us in the Audis, plus Pachulski and his partner. That leaves twenty.'

'I disabled three and killed one in the parking garage under the museum.'

'Nice work,' she said. 'That brings us down to sixteen.'

'Fifteen,' Victor corrected. 'The guy on the subway will be calling in sick.'

'What did you do with him?'

He said, 'I convinced him his time would be better spent not following me around the city.'

'You *convinced* him?'

'I can be very persuasive when I want to be.'

Raven said, 'So, he's still out there?'

Victor nodded.

Raven shook her head. 'Halleck picks people for their loyalty first and foremost.'

'Good,' Victor said. 'I'd rather go against the most loyal opposition than the best opposition.'

She frowned at him. 'What I mean is that guy you scared off will have had a change of heart.'

'No,' Victor said. 'Right now he's home or on his way home and thinking about what to do with the rest of his life.'

'Sixteen guys left,' Raven said as though she hadn't even heard him.

They stared at one another.

'Or would you prefer we underestimated the strength of our opposition?'

'Well played,' Victor conceded. 'Sixteen it is.'

She didn't gloat. Instead she bit her lip. 'That's a hell of a crew. Sixteen guys is too many. We've only been up against a handful at a time before now. Next time we'll be outnumbered eight-to-one.'

'I can do basic arithmetic, Constance.'

'I'm not sure what I dislike most: your sarcasm or your insistence on calling me that.'

Victor said, 'When all this is over I'll tell you my own name, which I've never liked either. Then you can have your revenge.'

'Really?' she asked, eyes widening in disbelief.

'No,' Victor said. 'I was being sarcastic again.'

She groaned and rolled her eyes. 'You're like an annoying older brother, you know that?'

He nodded. 'But an annoying older brother with a plan to get that number down.'

He placed Pachulski's radio on to the tabletop.

FIFTY-SIX

There were several clothing stores in the immediate area, all closed for the night. They broke into the one that sold camping and fishing gear too. Raven headed straight to the women's section while Victor selected garments from the men's racks, choosing dark-coloured items and ignoring synthetic materials.

They reconvened in a back room. Victor turned away as Raven began undressing. He didn't like having her out of sight whilst in close proximity, but figured he was safe enough while she undressed. No one would attack while half-naked.

'You don't need to protect my modesty,' she said. 'I don't have any.'

He didn't reply.

Raven said, 'Or are you trying to tell me you don't trust yourself?'

'Just hurry up.'

He couldn't see it, but he could feel her smile. He began undressing.

She wolf-whistled, then laughed when he sighed and shook his head in response.

He changed into his new clothes. They were a reasonable fit and suitable quality for what would come next. He would have preferred military fatigues with lots of pockets but he settled for dark blue cotton trousers, a black T-shirt and a dark grey knitted sweater. A midnight blue windbreaker and black lace-up boots completed the attire.

Raven said, 'Okay, Mr Chivalrous, you can peek now.'

She had chosen similar garments – charcoal trousers and a black sports jacket over a blue turtle-neck sweater.

'How do I look?'

He didn't answer. Instead, he checked the time. It was almost eleven p.m. He asked, 'Are you ready?'

She nodded. 'Do it.'

Victor thumbed the send button on Pachulski's radio transmitter and said, 'I want to speak with Halleck.'

He released the send button and waited for a response. Maybe he wouldn't receive one at all. Raven stood nearby, paying attention to their surroundings while he could not.

After a few seconds a voice answered: 'Code in.'

The speaker was a young man with levity in his voice despite the formal request. Victor pictured a lean Caucasian; not a smoker or drinker, maybe fresh out of the military – an idealistic recruit to Halleck's organisation.

Victor said, 'I don't have a passcode. I'm not one of you.'

There was a pause, before the young voice replied, 'Who is this?'

'Save us both some time and put Halleck on. He wants to speak with me.'

'Who is this?' the voice asked again, but with a deeper resonance. 'Or I disconnect right now. Identify yourself.'

Victor said, 'It's the killer.'

There was no response. Victor pictured the young man hesitant at first, then deciding and rushing or gesturing or calling Halleck over, explaining away argument or disbelief; appealing with innate integrity and convincing with urgency.

A crackle of static before Halleck said, 'Is this who I think it is?'

'Yes,' Victor answered. 'It's your best friend in all the world. How have you been?'

Victor heard Halleck breathing, then he said, 'What do you want?'

'I want to kill you,' Victor answered.

'Funny,' Halleck said. 'But I don't have time for jokes.'

'Does it sound like I'm joking to you? I couldn't be more serious. I wouldn't waste your time. I know you're busy. I know you don't have time for jokes. The blackout is only going to last until morning, right? You have a lot to do before then. That bomb isn't going to plant itself now, is it?'

'Raven told you everything then. Not that it matters. You're nothing to me.'

'I'm offended you can say that after all the trouble you've gone to to set me up as the bomber.'

'It really wasn't that much trouble. You did most of the work for me.'

'I can't deny that,' Victor said. 'Likewise, you can't deny the guys you've lost so far.'

335

Halleck exhaled. 'Natural selection. You're doing me a favour, weeding out those who aren't up to standard. You're strengthening the gene pool. So, thanks.'

Victor said, 'The fact remains, your numbers are reduced. Your manpower is down to seventy-five per cent. You didn't account for that. That's going to put pressure on your timetable. You're going to cut it fine.'

'What's your point?' Halleck asked.

'Raven didn't tell me as much as I would have liked, I have to admit. But there's still time to get more answers out of her if I require them. She's been a busy woman. She knows about the explosive. She knows Beaumont was your contact. She even knows what you like to eat for breakfast.'

Raven glanced his way and shook her head.

Victor raised an eyebrow at her.

'What exactly are you telling me?' Halleck asked.

Victor said, 'What I'm trying to say is that I have Raven here with me. I'm looking into her eyes at this very moment. What I'm also saying is that we have privacy and it means I have time to *convince* her to provide those answers.'

'I don't imagine she'll take much convincing, seeing as you two are getting on so well. Quite the double act, aren't you?'

'I think you're mistaken. I work alone.'

Halleck said, 'Yeah, right. I don't believe anything you're telling me.'

'I'm not trying to make you believe anything. I don't need a dead man to believe me, now do I?'

Halleck grunted. 'Spare the tough talk. You can't scare me.'

'That's where you're wrong again,' Victor said. 'I can scare you, because you're already scared of me. Unless you're saying to me that you brought twelve men with you to Dublin to keep you company? You're not the lonely sort, are you?'

Halleck didn't answer.

'I want to kill you,' Victor said again. 'That's not a bluff or a threat but a statement of fact. You set me up. You tried to kill me. You're going to let me take the blame for your bomb. It's in my best interests to watch you take your last breath, but I'm an accommodating kind of guy so I'll settle with cutting a deal. I want out of this mess. I want the cops and feds off my back, permanently. I want to get out of the country and never come back. In return I won't kill you, but I'll kill Raven.'

She couldn't disguise the second of uncertainty that passed over her face. He pretended not to notice.

Halleck didn't answer.

'Take your time,' Victor said.

'Why?' Halleck asked.

'Because I don't need her. Because you need her dead. She wanted my help stopping you. For a while I considered it, but I don't take attacks against me personally – I know it's only ever about business – and I'm no humanitarian. I don't care if a bomb goes off in downtown Manhattan. But what I do care about is getting through an airport without being bundled to the ground by security.'

Halleck said, 'You have Raven with you this minute?'

'That's what I said.'

'Then I want her for myself. I want her alive.'

'That's not going to happen. I'm sure you can appreciate she's too dangerous to transport alive.'

'Okay,' Halleck said. 'So put her on the line. I want to speak to her.'

Victor said, 'That's going to be difficult. She's a little tied up right now.'

'Then quit hanging around and untie her. I want to hear her voice. I need to know you have her. Otherwise there can't be any deal. Unless you're asking me to trust your word? Which would be hilarious.'

'Okay,' Victor said. 'Give me a second.'

'I'll be waiting.'

Victor released send so Halleck couldn't hear and held out the radio to Raven. 'Be convincing.'

She looked at him like he was an idiot – like she enjoyed the fact he was. She took the radio, cleared her throat and pressed send.

'YOU FUCKER,' Raven yelled. 'I'm going to fucking kill you both, you hear me? You're both dead. You're both—'

She rubbed the receiver against her chest to imitate a struggle to control it while she screamed in a varied pitch of emotions, rocking her head back and forth and smiling the whole time. She released send and handed the radio back to Victor.

'How did I do?' she asked, nonchalant.

Victor said, 'You missed your calling,' and she curtsied while he pressed send and spoke into the radio: 'Now do you believe me?'

Halleck said, 'I guess I do.'

'So, do we have a deal or not?'

'I want to see her body. I want to see her dead with my own eyes. Otherwise, no deal. Once I know for sure she's a corpse, I'll put out the word to Homeland Security, the FBI and the NYPD. You'll be taken off the terrorist watch list. You'll no longer be a fugitive.'

'That's exactly what I wanted to hear. In forty-five minutes go to FDR Drive. Raven's corpse will be in the trunk of a silver Impala, parked under the Williamsburg Bridge.'

Halleck said, 'No deal. The car could be rigged with a bomb or you could take me out with a rifle.'

'Indeed. Or better yet I'd have the car wired with explosives, and be waiting behind a high-powered rifle. But where's that going to get me? If I kill you then I'm still in the same mess.'

'You'd better believe that, asshole.'

Victor said, 'So it's in my best interests not to kill you.'

'That's right,' Halleck said. 'You need me alive far more than I need you. So you'd better not be fucking around with me, because if you are then you'll be in a world of hurt.'

Victor said, 'Strange threat, given my current predicament, but I believe you nonetheless. And you would do well to believe me when I say if you try anything you'll be able to count the days you have left on this earth with one hand.'

'Then it sounds like we both have enough incentive to play it straight with each other.'

'Doesn't it just?'

He released send and no further communication came from Halleck.

'Did he believe you?' Raven asked, handing him a Rapala fillet knife.

Victor thought for a second. 'I think so. I think you did a good job and convinced him you were at my mercy. He won't go himself, of course. But he'll send guys to check out the car. He can't afford not to. Either he'll send people in the hope of getting to me, or to confirm you're actually dead.'

'But how many?'

Victor thought again. 'Regardless of what I said to him on the radio, Halleck's not short of manpower. He brought enough guys to New York to deliver the bomb and to watch me and to look for you. He's lost some, sure. But he has plenty left. I'd say he'll send between five and ten, which leaves us between six and eleven to deal with at the airfield while the others are waiting at FDR Drive for a silver Impala to arrive.'

'That's some range.'

'I can only make an educated guess. I think he'll send a small unit because it doesn't take more than one pair of eyes to see a corpse, and if it's a set-up he won't want to risk too many getting blown up or sniped.'

'So now you're saying five?'

'I'm saying that's what I consider to be more likely. If Halleck really did believe us then he might send a whole crew there to deal with me. But I can't be sure. He's fooled me once already. Whether five or ten or whatever in between, we reduce our opposition.'

She nodded. 'Then we plan to encounter eleven men at the airfield. I prefer to assume the worst.'

'As do I.'

Raven smiled. 'Pessimists of the world unite.'

FIFTY-SEVEN

The bay was as black as the sky above. Moonlight glimmered off small waves swelling and breaking. The gentle swish of the surf grew louder. Victor and Raven paddled the inflatable the last few metres until it came to ground on a narrow strip of beach, churning up wet sand. They placed the paddles inside the inflatable and jumped out, avoiding the small lapping waves, feet sinking into the sand. Grassy dunes lined the shore. Waves lapped against sand and rocks. The dune grass seemed more brown than yellow-green in the darkness, swaying and rustling in the wind. In the distance he could see the unlit Manhattan skyline against the backdrop of the night sky, the dark buildings seeming to rise from the horizon as jagged teeth, small and broken.

A pale half-moon brightened the night sky above, highlighting torn strips of cloud that crept from east to west, pushed by a chill wind. Victor's breath clouded before him.

He exhaled through his nostrils to direct the vapour earthward, where there was less chance it would be noticed in the moonlight. He kept his chin down so his eyes were in the shadow of their brows in an effort to prevent the moonlight glinting from them.

His attire, like Raven's, had been chosen to provide other small advantages. Black gloves covered their hands and rolled-up balaclavas sat on their heads, ready to be rolled down to hide their faces when the time came. Victor was armed with Guerrero's SIG. Raven had the Ruger he'd taken from the passenger in the crashed Audi. He had two spare magazines of ammunition in the left-hand pocket of his windbreaker, each one wrapped in a sports sock to reduce unnecessary noise. The socks could also be used as tourniquets, should they be required. He had no plans to get injured, but he had never planned on getting any of the many injuries he had sustained during his life as an assassin. Before that, he had never been wounded in the military. His teammates had considered him a lucky charm in that regard, but that luck had run out the day he sold his soul. He told himself that these days he didn't believe in luck.

For a brief moment he allowed himself to remember their faces – alive and smiling, instead of distorted by death as he had last seen them.

They left the inflatable on the beach. It was a calculated risk. Victor would have liked to drag the inflatable into cover, but doing so would only leave a tell-tale trench across the sand that would be easy to follow for anyone who happened this way. Plus, Raven noted, if they had to retreat in a hurry, those precious seconds dragging the inflatable back to the water could prove fatal, making them slow and easy targets. They had no choice but to leave the inflatable exposed and obvious. If Halleck had sent between five and ten men to check Raven was dead in the trunk of an Impala, the remaining six to eleven would be far too few to patrol the whole of the airfield.

Victor didn't expect any men to be patrolling this far out, but he and Raven moved at a cautious speed regardless. Speed was useful here, but pointless if they walked into a hidden sentry. Minutes lost now might avoid a firefight.

A nearby section of old fence rattled in the wind. Terns squawked as he passed a nest.

A stretch of woodland lay between the beach and the air-field. The trees were sparse and not tall, but there was enough foliage to cast much of the undergrowth in shadow. They moved through it, from tree to tree, handguns up and ready. They stopped at intervals to peer around and listen. Victor heard or saw no sign of any of Halleck's men on patrol. Still they continued at the slow pace. The closer they came to the temporary headquarters, the more chance of running into one of the team.

Victor and Raven reached the edge of the woodland. Ahead, the runway was a pale sandy colour, uneven with cracks and potholes. The yellowing grass reached Victor's shins. Shrubs and bushes had sprung up along the runway.

In the distance he saw the old hangars silhouetted against the sky. Beyond them lay the old terminal building. Lights were on at some windows.

'That's where they will be,' Raven whispered.

Victor said, 'Then that's where we're going.'

FIFTY-EIGHT

He went to continue, but Raven raised a fist to tell him to halt because—

A soft mechanical click sounded nearby.

Victor pictured a hammer cocking and a muzzle pointing his way, but only for a split second because he then heard the scrape of steel teeth against flint and the whoosh of an igniting flame.

Raven lowered herself deeper into the undergrowth as Victor did the same. He pivoted on the spot. The origin of quiet sound was hard to pinpoint amongst the background noise of rustling foliage and overhead jets.

She pointed and he saw the floating dot of glowing orange first, and then the shape of a man came into view. He stood in the shadows, almost invisible until his arm moved as he brought the cigarette away from his mouth. Rising smoke drifted through a swathe of silver moonlight.

Victor remained still and silent, watching and evaluating. Considering.

He could kill the man without trouble. A double tap of rounds from Guerrero's SIG would be more than enough at this range, but the weapon was unsuppressed. Halleck's people in the terminal building would hear, even with the noise of low-flying airliners to help disguise it. Raven saw him thinking and gestured to her Ruger, which was as close to silent as any firearm could get. He shook his head. She had no spare ammunition, and if there was one sentry outside there could be others. They might hear even the Ruger's quiet bark. Victor had no way of knowing how many they numbered or their proximity to this position.

He watched her tuck the Ruger away and draw her filleting knife.

She stepped to the side, moving in a slow circle until she was four metres behind the sentry, who continued to smoke his cigarette.

Victor watched her approach, one careful step after the next, more dragging her feet along the ground than walking so as to reduce the chances of snapping twigs beneath her soles.

At two metres, Raven paused. She could see the sentry better now. The man was a fraction shorter than her. It would be simple to slap a palm over the mouth and pull the head back to slice the throat from ear to ear.

At one metre away, she stopped again, because the sentry said:

'This is Four, all quiet. Next check-in at o-one-forty-nine. Over.'

Victor checked his watch. It had just turned 1.39. If the sentry didn't report in ten minutes, the alarm would be raised. Ten minutes was not going to be enough time. But no password had been used.

Four light steps and Raven was behind the sentry. At the blade's touch, blood burst free and soaked the sentry's clothes. Her palm caught and muffled the man's gurgling scream. In less than ten seconds the sentry was unconscious.

Raven lowered him to the ground. By the time she had finished checking his pockets and taking his radio, the man was dead. Victor approached.

Raven said, 'Here,' and tossed him the man's weapon.

Victor caught it. It was a UMP sub-machine gun.

'Ammo,' Raven said, and threw him spare magazines.

They moved on. Victor didn't relish the idea of crossing the open ground that lay between the woodland and the old airport buildings, but they had no choice. They would be easy prey for any kind of half-decent marksman behind a rifle. There was nothing to take cover behind for almost five hundred metres.

He allowed himself to move at a faster pace. Outside of the darkness of the woodlands the moon provided plenty of illumination. They would be easier to spot crossing the space, but on the plus side they would see any other sentries from a long way off.

He tried not to think about a keen-eyed marksman lying on the roof of one of the hangars, armed with a high-velocity rifle equipped with an infrared scope.

No shot came, so no marksman.

They crossed the runaway, leaning forward in half crouches to reduce their profile.

Concrete slabs surrounded the hangars and the terminal building. Weeds bordered every concrete slab. A rusted steel hatch covered an entrance to a tunnel that ran from the terminal building, under the apron where they loaded the plane and out to the plane, avoiding the wash from propeller blades. It was sealed shut, and if not for the concrete floor that had been poured over the hatch at the other end, would have made an excellent entry point into the building.

Victor held the SIG down by his hip for speed. There was no need to have it ready to aim now. Any enemies were out of sight and out of range. If he had to open fire before he reached the safety of the hangars it would mean certain death, caught out in the coverless ground against multiple enemies.

Speed was their best ally now. He knew they were silhouetted against the horizon, but they had no choice. If they crawled across earth to reduce the chances of being spotted it would only increase the time they were exposed. They had to trust to speed to take the place of concealment and cover.

They had been waiting in the dark long enough for their night vision to be at maximum. The men inside the airfield buildings, having spent all evening in brighter interiors, would be blind in comparison. But only outside. The moment Victor and Raven emerged into light, their vision would suffer.

The old Naval Air Station building had two above-ground levels and one half-sunken storey. At the centre of the north-facing façade a hexagonal tower protruded and rose a further level, with the control tower itself perched on top.

They approached it from the south, rounding it until they were at the north side, between the building and the aircraft hangar.

A flatbed truck was parked between the two.

FIFTY-NINE

It was a big, old-model vehicle with a white cab and a long articulated bed that rested on eight wheels. The bed had been filled by a single intermodal shipping container. There were some seventeen million such containers in the world. This one was painted blue, but faded and marked over long years of use. Victor had never seen two tons of plastic explosives before, but he didn't have to look inside the container to know they were there. He could only imagine the devastation it would cause.

A noise alerted him to an approaching figure before he had come into view. The slow, shuffling footsteps told him it was a man, and that he was bored or tired. Not alert. Vulnerable.

Victor switched the UMP to his left hand and held it down by his hip, by the barrel, while he drew the fillet knife into his right fist. He stood with his back to the wall of the building and his right shoulder at the corner. He had his knife in a downward grip, positioned close to his left shoulder, arm across his chest.

He shut his eyes to better concentrate on the sound of the footsteps, as they grew louder, nearer, until they were near enough for—

Victor to snap out his hand through a fast one hundred and eighty degree arc until his arm was perpendicular to his body.

A gasp.

The resistance the knifepoint met told him he had stabbed the man in the chest, through the ribs, before he had turned to see.

He released the knife while the man was still gasping, pivoted, and swung the UMP, striking the man in the face with the weapon's stock and taking him from his feet.

He hit the ground, unconscious. He was never going to wake up.

Victor switched the UMP into a firing position and surveyed the area for others. No one in sight. No one in hearing range.

'We're good,' Raven said.

He knelt and kept the gun in a one-handed shooting grip while he worked the knife free with his left hand. It took some effort; the knife was buried up to the hilt. Victor wiped the blood from the blade on the man's jacket. Gaze still searching for enemies, he patted the man down, recognising the feel of a wallet, car keys and phone but ignoring them all. He was checking only for items that might help him in his mission. He was here to kill, nothing more.

He tucked the man's handgun into his waistband. There was no such thing as too many guns.

Raven was looking at the truck.

'What are you waiting for?' Victor whispered. 'Hot-wire it and go.'

'They'll have other, faster, vehicles. I'll never make it out of the airfield.'

'Then you'd better help me, hadn't you?'

Her eyes narrowed at him and he kept to the wall and the shadows as they passed between the buildings. He heard laughter and sounds of merriment coming from an open window on the second floor. They were relaxed and un-prepared. He noted the location on the map inside his mind and moved on. If he could catch them while they were still in the room, he could take out half the opposition in a matter of seconds.

Light up ahead framed a closed door.

Victor gestured for Raven to halt and he approached, careful and quiet. He heard noise from inside. It sounded like someone cooking; he could hear the hiss of steam and the clang of pans.

The door opened to the left, so Victor stood on that side of the doorframe and rapped on the door with his knuckles three gentle times.

It was enough to gain the curiosity of the person inside, who came to the door and opened it wide enough that the outside handle touched Victor's stomach.

He saw the man's shadow on the ground and the head turning in confusion.

Victor watched the shadow change and the door begin to close.

He stepped out and around it, grabbed the man's

outstretched arm that was trailing behind him to pull the door shut as he was turning away, and yanked him backwards.

The man fell, knocking open the door, and crashing to the ground outside of it.

Victor leapt on him while he was still prone and shocked, going into full mount with his knees tucked against the man's armpits, and forcing the stock of the UMP against the man's throat. He pushed down with all the strength of his arms and back. The man gasped and spluttered and suffocated below him.

Three down without discovery had been Victor's minimum assessment for operational success if they were going up against six. Which meant there were still at least three alive and armed if Halleck had sent ten men to FDR Drive, but there could be up to eight more if Halleck had dispatched fewer. If Halleck hadn't fallen for their deception there would be even more.

If Halleck had not fallen for the ruse and all thirteen remaining men were here, then things would get messy.

They entered the kitchen. The building had long fallen into disrepair. Cracks ran through the plaster. Paint was chipped. Wood had warped. Tiles were cracked. The dead guy had been preparing the evening meal for the others. Before he reached the exit, he switched off the stove as he went. The ragu sauce was starting to boil and stick to the pan.

They passed through the kitchen to a corridor. One by one, he cleared the adjoining rooms, fast, easing open each door and then charging in, sweeping with the UMP from left to right, Raven following a step behind and sweeping right to left.

Ahead was a doorway. Peeling paint covered the doorframe. Empty hinges were all that was left of the door itself. On the other side of the doorway the paint and plaster on the walls was cracked and chipped and had fallen or been pulled away in large chunks. Exposed wires ran around the walls where skirting boards had once been. The room was empty. It appeared to have been an office space or a dormitory for pilots from the days when there were no night flights. An open door on the south wall led to a small toilet.

Another open door led to a room of similar size that occupied the building's southwest corner. The walls in here had been stripped of their plaster, exposing bare brick and vertical wooden runners. Black-and-white tiles had once covered the floor, but now the black tiles were grey and the white tiles had turned yellow with dust and grime. Some had become loose. Others were missing.

Beyond the room was a corridor and a staircase that led both up and down. Victor had no desire to leave areas behind him unchecked for threats, but clearing it would burn time they didn't have. Each passing second increased the chances of being discovered – either them or the corpses – and enemies were unlikely to be in the basement. It was a risk, but most plans were based on compromise, and most fell apart when the first round was fired.

So far, no rounds had been fired.

The plan was working.

SIXTY

They ascended the stairs at a normal pace. They had no need for stealth – their enemies would expect to hear footsteps inside the building – but Victor kept his gait careful so as not to rush into danger.

At the top of the stairs, he emerged on to the building's first floor. The stairwell door opened on to a corridor shrouded in darkness. No lights were on overhead and no light emanated under doorframes leading off the corridor. He waited, listening.

As with the basement, he decided not to clear it for the sake of time spent against the chances of enemies present. He knew for certain enemies were on the floor above him as of two minutes ago. He turned to Raven and pointed up with a thumb.

They backed off and climbed the last set of stairs to the building's top floor, hearing the sound of movement and talking before they had reached the stairwell door.

With the stock of the UMP firm and comfortable resting in the crook in his chest where his pectoral muscle met the anterior deltoid, eyes peering along the iron sights, he used his left hand to work the door handle and ease the door open.

He could not disguise the noise of the jamb clicking or the hinges creaking, but both were quiet enough to not draw attention from the two men he saw.

They were standing five metres away, side on to him, talking to one another. One was leaning back against the wall behind him, arms folded. The second stood opposite, holding a UMP by the barrel while the stock rested against the flooring.

Victor shot the first man above the ear with a double tap, switching aim to the second as he recoiled in shock and horror, the contents of his teammate's skull pan splattered over his face, and dropped him with another two rounds before he had even processed what was happening.

The UMP fired heavy .45 calibre rounds. The mess was considerable.

Victor dropped to one knee in the open doorway. He would not have done so if it hadn't been for Raven covering the rear, but he wanted to be low and in a firing position should any other enemies appear ahead.

The gunfire would generate surprise, then fear. The men inside the room would be shocked into inaction, but someone would investigate – either the bravest man or the weakest-willed, pressured by his comrades.

Victor wasn't sure which quality the man possessed who opened the door to check, but a double tap blew off the top of his skull.

The body dropped in the doorway, creating a useful obstacle to prevent those inside closing the door.

'*Go*,' he called to Raven.

She rushed ahead of him while he covered her advance, keeping close to one wall and out of his line of fire.

Victor dashed over as soon as she had reached the doorway and charged in, UMP entering the room first, already firing on full automatic before he had acquired targets, Raven an instant behind him – he went left; she went right.

The two guys inside the room were stunned by panic. The closest had been caught by the blind shots and was stumbling backwards when Victor saw him. The second, further away, was bringing up his gun. Raven dropped him with a triple tap of rounds to his centre mass.

Which gave Victor an extra split second to deal with the shot guy, who had dropped his primary weapon and was reaching for a backup. One squeeze of the UMP's trigger made sure he never reached it.

'That's eight,' Raven said. 'So Halleck sent exactly half his crew to collect my body. I'm going to take that as a compliment. Or maybe it's one to you. When will they realise you aren't going to show?'

Victor said, 'Soon.'

A radio worn by one of the dead guys crackled to life and a disembodied voice said, 'This is Courier, how's it looking at the LZ? Over.'

Raven looked at it, then him. 'What do we do?'

He shrugged. 'I didn't hear any of them speak. They might have a code.'

'We can't ignore it.'

The voice said, 'This is Courier. Respond, please.'

'What do we do?' Raven asked again.

Victor took the radio from the floor and pressed send. 'You're clear for landing, Courier.'

There was no response.

'Does that mean they bought it?' Raven asked.

Victor shrugged. 'I don't know. If they believed me, they'll land out front. But if they didn't they'll make sure they're out of range; they'll hit the deck about a hundred metres from the terminal building.'

The radio crackled into life and Halleck said, 'Nice try, but no sale.'

Raven took the radio from Victor and replied, 'How are you, Jim? It's been a long time.'

Halleck said, 'Go to hell.'

'That's no way to talk to a lady. Where are your manners? I'd have expected humility, or maybe some begging. It's over, Jim. I've won. I have your bomb.'

Halleck laughed. 'It's a little early to gloat, Constance. You have nothing.'

'What are you flying in?' Raven asked. 'The bomb is outside. The blackout has cut the power to the city. What have you been waiting for? You already have enough explosives to take down a skyscraper. You can't possibly need more.'

'What do you think I am, a lunatic? I'm not going to take down a skyscraper. I'm no terrorist, whatever you think of me.'

Raven said, 'Two tons of plastic explosives on a truck says otherwise.'

Halleck said, 'Let me talk to your new partner.'

'I'm here,' Victor said, taking the radio.

'I didn't know you were so stupid as to fuck with me,' Halleck said. 'Now, you're never going to get out of this country. You'll be hunted to the ends of the earth forever more.'

'Why?' Victor asked. 'Eight of your guys are dead. The other eight are the other side of Brooklyn. The bomb's outside. It's not going anywhere. When it blows up, it's going to damage nothing but soil. No one's going to spend resources trying to track down the most incompetent terrorist in the world, are they? You really should have just found a way to hire me to kill Raven in the first place and saved us all a lot of bother.'

Raven huffed, 'You charmer.' Then she frowned and said into the radio, 'What were you planning to do?'

Halleck didn't answer.

'What are you delivering?' Raven asked again.

'I'm surprised you haven't worked it out before now, Constance. You were always so smart.'

'If you're not using the explosives to bring down a building, then what's the point of it?' Raven said. 'Then it's nothing more than fireworks. You blow it up on an empty street and the damage will be minimal. We're talking a massive crater and a thousand broken windows. So what? That's not going to start wars. If the explosives aren't for demolition, then you planned to use them as a delivery system. What for? A chemical weapon? Biological? Radiological?'

Halleck didn't answer.

'It's the last one, isn't it?' Raven continued. 'That's why

you needed to cut the power to the city. That's why you needed the blackout: Manhattan has a whole network of sensors to detect radioactive material. With the power down, you can drive the truck straight into the middle of Wall Street and set off a dirty bomb.'

'You got there in the end, but too late to make a difference.'

Raven said, 'You're a maniac.'

Halleck's voice came through the radio, loud and angry. 'It's a goddamn dirty bomb, not a nuclear weapon. They're a world apart. Dirty bombs have been tested by the Department of Energy and you know what? They don't do shit. You would have to live within the original blast radius for months to have any chance of getting radiation sickness. They're a tabloid weapon. They've invaded the public consciousness, but no one in the know rightly fears them. Like I said, I'm not a monster. The explosive is going to do more damage than the plutonium. This is a scare weapon. This is a true *terror* weapon. I have no intention of butchering millions of my own people. I'm a patriot.'

Raven said, 'A patriot willing to bomb his own country at the behest of those looking to profit from war.'

'I'm no altruist, that's true. But who out of us three is? So don't play that card. I work for a consensus of powerful individuals and corporations. But no one can pay me enough to wipe out a city. That's not what this is about. Every month a terrorist plot is foiled. People have stopped caring. They care more now about having to wait in line at airports. People are idiots. They need reminding about the realities of the world and the people who don't like them.

Better I kill a few dozen and scare a few hundred million than the alternative.

'This is not a weapon of mass destruction,' Halleck continued. 'This is a wake-up call. The blackout isn't just to allow us to get the bomb into position. It's to stop people coming on to the island, to keep them at home. It's to limit the casualties. We're going to see panic; we're going to see people scared; but the only long-term effects will be psychological. The price tag for clearing up the mess will be huge, but there are private operations ready and willing to step in and sort it all out in record time. For a nice fee, of course. But that's capitalism. It's the reason we're not living in caves. People want redistribution of wealth, right? You know what that's called? It's called subsistence. It's called your family starving to death if it doesn't rain enough. Capitalism brings prosperity and it brings stability. Without it, it's anarchy. So yes, I'm doing my own version of good. Everyone benefits this way. That's democracy. That's freedom.'

'You're insane,' Raven said.

'You may not agree with me, but everything in this life is a question of balance. If everyone with a smartphone traded it in for a cheap handset and donated the rest of the money to charity, there would be no world hunger. Are those people responsible for world hunger if they don't? Of course not. Their fathers' fathers paid in blood and death for them to enjoy their lives. You get nothing for free. Either you earn it or someone earns it for you. There are finite resources; there is finite time; there is finite will. For one person to be fat and happy, another must be thin and miserable. We've done too well in the West. We've poked the hornet's nest of the Middle East several times and we've only had to deal with the occasional sting in return. My sponsors want to sell their bombs and planes and tanks and bullets. For that, we need war. And war is a good thing. Human progress has followed war. If we live in peace and harmony we grow weaker and weaker until someone strengthened by conflict comes along and takes over. Then we become a footnote in history. It's happened to every empire. It's my job to make sure it doesn't happen to us. We will not go gentle into that good night. We will make the night hide from us.'

Raven said, 'But you won't. You've failed. You're a—'

Victor took the radio off her and said, 'Quiet. Listen.'

The thrum of helicopter blades reached Victor's ears. Raven heard them an instant later. He walked towards the window, and peered out. He saw no sign of an approaching helicopter, but it was near.

Victor said, 'Halleck was stalling.'

SIXTY-ONE

Raven said, 'We need higher ground.'

They left the room and found metal stairs thick with dust and grime that led upwards. A metal railing bolted to the wall offered support, but only for half the ascent. The rest had been bent and snapped away at some point long ago. The walls were rough and painted white, as dirty as the stairs, and a short, narrow corridor led on to more stairs through a doorless doorway. The door itself lay on its side in the corridor.

Victor passed a window comprised of semi-opaque glass blocks and climbed up again, Raven following. These stairs were wooden, warped and cracked through wear and rot.

The control room at the top was painted in utilitarian grey paint – the walls, the pillars, the floor, even the folding metal chairs and sink. The only thing that had escaped the grey was a desk fan, once white but stained to an unpleasant yellow. A door led out to a walkway that ran around the control room. A ladder led further up.

There was no air traffic control equipment in the room. The only evidence the room had ever been used as such were the holes for cables and dials that were cut into the boxing protruding from the walls.

To the west, over the neighbouring building's roof, he could see the road and the harbour beyond it. East and north lay hangars and runways.

But to the south, visible at last because of its aviation lights, flew the helicopter, growing larger and more distinct with every passing second. It was a big commercial model, painted graphite grey.

'That's a Eurocopter Dauphin. I've been in one just like it. Maybe even the same one,' Raven said. 'We should get out of here.'

'We're in a defensive position. We can take them here.'

She shook her head. 'They'll outnumber us. It can carry eight passengers. There are several points of entry. We can't cover them all. They'll box us in. We can take the truck and get the hell out of here.'

'We stay here and deal with whoever gets off that helicopter.'

'You mean you want to wait and get Halleck?'

Victor said, 'If they see the truck moving, they're going to go after it. We can't outrun a helicopter. They'll fly over us and land to block off our escape from the airfield, whichever route we try and take.'

'Good,' she said. 'The instant the chopper is directly overhead we're going to jump out – and they won't see us do it.'

'Let me guess: we'll have set the bomb to blow shortly after we do.'

'How fast can you cover a football field?' Raven asked.

'Because the lethal radius of two tons of high explosives is going to be about one hundred metres.'

She nodded. 'Give or take.'

'I'm fast,' he said. 'But that's no kind of plan. We can't assume they'll fall for it.'

She relented. 'Okay. We do it your way.'

'I'll stay here,' he said. 'I'll take shots at them as they approach. They're bound to split up – some putting down covering fire at me while the others close the distance and enter. Go to the first floor and ambush those guys when they come within range.'

She nodded again. 'Good luck.'

The thrum of rotor blades grew louder and the shape of a helicopter came into view, silhouetted against the night sky.

'Go,' Victor said.

She descended the stairs, and Victor watched her go. He then waited in the control tower, watching the Eurocopter grow nearer. It was flying in fast; and the pilot was bringing the bird in for a hard landing and rapid deployment of the men on board.

He thumbed the selector switch on the UMP to full automatic and opened fire on the helicopter.

The sub-machine gun roared, spitting bullets skyward from his spot in the control tower. He aimed in front of the chopper to account for its speed and the distance the bullets had to travel to reach their target.

A one-in-a-million shot might hit the pilot and bring the chopper crashing to the ground, but Victor's intent was to persuade those inside to deal with him in the control tower, making them easy targets for Raven downstairs.

The helicopter hit the ground outside the terminal building with force, rotor wash flattening grass, about one hundred metres out, and eight figures leapt out. He saw Halleck among them, ordering his men to split up and move forward. He was carrying a large aluminium case. It was heavy, no doubt lined with lead.

The seven men and Halleck began their approach.

SIXTY-TWO

Victor let all thoughts empty from his mind, passing control of his actions over to his unconscious, to the part of the brain evolved over millions of years, which some called the lizard brain. The conscious mind was slow and young and too prone to distraction and bias; the lizard brain was old and wise and could detect and analyse and process and calculate and act far quicker than any deliberate conscious thought. He felt the release of over one hundred and fifty different hormones into the blood, of which adrenaline was perhaps the most powerful. The others would be working in a variety of ways, shutting down non-essential bodily functions, focusing vision and deprioritising hearing – sound provided less clear messages than sight and warnings that were slower to receive and analyse and react to; the relative delay between processing sight and hearing might be minuscule, but it could spell the difference between survival and death.

He stood to peer down on to the open space before the terminal building and opened fire, wasting a whole magazine of .45 calibre rounds shooting blind into the darkness. Three seconds later he had dropped back in cover.

Victor crouched down on his haunches, back against the wall next to the window. Automatic fire exploded the pane and ripped chunks from the wooden framework, punching holes in the far wall. Plaster clouded in the air. Shards of glass shattered and skidded across the floor. As powerful as a .45 calibre round was, it could not penetrate solid brick, nor was anything inside the room solid enough to cause a bullet to ricochet.

He waited. The shooting was ineffectual. The gunmen were wasting rounds just as he had, but he still had an objective.

He reloaded the UMP and popped up to shoot again. This time at muzzle flashes, but without accuracy as he couldn't afford to spend the time aiming when he was outnumbered eight-to-one. But he was gathering intelligence, not trying to kill his enemies. Even with the higher ground and cover, he wasn't going to win this firefight.

But now he knew how far away his enemies were, and he had convinced them he was staying in the tower.

Further rounds took out more windows, scattering glass across the floor. It crunched beneath Victor's heels as he ducked low, back against the wall to maximise the cover.

In seconds the gunmen would be easy targets for Raven, but he realised the plan wasn't going to work because Raven wasn't downstairs as instructed, but driving the flatbed truck.

He glimpsed it in his peripheral vision. The noise of rotor blades was enormous and had drowned out the sound of the truck's engine. Victor saw it from the corner of his eye as it pulled out from between the two buildings and on to the runway, accelerating north towards the exit.

Raven was doing it her own way.

Halleck would have seen it too. Victor could almost see and hear the reactions and then instructions and action.

He risked looking and saw three of Halleck's guys rushing back to, and boarding, the helicopter. It was in the air a moment later and flying after the truck, leaving Halleck and four of his guys approaching the terminal building.

In less than thirty seconds the helicopter had passed over the flatbed truck. Victor watched it bank and slow and land again in the distance.

The truck continued in a straight line, heading straight for the landed Eurocopter. The pilot would be expecting it to slow and stop, but it didn't and Victor saw tiny specks of light as guns opened fire in the distance, shooting at the truck in an attempt to kill the driver and bring it to a stop.

When it was obvious the truck wasn't going to be brought to a halt, the helicopter took off to avoid being hit and the guys on the ground stopped firing to clear out of the way.

Both of which were pointless because two tons of high explosives detonated.

The night sky illuminated in a brief instance of dazzling white light that blinded Victor. The sound was a monstrous boom that hit him an instant later, the overpressure wave exploding windows and popping his ears and knocking him off balance, broken glass raining down on him.

The chopper had ascended to maybe fifty metres when the truck exploded and was caught in the massive mushrooming blast. The helicopter was ripped in half, the back end falling away as flaming wreckage as the front section spun in crazed patterns until it came crashing to ground, out of sight in the woodland.

SIXTY-THREE

He didn't know if Raven was alive or dead and it didn't matter because there were still five live enemies outside. He shook and swept the glass from over him and climbed to his feet. His eyes stung and his ears were ringing.

He peered outside through the gap where the control tower window used to be. Halleck and his men were still there – stunned by the explosion, but all functional.

Victor let off some more rounds, then crawled along the floor, feeling the coldness of the tiles and broken glass beneath his palms and smelling the cordite from expended brass shell casings.

A stationary target, no matter how well defended, was vulnerable against a numerically superior force. Mobility was his best ally. A larger force was a slower force.

He exited the control tower and used the solid metal butt of the UMP to knock out the opaque glass blocks from the window next to the stairs. They had been strong enough to survive the overpressure wave, but five good strikes were enough to clear a large enough space for Victor to squeeze through and fall out on to the terminal building's flat roof.

Ducking low, he crept along the roof until he could peer over the edge.

He saw four figures. Two were approaching the building, while Halleck and a companion stayed put, ready to provide cover.

Victor held off shooting. If he shot at the two closest, he would no doubt kill them, but would be cut down by the two further away. If he went for the two providing cover, the closest would have easy work killing him, maybe even before he had killed one of his targets.

Instead, he watched.

The man in the lead wore a dark nylon sports jacket, zipped up to the neck, boots, and faded black jeans. His head was shaved to the skin, bone-white scalp contrasting with the tanned face. He was in his mid-thirties, of average height but heavy with excess muscle and fat. He moved like he was used to the weight – quick and assured.

The second man was younger, with dark skin and longer hair tied back in a short topknot. A neat black beard framed a jaw set with aggression. He wore jogging bottoms, trainers and a hooded sweatshirt.

They were dressed like civilians, casual and nondescript, but they were professionals.

They didn't look much like killers. But the good ones never did.

Victor watched them approach and communicate with

hand signals. He didn't see the fourth of Halleck's remaining men, which meant either Victor had shot him by some minor miracle or the man had circled the building to enter through the back or to guard it as an obvious escape route.

He backed away from the edge before the two closest moved out of his line of sight. A moment later the sound of glass breaking reached his ears. It had been broken with as little force as possible to lessen the noise, but it would be impossible to smash glass from a door without a sound. He pictured one of the men reaching through and unlocking the door while the other had his gun drawn in cover.

He failed to hear the door open, but detected their footfalls as they passed through the open doorway and into the hallway beneath him. They would spend a minute or more clearing the rooms on the ground floor, one by one. They believed him to be in the tower, but they could not head straight there and risk giving him their backs if he had descended.

Hurried footsteps told him Halleck and the other man were approaching and entering the building too.

Victor waited thirty seconds so the second two would be deep within the building, then slung the UMP over one shoulder.

With his back facing the edge of the roof, he lowered himself until his arms were extended and he was holding on by his fingertips.

He dropped one storey and hit the ground and bounced on the balls of his feet to disperse some of the fall's energy before going into a roll to absorb the rest.

Halleck and the three men had left the door open for

him. Fragments of broken glass lay on the inside of the threshold. Victor stepped over the glass and into the building. The aluminium case sat inside the doorway, containing uranium or plutonium or whatever else made an effective radiological weapon. Halleck had set it down because it was heavy and bulky and a hindrance – and because he believed he was the hunter and Victor the prey.

He was wrong.

SIXTY-FOUR

Victor heard boots ascending stairs. They had cleared the ground floor faster than he had estimated, maybe because the fourth man had joined them and helped speed up the process, or because they were not as thorough as they should be, or they were even better than he thought.

When the boots had left the stairs, he crept through the darkness, but the floor was covered in hard tiles. His enemies were making enough noise to disguise his footfalls; if his enemies heard him it would be because he was right next to them.

They were close. He could hear the men moving around on the floor above him – even less concerned about making noise than he was – but the echoing effect of the quiet, empty building made it difficult to pinpoint their positions.

He kept his boots on, despite the additional noise they made on the hard floor. In bare feet – because socks lacked traction on tiled flooring – he would be able to move in near silence, but in the confines of the first-floor rooms he might not be able to take them all out without a physical confrontation. For that, he needed shoes. He wanted the extra power a solid heel added to his kicks and stomps, and likewise wanted the protection of tough leather covering his feet from similar attacks and from broken glass scattered by the explosion in rooms with windows.

He emptied his pockets of anything that might rattle or fall out and give away his position. Triumphing against the odds often came down to such small details often overlooked by those whose life did not rely on considering everything.

He climbed the stairs, stopping midway to listen, hearing noise from both his left and right, originating from opposite sides of the building. The four men had split up to search for him.

Perfect.

He headed to the left. It was an arbitrary decision.

He approached an open doorway at the end of the hallway, hearing the rustle of nylon, and knew the man inside the room was the white guy with the shaved head. Victor stopped a metre from the doorway and kept his gaze directed at the floorboards ahead of it, because the first part of his enemy he would see would be the man's foot as it crossed the threshold.

When that foot appeared, Victor stamped on it with his heel, then stepped in front of the man and snapped one palm over his mouth as the other hand struck him in the throat.

The man stumbled backwards, shocked and injured and overwhelmed and unable to fight back as Victor disarmed him and twisted him one hundred and eighty degrees and into a rear naked choke.

He locked the guy's head against his chest as he applied pressure with his biceps and forearm on the carotid arteries either side of the man's neck, and increased that pressure by tilting the head forward into the choke. The blood supply to the man's brain was cut off.

Within five seconds the man stopped struggling. He was unconscious after another three.

With other enemies nearby Victor didn't have time to keep the choke on long enough to ensure the man never woke up, so he adjusted his arm until the blade of his forearm was against the guy's trachea. One of Victor's old instructors had told him: *If you can crush a soda can, you can crush a windpipe.* He squeezed, feeling the momentary resistance of cartilage before the trachea collapsed inwards.

Victor lowered the unconscious, and soon-to-be dead, man to the floor.

Four enemies remaining.

Three of whom appeared as Victor turned round.

He snapped up the UMP and opened fire, seeing Halleck among the three but aiming for the closest threat. The sound of the UMP's gunfire was a loud, dull bark that echoed in the confined space. The muzzle spat out bright bursts of exploded gases. Expended brass shell cases, hot and smoking, arced out of the breech, clinking off the walls and floor and crunching underfoot. The recoil thumped against his shoulder and reverberated through his body.

The closest man took a burst to the torso, shielding Halleck and the other man, who both backed off in surprise, seeking cover as Victor stalked forward, shooting in short, controlled bursts of two or three rounds. He moved in a crouch, half-squatting for stability and to reduce his height and silhouette.

He was reaching to change the magazine before he had squeezed the trigger for the last time, having counted bursts. Within four seconds he was shooting again.

They returned fire from doorways, but without accuracy because they were on the defensive. He squeezed off shots at each target, not expecting to hit any of them while they were buried in hard cover, but aiming to buy himself time to move while his enemies ducked and flinched and kept their heads down.

The response to fire went against every instinct evolution had instilled into Victor. He approached the danger, increasing the risk of death or dismemberment with each step, but in doing so he fought his enemies' will as he fought their physicality. They outnumbered him. They were in the position of strength. For Victor to attack instead of retreating disrupted their psychological narrative. He thought of Sun Tzu: *When strong, appear weak; when weak, appear strong*.

It worked.

The continuous fire and advancement made his enemies doubt their strength. They backed off and retreated. The wrong thing to do. The gunman fell amid the storm of gunfire. Halleck managed to scramble away, losing his gun in the process, but kicking open a doorway and charging into safety as Victor's last round buried itself in the doorframe.

He released the empty magazine and went to reload but a door burst open behind him and the fourth gunman appeared.

SIXTY-FIVE

He had come from the control tower, flanking Victor by climbing up while he had sought to flank the men by climbing down. Victor charged into him, releasing his own empty sub-machine gun to grab the gunman's UMP and drive it and the gunman against a wall. He grunted from the impact and Victor wrenched the weapon closer, pulling the man off balance and into an elbow.

His grip on the weapon loosened and Victor tore it from his grasp and swung it like a club at the guy's head.

The fourth man ducked to avoid it and caught the gun by the barrel. They wrestled for control of the weapon, strength versus strength, Victor winning but only continuing the struggle to focus his opponent's attention on fighting back instead of what Victor's legs were doing.

He kicked the guy, missing the side of the knee and striking him on the thigh. The force was enough to make him grimace and pull the leg back, transferring all of his weight to the other leg.

Victor swept the load-bearing ankle and the guy dropped.

Victor put a burst of rounds through the man's face.

Before he could turn round, a thick forearm snaked in front of Victor's neck, going for a choke hold.

At that moment he couldn't know whether Halleck intended to apply a blood choke or an air choke, but Victor's reaction was the same. Before Halleck could get into either position, Victor tensed his neck to harden the muscles and flare the strong tendons. At the same time he released the UMP and shrugged his right shoulder to raise Halleck's arm and create room to manoeuvre. Then he turned his head away to the left, so the attacking arm applied pressure to the muscle and tendons at the side of his neck.

Any delay in response would have decreased his chances of survival to almost zero. Halleck's years in the military had taught him how to fight and kill, but he was not fast enough to apply the more difficult blood choke in time. He went for the air choke, locking his hands off in a gable grip, the bony part of the forearm applying the pressure. He pulled Victor tight against him and put the side of his head against Victor's back, both to increase the pressure of the choke and to keep his eyes away from Victor's reach.

The flared neck, raised shoulder and turned head combined to give him extra time to fight back. Attacking eyes was problematic at the best of times in Victor's experience, let alone while suffocating, so he concentrated on Halleck's arm.

He grabbed at the forearm in both hands. An attacker

didn't have to be strong to be able to resist an attempt to pull the arm away, but Halleck had dense arms, packed with powerful muscle, so as Victor wrenched downwards he also lifted his feet to drop his weight.

Halleck was strong, but not strong enough to resist now.

The forearm edged away from Victor's neck.

Not far, but far enough to dispel the agony and let Victor draw in a big lungful of air, giving him more time and space to twist his body so that he was at a ninety-degree angle from his attacker. The choke was now a headlock. Halleck still held on, his grip tight and secure, but the danger of suffocation had gone.

With his left hand, Victor grabbed a handful of Halleck's jacket and the love handle beneath it and squeezed. The pinching effect caused significant pain, but also secured Halleck in place. Otherwise, if he opted to move, Victor would have no choice but to be dragged along with him. Now, with a firm hold on Halleck, Victor kept him where he wanted.

He slammed his right palm up between Halleck's legs for a groin strike.

Halleck grunted but his grip stayed secure. His pain tolerance was Herculean, but could not withstand a second palm strike.

His hold weakened and Victor lifted him off his feet and slammed him on the floor, scrambling on top of Halleck and pinning him in place, the blade of his forearm compressing the man's Adam's apple. He wheezed, breathless, strength fading. Victor smashed Halleck in the face with his free elbow again and again until he stopped fighting back and Victor's sleeve was soaked in blood and frayed where it had ripped on broken bone.

Victor took a few seconds to get his breath back then reloaded his weapon and exited the building. In the distance, flames licked the sky from the burning truck and helicopter wreckage.

The aluminium case was no longer by the door.

He peered into the distance for a sign of Raven, but there was only darkness.

SIXTY-SIX

One month later

The hotel bar was about thirty metres square. The thick grey carpet in the centre of the floor was ringed with limestone tiles. Leather chairs, sofas and stools surrounded glass tables. Against one wall sat a woman playing an ornate sandalwood harp. Her hair was red and straight, and so long it hung past her waist. The graceful, dextrous movements of her fingers impressed Victor as much as the music soothed him. She never opened her eyes, lost in the concentrated rhythm, and Victor fought to remember the last time he had chosen to impede his own sight in public and found pleasure in the experience. No memory came to him.

Behind her, the wall was covered in glass, behind which blue lights cast her in a soft, almost metallic glow. Waitresses wearing red dresses drifted around the room, taking table orders or delivering drinks and snacks. Their movements were as effortless as the harpist's. Bartenders wearing waistcoats and bow ties mixed cocktails, their faces etched with focus. They looked like men who would refuse to pour Scotch over ice or mix bourbon with soft drinks.

'Woodford Reserve,' Victor said to one, who looked old before his time.

The bartender poured a double measure of the bourbon into a tumbler as he said, 'Singles are for daylight only.'

Victor took a seat at the bar and ignored the noise of chatter and merriment to listen to the harpist.

He had fled Floyd Bennett Field long before the first responders had shown up and sealed off the area. Using the chaos of the blackout, he had slipped out of the city and headed across the border into Canada.

After lying low in Nova Scotia for a week, he had contacted Muir. She had heard nothing of the incident at the airfield, despite rumours of gunfire and an explosion. The Consensus at work, Victor assumed. He was still a wanted man, but as an assassin, not a terrorist. No terrorist attack had been committed. Halleck's death had been recorded as a suicide. He was suspected of killing Guerrero.

Victor had neither seen nor heard anything from Raven until she appeared alongside him at the bar.

'Ten thousand hours,' she said, looking at the harpist. 'That's how long they say it takes to master a skill like that.'

Victor sipped the whisky. 'I've heard the same.'

'Sounds about right to me,' Raven said. 'Do you play any instruments?'

'Like that? No.' Victor gestured to the harpist. 'But I know my way around the piano. Well, used to.'

'Why the past tense?'

'A piano needs a home.'

She turned to face him, leaning one elbow on the bar. 'And you're homeless? Poor baby.'

'I prefer to think of myself as a nomad.'

The old-before-his-time barman approached. 'What can I get for you, ma'am?'

She pointed at Victor's glass. 'What's he drinking?'

The barman said, 'Woodford.'

'Bourbon?' She frowned at Victor, then looked back to the barman. 'No, no, no. Scotch, please. An Islay. Caol Ila, if you have it.'

The barman nodded. 'We do.'

'But don't even think about putting ice in that glass.'

The barman smiled and looked young again. 'I wouldn't dream of it.'

'What are you doing here?' Victor asked.

'Maybe I just wanted to see you.'

Victor raised an eyebrow.

'What?' Raven said. 'Why is that so impossible to believe?'

'Because you deserted me at the airfield,' Victor said.

She shrugged. 'Don't forget you're the one who said we weren't a team.' She smiled. 'That doesn't mean we can't be friends.'

'I haven't had too many friends,' Victor began, 'but I'm pretty sure trying to kill one's friends is the antithesis of friendship.'

'Ah, but that was then. That was before. Now that's all out of the way, we can be friends.'

'Can it ever truly be out of the way for people like us?'

She regarded him, acting as if she was only thinking about it now in this moment, but he knew she must have thought about it countless times. As he had.

The barman returned with Raven's drink and placed it down before her. She smiled at him and looked at Victor.

'Aren't you going to offer to buy it for me?'

Victor held her gaze and allowed her to play her game with him.

He nodded to the barman. 'Please put the lady's drink on my tab.'

'Certainly, sir.'

Raven beamed. 'You called me a lady. How nice of you, Jonathan.'

'My name isn't Jonathan.'

She lifted her glass to smell the whisky. 'It will be unless I know your real name.'

'Then I guess I'm Jonathan.'

She winked. 'I knew you would see it my way. What shall we drink to?'

'World peace.'

She laughed. 'Then we'll both be out of business.'

'Would that be so bad? Retirement sounds like fun from where I'm sitting.'

'Now I know you're joking. You're never going to retire, Jonathan. You'll be the world's only ninety-year-old hitman.'

He frowned. 'I really don't like that word.'

She grinned. 'I really don't care. Don't be a bore, Jonathan. Come on, clinky clink.'

They touched glasses and sipped their drinks. Raven closed her eyes to savour hers.

When she opened them, she said, 'Try some. You'll never go back to that junk again.'

She held out her drink. He looked at the smudge of lipstick on the glass.

'I'll stick with this, thanks.'

She saw that he had looked and sighed. 'That offends me. We're past all that. As I said, we're friends now.'

'If we're friends then you won't be offended accommodating my precautionary nature.'

Her eyes narrowed, but she smiled. 'Slippery. But I like it.'

They held each other's gaze.

'So,' she said, using her chin to gesture at Victor's drink. 'How many of those do you need inside you before you invite me up to your room?'

SIXTY-SEVEN

He used his keycard to unlock the door and said, 'After you.'

She smiled and pushed it open and stepped into his suite. 'Oh, very nice. I see you're treating yourself well.'

He followed her inside. 'Someone has to,' Victor said. 'What did you do with the case?'

'I left it in the office of the non-proliferation department of the United Nations.'

'You're kidding,' Victor said.

'Probably.' She winked and walked around the suite. 'Well, I guess you deserve all this after you helped prevent a dirty bomb going off in the middle of New York City. You are something of a hero, even if that is only a byproduct of looking after yourself.'

Victor remained silent.

'Showing some emotion won't kill you, you know?'

'I've stayed alive this long, so I must be doing something right.'

She raised her hand, as if holding a glass. 'I'll drink to that.' She turned, looking. 'Talking of which . . .'

She approached the sideboard where a bottle of dessert wine sat. 'Shall we?'

He didn't answer, but she didn't wait for one. She tore off the seal and used her knife as a makeshift corkscrew. Not the easiest thing to do without corking the wine, but she did so with speed and deftness. Once again he was impressed with her dexterity. He watched the whole process because she did so facing him. He knew this was not arbitrary. She wanted him to see she wasn't tampering with it and that she hadn't already.

With the knife embedded within the cork, she set it down on the sideboard along with the wine bottle and fetched a couple of glasses from the kitchen. He was still standing in the same place when she returned. She smiled at him, friend to friend, and poured into each glass. Even from across the room, he could see she hadn't corked the wine.

She took a glass in each hand and stepped towards him, still smiling. 'Here.'

His hands remained by his hips.

He knew it had taken her but a second to understand, but she ignored it and persisted, the smile on her face warm and inviting.

When he made no further move to take a glass, she said, 'Don't be foolish.'

'Foolish would be accepting a drink from a professional assassin who has tried to kill me once already.'

'You saw me uncork the bottle. You saw me pour it.'

'You allowed me to.'

Her eyebrows arched. 'So you would have no need to worry.'

'I never worry.'

'Then drink the wine.'

He remained silent.

'Is it because I fetched the glasses? You can pick whichever one you want.'

His lips stayed closed. He felt no awkwardness or pressure. He was good at waiting. If it came to it, he could wait until he collapsed from dehydration.

'Fine,' she breathed and drank a mouthful from one glass, and then a mouthful from the other.

She made a big play of swallowing and opened her mouth afterwards so he could see it was empty. Her teeth were white and perfect, her tongue smooth and pink.

'Happy now?'

'Deliriously so.'

She held out the glass in her left hand, so he took the one from her right. She laughed.

'For a robot, you're really quite fun.'

'I know,' he said and raised the glass.

'Make sure we maintain eye contact or it's seven years' bad luck. Or is it seven years bad sex?'

'Isn't that the same thing?'

She smiled, her eyes mischievous, and for a moment he thought of someone else.

Raven said, 'Salut.'

'Cheers.'

They clinked glasses, holding eye contact, and sipped.

'God, that's delicious,' Raven said, taking another, longer swallow. 'I didn't expect you to have such good taste.'

She swallowed another mouthful. Smiled at him. Victor took another sip. She returned to the bottle to top up her glass. 'Another one?'

Victor brought the glass to his lips and let the wine he had been holding in his mouth flow back into the glass.

Raven's dark eyes widened.

She looked at him, at the glass, at her own. He could almost feel her pulse spike from the adrenaline dumped into his bloodstream. He could almost hear the thump of her heart, as if his subconscious could detect the reverberations through the air.

Fear was the strongest of all the emotions.

All she could say was, 'Why?'

He set the glass down. 'I told you before, I only kill for two reasons. And no one hired me to kill you.'

'I'm no threat to you.'

'That's right, because you're going to die. You were never going to walk away from this and leave me out there. You're like me. You don't want a weak link in your armour any more than I do. Maybe you would have done it before we parted ways, or you would have tracked me down at some other point. But that whole show with the bottle was to make me trust you so I would leave myself vulnerable later. That's when I knew for certain you still wanted to kill me. I'm guessing you would take me to bed and kill me when I'm at my most defenceless. You tried too hard to make me trust you. You should have listened when I said I don't trust anyone.'

She looked at the knife on the sideboard, and again he felt as if he could sense the workings of her mind. She wanted to kill him in that most base of needs: revenge. For a beat he thought she would grab it and attack. But she looked away.

Like him, she was a survivor, first and before anything else. If she killed him now, she would die. While she lived, she still had a chance, so she looked away from the knife and said:

'What do I need to do?'

'There's nothing you can do. Maybe if you hadn't made the show with the bottle I would have told you not to drink the wine. But we'll never know, will we?'

'There has to be something.' Not desperate. Determined.

'I have no antidote. I didn't poison you only to save you.'

'Help me.'

'Why?'

'Because then I'll owe you.'

'The debt of a corpse is of no use to me.'

'But if I live.'

'You won't. That's the point.'

She shook her head. 'There's always a way. There's always something. You poisoned me. So you know everything about the drug. You know how to stop it or slow it down.'

He did. He never used a weapon unless he understood how it worked.

'Why?' he asked again.

'Because you're a loner, and you know you're a harder target that way, it also makes you vulnerable. One day you'll need someone to back you up. There's no one better to do that than me. Who else has proved themselves like that? You don't trust anyone, but you know, when it comes to it, you can rely on me like you can rely on yourself. You'll never have that again.'

She spoke like a sales person making a compelling pitch, demonstrating to the client why they needed the product or service. But she needed to sell it more than anyone working on commission because she was trying to stay alive.

'Well?' she said, unable to stand Victor's silence any longer.

'I'm thinking about it.'

'Think faster, please.'

'How do I know you'll keep your word? You could be lying.'

Her eyes lit up, because she knew she had got to him. She had hooked the client, now she needed to reel him in, to reassure, to get rid of the buyer's guilt before it impeded a sale.

'You don't,' she said. 'But we have the same principles. If our roles were reversed right now, would you be lying or would you honour your word?'

He said nothing, because it was a rhetorical question. They both knew the answer.

'Eat,' he said. 'Eat as much as you can as fast as you can. Anything sweet. The more sugar the better. Drink as much soda as you can stomach. You need to spike your blood sugar. Insulin will slow the effects of the neurotoxin. Then get yourself to a hospital. You might buy yourself enough time to make it before the paralysis kicks in. If you haven't got there by then, you're done. After paralysis comes heart failure. At the hospital, you're going to die. There is no anti- dote for the toxin. Your heart will stop. There is nothing you can do to prevent that. But if you're strong enough, they'll bring you back.'

'I'm strong enough,' she said, heading for the kitchen.

He opened the door to leave her to her fate, one way or the other.

DISCOVER THE MAN
BEHIND THE ACTION

TOM
WOOD

Author photograph © Charlie Hopkinson